'Doubt thou the stars are fire,
Doubt that the sun doth move.
Doubt truth to be a liar,
But never doubt I love.'

William Shakespeare
Hamlet, Act II Scene II

DRAFT

PROVENCE STARLIGHT

by

Kate Fitzroy

Kate Fitzroy

1   *'a good voice and an interesting name'*

Alice watched, waved and smiled as the last wedding guests finally departed. She had been smiling all day and her face felt stiff with the effort. Then, her false smile turned to a giggle as she watched Auntie Jessie trying to persuade Uncle Joe to get in the passenger seat of their car. She hesitated and then relented and ran out to help.

'Bye then, Uncle Joe, hasn't it been a great day!' Alice put her arm around the large shoulders of her mother's brother and managed, with a little push, to get him into the car. Her Aunt looked across the car roof at her and smiled.

'Bye then, Alice, thank you for a lovely day. You did your mother proud!'

They drove away and Alice walked slowly back to the house. Her shoulders dropped and she felt incredibly tired. Well, maybe Auntie Jessie was right and all her efforts had been worthwhile. Alice went into the small, front room and looked at the remnants of the wedding party. She began to stack the dishes and glasses on a tray and then, suddenly, she put down the tray and flopped onto the sofa. Enough was enough. She had done her best all day, but now she just wanted to have a shower and rest.

An hour later she returned to clearing the party debris but in a better mood. Her mother had long deserved the happiness of this day. She had always been there for Alice and now, after twenty-six years of life as a single, unmarried mother, she had found love. Alice sighed as she thought about her new step-father, the very nice Michael Jennings… or rather, Dr. Michael Jennings. He was nothing if not nice. Or was he nicely a nothing? Alice imagined him with her mother, now, driving to Southampton to board a cruise ship. A holiday of a lifetime, he had called it. Fair enough, a cruise around the Mediterranean was certainly the most exciting holiday her mother had ever had. She had taken Alice to Calais once for a day trip, but there had been a lot of saving up for that. Was that when Alice had decided to study French at university or was it the other way round? All Alice could remember was the cold ferry boat and the excitement of seeing France for the first time. They had taken a bus into Calais and eaten in a brasserie with no idea of how or what to order. Now, as Alice stacked the last plates into the dishwasher, she felt a moment of gladness. Yes, her mother deserved this new life. All Alice had to do now was sort out her own. Certainly, it should have been the mother's job to be arranging her daughter's wedding rather than the other way round but… well, who ever had a normal life? Certainly not Alice Shakespeare. Sometimes she worried that whenever an easy solution came along, that she automatically chose the other route. Witness today… she could so easily have still been with Simon. Yes, organised, straight-forward Simon Stafford. He would have been the ideal back-up partner, helping her all day and, right now, neatly stacking the dishwasher. As it was, as soon as their degrees at university were handed out, she had broken off with him. She knew she had hurt him, but something in her had known that to carry on would only have led to a bigger hurt in the future. They had studied and loved and had fun for nearly four years at Bristol uni… but now, now she wanted something different.

After a final Hoover of the ground floor, she looked around the small house that had been her home base for as long as she could remember. Coming back here in the university holidays had always been good… secure and easy. Her holiday work at the local language school was part of the pattern. Now, they had offered her a full-time job and, of course, her mother was hoping she would take it. Alice turned off the Hoover, carefully wound the cable around the handle and stacked it neatly away in the cupboard under the stairs. Once again, she thought to herself, now, she wanted something different, very different. Alice looked around with satisfaction at the tidied house, grabbed a copy of the Guardian that she hadn't had time to read and went up to her room.

An hour later she had read most of the paper and had started on the situations vacant columns. With her honours degree in French and History she knew she could do better than the local language school in Esher. She read carefully through the vacancies abroad. Even a language school abroad would be an improvement… and she already had her Tefl qualification… then her eyes strayed to a small private advertisement.

Private secretary required by single lady living on the Côte d'Azur. High level of literacy and excellent French required. Car driver and dog lover essential. Private cottage plus good wage offered. Please telephone 0033 4945682 . Serious applicants only.

Alice read it through again… and then again. Such a short advertisement but for some strange reason there seemed to be more in what it didn't say. Private secretary, that somehow sounded so old-fashioned… didn't everyone have a PA now or… Alice looked at the time on her mobile. Eight pm so it would be nine pm in France. Was it too late to call now? Alice yawned, it had been a very long day and she decided to leave it until tomorrow. She threw the paper onto her bedside table and reached for her book. Somehow, she just couldn't concentrate on reading and she snatched up the newspaper again and quickly rang the number.

'Grace Devine's residence.' The voice that answered was very English and distinctly frosty.

'Good evening, I hope I am not disturbing you too late. My name is Alice Shakespeare and I am calling in response to your advertisement in today's Guardian.'

'I'll pass you to Miss Devine, hold the line please.' There was a short silence and Alice waited nervously, quite unsure of how she would continue and beginning to regret calling.

'Hello, Grace Devine here, I understand you have read my advertisement?' This voice was very different, warm and smooth as honey.

Alice answered quickly, 'Yes, that's right. My name is Alice Shakespeare. I have just finished my degree at Bristol university and I am looking for new and interesting work in France. I was attracted to your advertisement.'

There was a small pause before the voice replied. 'I see, hmm, well why don't you hop on a plane and come to see me. It would be so much easier to talk face to face. I'll pass you back to my secretary, Monique, and she will take down your details. I insist you let me pay your airfare. Absolutely insist. I think we may get along very well… you have a good voice and an interesting name. I always go by my instincts. Hmm, yes, do come and meet me!'

The plane was an hour late departing and didn't make up much time on the journey. Alice tapped her foot nervously as she waited at the luggage carousel in Nice airport. Finally, her small suitcase emerged and she grabbed it quickly and made for the passport control queue. Once through, she followed the line of people through the security gate and as the doors swung open she immediately saw a man in chauffeur's uniform holding a large, white card with her name. Of course, this would be Gerard, the man she had been told would meet her. She was surprised to see the formal uniform and the rather sullen look on the man's face. She walked up to him and, in an attempt to appear confident and accustomed to being met by a chauffeur, she spoke a little too loudly,

'Bonjour, vous êtes Gerard? Je m'appelle Alice Shakespeare.'

The man looked mildly surprised and then bowed his head quickly instead of answering, took her bag from her and marched out of the airport doors. Alice followed close behind and nearly giggled aloud at the thought that Gerard was living up to the reputation of the French being rude to foreigners. Alice had studied six months in Bordeaux for her degree and had always thought everyone most polite and helpful. Perhaps she had now found the exception or the rule. In any case, this was no time for a study on national characteristics. Gerard was way ahead of her and holding open the rear door of a very large, very old silver-grey Bentley.

'*Quelle belle voiture*!' Alice said to the surly chauffeur, as she caught up with him.

'A Bentley R type, Miss Devine has had it since brand new and it's still in good nick.'

Alice looked at him in shock. Gerard was not French at all… in fact, she would guess, he was a Londoner, born well within the sound of Bow bells.

'I'm sorry, I thought you were French… that's why I spoke to you in French…' Alice stammered to an awkward silence, feeling she had made a very bad start. Gerard was still holding open the huge door, so she slipped quickly into the back of the car. The door closed with an expensively heavy thud and a moment later they were pulling slowly away into the traffic around Nice airport. Alice decided it would be more tactful to remain silent until Gerard spoke, so she devoted herself to taking in the scenery. The limousine swung through a series of roundabouts and every turn brought another surprise. Steep snow-capped mountains in the far distance, a palm-lined avenue, then suddenly a glimpse of the dark, blue sea, glinting in the bright winter sun... the Mediterranean. Her first glimpse of the Mediterranean. Alice slid across the wide leather seat and looked backwards as the car gathered speed and went between high buildings. Next she turned her attention to an inspection of the car interior. Never had she seen anything like it... the soft, cream leather, the deep pile carpet, the grey velvet roof... she was enclosed in old world luxury. Inset in the back of the seats in front of her were two walnut panels with gold clips. She felt tempted to open them and find out what was hidden behind but then a ray of sunshine filled the car. They had left the built up area and now she could see a wide marina with tall masts bobbing in the light breeze. Here, the sea was not just dark blue but streaked with brilliant turquoise. Small yachts scudded across the white ripples of surf and, far out at sea, a cruise ship shimmered on the hazy horizon. Alice thought for a moment that her mother was out there somewhere in the blue, on her honeymoon with the nice new Michael. She smiled at the thought and silently wished them a nice time, no, she corrected herself, she wished them an absolutely fantastic time.

The car was now speeding along in the fast lane, overtaking smaller cars and vans. Alice felt a rush of excitement as the foreign names sped past her, St Laurent du Var, Cagnes sur Mer... then Villeneuve Loubet and a sign to Antibes. Alice drew in her breath... Antibes, the fabulous Cap d'Antibes. The length of the famous Riviera stretched away from her in both directions. Mountains, the Alpes Maritimes, looming high on the right-hand side and the sea spread out on the left. The Côte d'Azur, a sparkling coast as blue as its name. ... she could hardly believe she was here. It had all happened so fast since that first phone call. A special courier delivery of return flight tickets followed by an email giving a formal invitation to attend an interview at the Villa La Vie en Rose. Alice had spent the next day on Google, finding out all she could about Grace Devine. There was a lot to find... a long page on Wikipedia was just a start.

Grace Devine, (b. 25th May, 1945) in Walthamstow, London. Her career began as a ballet dancer, but she was soon...

Alice was brought out of her daydream as she realised the car was slowing down and leaving the motorway. Gerard had remained silent and Alice resisted asking him about what lay ahead… or even if he was from the east end of London. The entire journey passed in silence.

"Giddy Fortune's furious wheel"

Alice sat sipping tea from a fine, white porcelain, teacup and nibbled at a thin slice of delicate sponge cake. She had a surreal Alice in Wonderland moment. Had the cake made her grow larger or was the tiny woman sitting in front of her real? Grace Devine was probably a little over five foot high but so thin and delicately boned that Alice felt enormous. She placed her teacup and saucer carefully on the low glass table in front of her and tried to hang on to reality. From the moment the Bentley had swept in through the large iron gates of La Villa La Vie en Rose she had surely been in a dream? But Grace was talking… for such a small woman she had a strong, resonant voice.

'Welcome, my dear, I hope your journey was not too exhausting?'

'Not at all, and I loved the run up from the airport in your wonderful car.'

'Ah, the old Bentley is Gerald's pride and joy. He has been cleaning it for years and years.' Grace gave a low, husky laugh and waved an elegant hand in the air. A very large diamond ring sparkled in the low beam of sunlight that crossed the room. Almost a spotlight… had Grace planned the whole scenario? The vast open plan room was … white, so white that it completed Alice's sensation of being in a dream. They sat facing each other on huge white leather sofas, the floor was of pale white marble, three walls were white and without paintings or any decoration - the fourth wall was completely glass and gave a wide panorama over a sloping olive grove and down to a fine blue line… which could only be the distant Mediterranean. To complete the scene, the final touch of elegance, were the two pale grey Weimaraner dogs sprawled at Grace's feet. They looked at Alice as Grace spoke,

'I don't want to press you as soon as you have arrived but can we talk a little about the work.'

'Why, of course, and I'm not at all tired.'

'Good, how wonderful it is to be young. I hardly remember it!' Grace gave another low-pitched laugh and there was a small pause where Alice felt she was expected to compliment Grace on her youthful appearance. Before she could think of the right thing to say, Grace was continuing,

'I'm so glad you haven't attempted some trite reply about how young I look. I do have a mirror. Anyway, I consider myself very fortunate to have once been beautiful… although, maybe if I had been a plain girl my life would have been different…' Grace looked sad for a moment and Alice decided it was time to speak.

'It's a strange thought, isn't it? How one's life can turn at any moment. The smallest event can change everything. That feeling of… I don't know… if…or if only… what might have been.'

'How philosophic for a young girl… but what can one do about fate? *Giddy Fortune's furious wheel.*'

'*That goddess blind…* Henry the Fifth!' Alice replied, laughing. But I prefer '*It is not in the stars to hold our destiny but in ourselves.*'

'Ah yes, Romeo and Juliet, of course. My, my, pretty and educated, why Alice if you want the job then it is yours!'

They both laughed and resumed drinking tea. From that moment it was decided between them. All that Shakespeare or Grace or Alice herself could say about destiny was in the air between them.

'So, do you want to know what the job involves?' Grace sat forward, clasping her hands together and looking more serious.

'Please, at the moment there is a dream-like quality to my whole day. Your secretary, Monique, said on the telephone that you are writing a book?'

'Hmm, did she? At the moment I am just pretending.' Again, Grace laughed, 'My agent, poor man, thinks it would be a good idea. He dreams of getting me back to work and squeezing his last percentage out of me. I keep telling him it's too silly and too late.'

'Also, the advertisement asked for a dog-lover. I want to say that I am definitely a dog-lover. I've never ever seen two more beautiful dogs than yours, what are their names?'

'How nice of you to ask. This is Cloud and this Smoke,' At the sound of their names both dogs lazily wagged their tails and then dropped their heads back on their paws and went back to sleep.'

'They seem very quiet, I always thought Weimaraner would be nervy dogs.'

'Not these two, they live a life of quiet luxury. The whole estate is securely fenced so they roam around all day, inspecting every inch of their own patch of Provence. They are beautiful, aren't they?'

'Oh yes, superb. As I said, I've never seen more beautiful dogs in my life.' Both dogs looked up again, straight at Alice and wagged their tails again. 'Oh my goodness, I think they understood me,' Alice laughed, 'and their eyes are amazing, such a strange, light blue.'

'I think that's why I chose them, dogs with blue eyes are an extraordinary phenomena. You will discover I have many prejudices and liking beautiful things around me is one of them. And, of course, their eyes are the same colour as mine… and, indeed, yours too.'

'I'm not sure if appreciating beauty is actually a prejudice,' Alice said thoughtfully, 'I would need to think about that. But I just love dogs, any dogs really. I could never have one when I was a child, but I used to look after neighbours' dogs… they certainly weren't all beautiful to look at, but each had a character that one grew to love.'

'More philosophy from one so young. Did you read philosophy at university?'

'No, no… I read French and History.'

'I can't imagine why anyone would want to read French whereas History… ah, how I envy you that. So how is it you can quote Shakespeare?'

'Oh, that was just A level at my grammar school. I always loved the bard, maybe I was drawn to it because of my name. Which reminds me, there was mention of reading aloud?'

'Ah yes, my eyes get so tired and it would be a great luxury to listen to a story now and then… maybe a drama… some poetry…' Grace waved her hand again vaguely around her head, 'and you do have a very good, very melodic voice. I interviewed a young woman last week, but it was hopeless… I hate to reveal yet another prejudice, to be regionally prejudiced… but a Welsh accent is only bearable on Richard Burton or Dylan Thomas.'

Alice laughed aloud at this and knew with absolute certainty that she was not dreaming but had found a dream job.

Grace then rang a small, white china bell and immediately the door opened at the end of the long room and a small woman hurried in to remove the tea tray.

'Ah, Minnie, I want you to meet Alice Shakespeare who will be joining us here at the Villa. Do you think you could show her over to the cottage?'

'Of course, follow me, Miss Shakespeare, Gerald has already taken your bag over there.'

'I'm afraid I called him Gerard as I thought he was French. I must have misheard over the phone.' Alice turned to Grace and then to Minnie and was surprised to see them both laughing at her.

'Oh dear, he won't have liked that.' Grace was actually giggling behind her hand, 'As you may have guessed we are a small colony of Londoners hiding in this glorious land that is Provence. Minnie and Gerald are both from Stratford, not the one upon the Avon, and many years ago I was born in Walthamstow. We share a dislike of the French language, a tolerance of the French themselves and completely adore their country. Unreasonable, I know, but I feel I have worked for the right to live where I wish. I bought this villa at the height of my career and have never wanted to leave.'

'I can certainly understand that,' Alice said, looking around at the subdued opulence of the large room, 'it's a stunning building and with such a magnificent view.'

'Indeed, now run along and see what you think of the little cottage. I need to rest now and we can meet again for dinner at eight?'

Alice nodded quickly in agreement and then followed Minnie. First they went into the kitchen, a large and functional modern room with an impressive white, bleached oak dresser stacked with white porcelain plates and tureens. Before Alice could take in more, Minnie was hurrying out of the back door.

'Grace calls it a cottage,' she said, looking back over her shoulder to see if Alice was keeping up with her. 'But it's really quite large and very comfortable. I'm sure you'll like it and then it does have a nice veranda straight on to the pool. Young ones like you enjoy a swim. I've never fancied it myself.'

Alice was distracted by the splendid sunset that was dramatically taking place behind the olive grove. Now, there was Minnie telling her that she could use the pool. It suddenly seemed a very long way from her semi-detached home in Esher.

'he looks like an angel but he is a bad boy'

A few minutes before eight o'clock Alice walked back up to the Villa la Vie en Rose. It was dark, now, but the moon shone high in the sky and touched the olive trees with silver. The stars looked nearer than she had ever seen them before. She took in a deep breath of the fresh, cold air and pulled her cardigan closer around her. The cottage which had been allotted to her was warmly heated and the night was much colder than she had realised. Alice had spent the last few hours examining every detail of the cottage. Minnie was right when she had said it was quite large. It was a scaled down version of the large villa… modernistic in every way. An open plan living area with a galley kitchen divided by an island unit. All white. The separate bedroom was roomy and had a large fitted wardrobe that Alice could never imagine filling. Again, all white. There was definitely a calm peace in the whiteness, as in a fall of new snow. Alice thought about the bright mix of colours of her own room in Esher and smiled to herself. She had spent the last half hour texting back and forth with her mother, but it was impossible to even begin to describe Grace Devine, the villa and all that had happened since she had landed in Nice. Alice looked up to the Villa, the long glass wall now radiated light over the sloping olive grove. It was a stage set, as bright and fascinating as the moment when the curtains first raised. Alice hurried up the path, impatient now to enter the next scene.

She tapped on the back door to the kitchen and waited a moment before opening it and peering in. Minnie was working at the large, scrubbed wood table, slicing tomatoes. She looked up and gave a quick smile.

'There you are, dearie, right on time. That will please our Grace, she hates to wait for anything. You go on through and I'll just finish this salad.'

Alice walked through the kitchen, breathing in the smell of fresh herbs and buttery garlic, realising that she was very, very hungry. Again she tapped on the next door but this time waited. She could hear music playing and voices, then Grace's distinctive tone,

'Come in, come in… are there you are, Alice. How good of you to be so punctual.'

Alice felt a moment of shyness or was it stage fright? She walked into the centre of the room and then over to a log fire that was burning brightly. Grace was seated on a white, leather recliner, holding a glass of white wine in her elegant and diamond-weighted hand. Gerald was standing beside the fire and gazing into it but turned to look at Alice as she drew near. The other side of the fire stood a young man. Alice drew in her breath at this unexpected and well, definite pleasure.

'Let me introduce you, Alice, you have already met Gerald, lucky enough to be married to my Minnie and this is Jason, their pseudo nephew. Alice smiled and nodded, unsure whether she should shake hands in the French manner or even if she dared make contact with the young man called Jason. He stood with his back to the fire, the flickering light from the flames silhouetting every inch of his large, muscular frame… heroic as the Greek god of his name. Alice seemed rooted to the spot and, as though she had read her thoughts, Grace continued, laughing as she spoke, 'Don't go too near Jason, he looks like an angel, but he is quite a bad boy.' They all laughed and then Gerald said,

'Not all bad,' his voice was friendly now and to Alice's surprise he turned to her with a crooked grin, 'You'll see that our Jason is really a good lad. He's made a fine job of strimming around the olive trees today… it's hard work on the slopes and I'm glad of the help.' He patted Jason on the back and then began to poke the fire. Jason remained silent and looked down at his feet in embarrassment.

'Such a wonderful, ancient olive grove… it must be a pleasure to work there on a day like today.' Alice spoke directly to Jason, but he made no reply. Grace spoke, filling the awkward silence with the resonance of her voice.

'Hmm, the wonderful olive grove… do you know Alice, we have just over two hundred trees and produce enough olive oil for Minnie to use all year round. Of course, by the time I have paid these two villains to trim around and then a team of olive pickers… and the pressing…well, it has to be the most expensive extra virgin oil in the world… but what can I say, it's our oil and we love it. And, of course, Minnie creates such wonders in the kitchen. Now, Jason, you could at least pour Alice a drink. Would white wine be acceptable, Alice?' She raised her own glass in the air as she spoke and Alice suddenly wondered if she had found the snag in this new, dream-white world. Was Grace an alcoholic? Before she could think any further or begin to worry, Grace was speaking again,

'Don't worry, dear girl, I'm not an old lush!' Once more it was as though Grace had read Alice's thoughts, 'In my long career I have seen too many women take that route, not to mention my own dear mother. No, definitely not to mention her! I like a glass of wine as an aperitif and another glass with my food. For goodness sakes, Jason, do pour the girl a glass.'

Alice watched as Jason shuffled his feet and looked even more embarrassed. His hair was so blonde, maybe bleached by the sun, and his skin, although tanned, was so fair that it was easy to see his cheeks had reddened. Alice wondered how old he was, possibly her age but maybe younger? Why had Grace called him a bad boy and why was she teasing him? Alice felt a moment of sympathy for Jason and the next moment thought how dangerous that could be. Fortunately, before she could take the idea too far in her head, Minnie opened the door from the kitchen and called out,

'Come and get it then!'

Gerald and Jason hurried over to the kitchen and Alice followed. Were they to eat in the kitchen? Then she was given a large, heavy tray to carry, loaded with white china and cutlery and she followed Gerald and Jason, both carrying large trays of food. They went through a door that Alice hadn't noticed before. To her surprise the next room was a long dining room, lit entirely by tall white candles. Another length of glass wall and, as to be expected, a table covered with an immaculate, white table cloth. As though by magic, Grace was already sitting at the head of the table, perfectly lit by the candles on each side of her place-setting. Alice smiled to herself as she helped to lay the table and spread out the large dishes of food. Grace Devine didn't need to make an entrance, it seemed she was always centre stage.

5   'to fly off into the wild blue yonder'

In the week that followed her interview at the Villa la Vie en Rose, Alice found out, for the first time in her life, how easily money could make everything happen. Accustomed to a life of scraping and saving, suddenly she had entered a world of the rich and, if not powerful, then certainly influential. Working silently in the background, Grace's secretary, Monique, had smoothly arranged everything. Alice had flown back to England and been given a week to pack and sort out her own life. She was surprised to find there was surprisingly little to do. The invisible Monique had arranged medical care and insurance, a one-way flight on Sunday, 12th January… and all the small details connected to moving from England to France. The days passed quickly and yet somehow slower than she had ever known a week to pass. She was either in a panic of disorder, carting dustbin bags of clothes and books to charity shops or lying on her bed wondering if Sunday would ever come. Alice was looking, for the hundredth time, at her one-way ticket and felt a rush of excitement. This was the symbol of everything that was happening. Then, there were all the phone calls with her mother. The thousand and one questions that she had asked and the very few that Alice could reasonably answer.

'Are you sure, Alice? Have you thought about what you're doing?' Her mother's voice was high and tense, the phone connection poor and intermittent.

Alice turned down the music she had been playing on her old DVD player. 'Don't worry, Mum. Grace seems to be a very nice woman and, anyway, if I don't like it then I'll just come back. We've agreed a month's trial on both sides. And it's only France, not the other side of the world.'

There was an audible deep sigh on the other end of the line and Alice could hear her new step-father, Michael's, voice in the background.

'Michael says why don't you wait until we get back and then we can all talk it over.'

Alice grimaced and thought to herself that would be the most unlikely thing to happen. Nice as Michael was, and however pleased she was for her mother, there was no way she was going to discuss her future with him. She felt an irrational surge of anger, then she quickly suppressed it and smiled… Doctor Mike was only trying to be nice.

'No, I'm off on Sunday. I have the ticket now.' Alice waved the ticket above her head and danced madly around the room to the music still playing, 'Don't worry Mum, I am behaving very sensibly about all this.'

'Well, there's nothing we can do about it if you're determined to fly off into the wild blue yonder.'

Alice nodded and continued dancing, 'I'll be fine, I'll leave all the details of the Villa la Vie en Rose and a copy of my contract for you to see when you get back. I've told the Morrisons next door and they're going to keep an eye on the old homestead… anyway, you'll be back next week.' Alice turned the music up a notch and danced to her own image in the long mirror on her wardrobe. Her cheeks were pink, her ash blonde hair flying wildly… she was happier and more excited than she had been for a very long time.

And then, it was suddenly Sunday. Alice sat in the departure lounge at Gatwick and tried to think of all the things she might have forgotten to pack. Well, it was all too impossibly late now, she sighed and tried to read the magazine she had bought for the journey. She stared unseeingly for a while at the front cover. A close-up of a beautiful, young woman, photo-shopped to perfection, her hair blowing in the wind. Then, Alice read the caption and suddenly her attention was riveted to the page.

'Mara Browning, latest celebrity to buy property in Provence - read more on page 5.'

Alice quickly opened the magazine and began to read the article about the list of celebrities already living on the Côte d'Azur, Johnny Depp, Vanessa Paradis, the Beckhams, Angelina Jolie, John Malkovich… the list went on and on. Then, half way down the page there was a list of iconic stars of the 50's and 60s, Brigitte Bardot, Grace Kelly and then… Grace Devine… a short sentence about the enigmatic star of the past who left the screen and retired into hiding in the hills behind Cannes.'

Alice read the line twice and then realised it was time to board the plane. Half an hour later she was once again winging her way toward the South of France.

And, once again, Gerald was there to meet her. No named card this time and only a brief nod of recognition as he took Alice's large suitcase from her and made his way to the exit. Alice smiled, already feeling a small familiarity with her new life. Outside on the tarmac the air was colder than she had expected and she clutched her scarf as a strong gust of wind came at them from the west.

'Bloomin' Mistral!' Gerald had spoken as he opened the back door of the Bentley. Alice hesitated for a moment, wondering if she could suggest that she sat in the front.

'Jump in, ducks, the old Mistral chills you to the bone.' Gerald stamped his feet and rubbed his hands together, hunching his shoulders against the wind. Alice jumped in quickly, 'Thanks, Gerald, it certainly is cold but not as bad as London. And the sky is such a deep blue, even though it's winter.'

Gerald closed the door and walked round to the driver's seat. 'Don't talk to me about London, you'd never catch me back in the old Smoke. Nah, you'll soon find out…this is the place to live.'

'I am excited, I can't wait to find out what it's like to live here. Have you been here long?' Alice leaned forward as she replied, pleased that Gerald had begun to talk to her.

'Long enough, now then, you sit back and belt up, enough chat… I'm driving now.'

So that was that. Alice caught a glimpse of her own reflection in the driving mirror and smiled. There would be plenty of opportunities ahead to find out more about Gerald and his wife, Minnie… not to mention Jason, their interesting but silent nephew. Interesting, definitely interesting to the point of intriguing and… what was the other adjective she was searching for? Desirable? And what was his secret past… or was he too young to have much of a past? Why had Grace felt it necessary to tease him and call him a bad boy? The unanswered questions flew through Alice's mind and suddenly she realised they were already approaching the gates to the Villa. As before, the large wrought iron gates swung open automatically and Gerald drove slowly up the steep sloping gravelled drive, winding between the olive trees. As they rounded the final bend, the two Weimaraner dogs bounded into sight and ran beside the car. Alice sighed in delight. The red sun was dropping into the horizon of the sea, casting a golden light over the silver, grey olive trees and glinting across the long glass walls of the Villa. Was there anywhere more beautiful to find a job…and to be actually working for a celebrity, even of a past decade, named in her favourite magazine? This question, at least, she knew the answer to and she almost clapped her hands in excitement as the car drew to a smooth halt. She had definitely arrived into what her mother had called the wild blue yonder.

'a ballet school in Bow'

Alice had already unpacked her large suitcase and begun to place her few books and belongings around the cottage. Her clothes only filled a quarter of the long wardrobe. Maybe, on the salary that had been given to her, she would soon be able to do something about that. Alice sat on the bed, a king-size bed that would have filled her entire room at home, and read again the neatly printed job brief that had been left for her.

Monday:	Grace/yoga-meditation 10-11 am
	Grace/Alice 14.30-17.00
Tuesday:	Grace/massage 10-11am
	Grace/Alice 14.30-17.00
Wednesday:	Grace/manicurist-astrologer 10-11am
	Grace/Alice 14.30-17.00
Thursday:	Grace/Monique 10-11am
	Grace/Alice 14.30-17.00
Friday:	Grace/hairdresser 10-12 noon
	Grace/Alice 14.30-17.00
Saturday:	various
Sunday:	once a month lunch party/various
Daily:	lunch 12.30 am/dinner 19.00
	please give notice one day prior if you are not attending lunch or dinner, including Saturday and Sunday

Alice stared at the simple timetable, wondering if she really was only to work with Grace for two and a half hours a day, and then only weekdays. Her salary was more than twice any language school would have given her for a full-time week. Then there was the free accommodation. Alice looked round the spacious bedroom and into the open-plan living room and kitchen. The whole affair was too good to be true… and what was it said about that? She shrugged and smiled to herself as she thought how her mother and Michael would be looking for hidden traps. Maybe she was being naive, but, for now, she would just enjoy the luck and the luxury. She flicked on her iPad and checked her emails, mostly junk and a few from friends… Esher, Bristol university… all seemed to belong to a different world. She quickly answered a few but felt too impatient to spend the time needed to give a complete update on her new life. She looked out of the window and saw the lighted path to the Villa, twinkling an invitation to dinner. It was nearly time to go. She checked in the mirror and was reasonably pleased with the new pale, grey linen dress that she had bought in Kingston. She had chosen it to blend with the cool, sophistication of Grace's pure white surroundings. Her hair was smooth and she wore a minimum of make-up... all external effects showed her to be a calm efficient woman... it was such a shame that inside she felt like a scared teenager. How on earth had she thought she could be a secretary? She hardly knew what it meant... could it involve old-fashioned shorthand and dictation or some-such mystery? Well, it was too late to worry about it now and with a final twirl in front of the mirror she waved herself farewell and ran up the path to the lighted villa.

The dogs greeted her as soon as she reached the terrace. They danced around her, giving little hops of delight but obviously well-trained not to jump up.

'Good dogs, my, aren't you so beautiful. Now, let me remember... yes, you're Smoke and you're Cloud.' Alice leant over the dogs and stroked their silky smooth heads. She was so involved with them that she jumped when a voice behind her spoke quietly,

'How did you know which was which, like, just like that?'

Alice turned and saw Jason standing under the lantern that hung over the back door.

'Hi Jason, you made me jump. How are you? Oh, the dogs... well, I remembered that Smoke had a narrower forehead, more pointy-headed than Cloud.'

'Wow, impressive... took me a while to tell one from the other. They both have the same wide leather collars and no name tags... I asked Grace is one could have a different colour collar but she didn't go for it. Smoke's the wild one though... you can tell when they're running. She's like a greyhound out of a trap!'

Before Alice could reply, Jason had turned on his heel and opened the kitchen door for her. Not so fast that Alice didn't have time to notice his very attractive rear view. She went past him and into the kitchen and found Minnie, once again, preparing food. Alice expected Jason to follow her but when she turned round he seemed to have disappeared.

'Ah, there you are dearie, punctual again.' Minnie looked up with a welcoming smile, 'That's what I like. I always think if I can cook then it's only right that everyone else can sit down on time.'

'That dinner we had last week was fantastic. You're a great cook… I wish I could cook even half as well.'

'Oh, I wouldn't worry about that yet. Plenty of time ahead of you, if you want to cook. Anyway, it's just common sense and timing. I like to keep it simple.'

That's the trick, isn't it… keeping it simple is really so very difficult.'

Minnie laughed, 'Get on with you, now hop it while I finish off grilling this aubergine. You go and chat with Grace and I'll be through in a minute.'

'Well, I hope you'll let me help you one evening.'

'Maybe, we'll see. But I'm set in my ways. Off you go now.'

Alice left the kitchen feeling like a troublesome child who had been sent off to play. She thought about it for a moment and then decided that she rather liked it

Dinner was taken, as before, in the long candlelit dining room. Grace sat at the head of the table, Jason, who had reappeared, was on her right and Gerald on her left. Alice was seated next to Jason, Minnie next to her husband, Gerald. The food was as wonderful as before but the conversation faltered and flagged. They were a strange combination of dinner guests. Alice complimented Minnie on the food and then was searching for a new subject to open when Grace spoke,

'It is very good to have you back with us, Alice. Don't feel you always have to eat with us, I know we can be very boring but the food is so very, very good. One could almost eat in silence as though at church.'

'How true,' Alice replied, 'This aubergine is like nothing I have ever tasted before… it is divine!'

'Now, there's a word!' Grace laughed her deep, vibrant laugh, 'Divine… whenever I hear that word it makes me laugh. Do you know, Alice, my dear mother changed my name to Devine but she was so ignorant she mis-spelt it! So, at the tender age of twelve I changed from Grace Watts to Grace Devine.'

'Really? That must have been so strange and confusing… and only twelve years old. So did she intend you to go on the stage?'

'Oh my goodness, didn't she just! I was enrolled at eight years old to a ballet school in Bow. That was the start… oh, how my little legs used to ache after hours practicing at the bar. Maybe we really will write my life story together, Alice… little by little. But right now, I can see that Minnie is ready to serve the dessert. What are you going to treat us to tonight, Minnie?'

Minnie began to clear the dishes and looked up fondly at Grace. 'Your favourite tonight, Grace, and to celebrate the arrival of Alice… *tarte tatin à la di da* Minnie!'

They all laughed and Alice looked quickly at Jason who had remained silent all through the meal and even now was not joining in the laughter. What was his problem and why did he have to be so very cute? Alice was very conscious of his large, muscular body next to her. He sat straight and square, unbending and totally removed from the conversation. Alice stood up and helped Minnie load the tray, then she turned to face Jason,

'Will you carry the tray to the kitchen, Jason, it's so heavy.'

Jason jumped as though he had been shot and silently picked up the tray and carried it into the kitchen. Alice caught Minnie and Gerald exchanging amused glances and then she saw that Grace was trying not to laugh. Unabashed, Alice picked up the rest of the plates and went through to the kitchen. Jason was still holding the tray as though uncertain where to place it. Alice sighed, as she thought that maybe looks weren't everything.

'Thanks, Jason, can you put it on the table. Now I'm here, I thought I'd like to help Minnie as much as possible… but of course, you help your Uncle Gerald all day, don't you?'

'Yeh, I don't mind though.' Jason carefully laid the tray on the table and stood straight in front of Alice and added, 'I'm glad you like the dogs.' He then almost pushed past her and went back into the dining room. Alice stood trying to work out several things at once. Why was Jason so reluctant to communicate, what was it in his past and whatever did the dogs have to do with anything?

Right now though, Minnie's *tarte tatin* awaited.

7   *'Like Alice down the rabbit hole…'*

The next morning, Monday morning, Alice woke early with the sun streaming across the room from a gap in the blinds. She rubbed her eyes and blinked, taking a moment to believe where she was. This was to be a Monday unlike any other in her life so far. She stretched and went over to the long wall of glass that ran the length of the bedroom. She peered out and realised she was looking at a swimming pool. Only a narrow terrace divided her room from the water. Amazing, turquoise-bright water. Suddenly there was a splash and, like a Hockney canvas, the drops of water sparkled in the sunshine. Jason was swimming, moving through the water, like a dolphin. Alice watched through the slit in the blind, admiring his style and speed. Then, feeling like a furtive voyeur, she turned away quickly and went into the shower. As the hot water ran over her she tried to dismiss the disturbing feeling that Jason evoked in her. It was something like desire but tempered with mystery. As she shampooed her long, blonde hair she decided to dismiss him from her thoughts altogether. This was her first day at her new job and she was not to be distracted. Then, there was a tap at the door. She quickly wrapped herself in her bath robe and ran to open it, her heart thumping.

'Good morning!' There stood Gerald. Alice took in a deep breath, trying to adjust to the reality… Gerald and not the heroically handsome Jason. Maybe it was just as well.

'Hi, Gerald, I slept so well, I am only just up.'

'Sorry to get you to the door, I didn't think. I'm always up with the lark. Anyway, it was just to leave you the car keys… I forgot last night and Grace will give me a good ticking off if you don't have them for this morning. There's a Mini, all insured and ready for you to use, it's parked now round the back of the kitchen… don't forget to drive on the right, my girl!'

Alice took the keys that Gerald was holding out to her and he turned on his heel and, with a quick backward wave, he hurried off down the olive grove.

Alice looked at the keys and then called out her thanks. Gerald waved his hand again in the air and carried on his way.

So, Monday had begun with a bang… maybe there had only been a vision of the perfect Jason but instead she held the magic gift of the silver keys to explore Provence. Alice felt a rush of excitement at the thought of driving to all the places she had seen signposted on the drive up from the airport. She hurriedly dressed and ran outside, keen to find the car. The air hit her like a cold blast, even though the sun was bright and the wind had completely dropped. She ran back for her anorak and pulled a hat over her wet hair. Outside her front door again she was greeted by the dogs. Exhilarated by the fresh air, she ran toward the villa with the dogs loping along beside her. She followed the path round to the back of the kitchen and there was a white-hooded Mini convertible, parked and waiting. Alice looked at the keys and then at the dogs. 'Do you believe my luck?' The dogs looked up at her, their blue eyes bright and their long tails-wagging enthusiastically. 'I can't take you out just like that…' Alice continued, trying to resist their obvious intention to jump in the car. 'I don't even know if you're allowed out and…' The dogs' tail-wagging now developed into wriggling with excitement. Hesitating and unsure what to do next, Alice was relieved to hear the kitchen door open and she turned to see Minnie standing there.

'Good morning, Alice, are those dogs troubling you?'

'Oh no, not at all, it's just they seemed to want to come out with me… Gerald has given me the keys to the Mini and I was so excited I wanted to go for a short spin.'

'Course you do, and why not? Have you had your breakfast?'

'Er no, I forgot.' Alice replied, feeling once again rather childish.

'I've some coffee in the pot and some croissants… come and have a bite with me. Get out of the cold.'

Alice looked at the Mini and then at the dogs and hesitated.

'The car and the dogs will still be there if you have a bit of breakfast first. You're Alice in Wonderland, aren't you…not Cinderella with a pumpkin?'

Alice laughed and went into the kitchen with Minnie. The heat hit her and she pulled off her anorak and hat.

'Oh my, your hair's all wet, too. What shall we do with you? Sit by the Aga and get warm. Minnie pulled a chair over and Alice obediently sat down. Somehow, her attempt at being a cool secretary had been singularly unsuccessful so far. But how cosy it was and how good the coffee and croissants smelled.

'Did you see our Jason swimming this morning, now, nothing beats that in my opinion. Middle of winter and swimming outdoors, I don't know what next.'

'Yes, I did see him swimming…' Alice hesitated, 'I don't know how he could do it… it's a beautiful day but really cold.'

'Yes, cold as charity out there. The olive tree pruning starts today. You'll see a few men and women in the olive grove. I'd keep your door locked if I were you… they're a rough lot.'

'Really! I'll go down and lock it when I've finished my second croissant. You really spoil me, Minnie. I hadn't realised how hungry I was… although I don't know how I can be after that amazing dinner last night.'

'You're very welcome, ducks. That's my job, cooking and bit of spoiling now and then. I've put a few basics in the cottage kitchen but you're always welcome here.'

'Thanks, Minnie, I feel like I've fallen into some dream world.'

'Like Alice down the rabbit hole!' Minnie laughed.

'Cinderella in Wonderland, that's me!' Alice laughed, 'Thanks for breakfast, Minnie, can I help wash up or anything? I always help my Mum at home.'

'Goodness me, no… we all have our own jobs at the Villa. You'll soon find out how it all goes here… don't worry. Now, are you going for that spin in the Mini or not? And don't forget to lock your cottage door as you go past. Better leave the dogs here with me the first time you go out.'

Alice looked down at the dogs who were now sprawled out and fast asleep by the Aga. 'Yes, I will, they look happy now, anyway.'

'Yes, I'll keep them in while the men are pruning the olives. Never know the gates might be left open or something. Yes, leave them with me.'

'Anyway, I'll have to concentrate on driving on the right side of the road.'

'Wrong side of the road, if you ask me… can't think why they thought that up. Still,' Minnie picked up a large cauliflower as she spoke and looked at it admiringly, ' the Frenchies do know what's what when it comes to food.'

'So do you, Minnie. Right, I'm going to brave the cold out there and get going. Is there anything you want if I do get to a village?'

'No, it's not market day, today. Gerald and I go in once a week on a Friday, just like two old country locals, we are. Now, get on with you.'

Alice pulled on her anorak and hat and went out to the car, smiling to herself as she wondered whether Gerald and Minnie went to market in the Bentley and if so, whether they were quite like the other locals.

Alice backed carefully out of the kitchen courtyard and slowly down the drive to her own cottage. She parked and made sure the handbrake was secure, then got out and quickly locked the door. She carried on down the drive, getting used to changing gear with her right hand, and soon saw Gerald and Jason in the middle of a group of men with ladders. Again she pulled to a halt and got out. Gerald waved to her and she went across the rough, stony land to meet him.

'Are you off out then?' Gerald asked as soon as she drew near.

'Yes, I thought I'd try and get my bearings and have a test drive. Is there anything you want?'

'No, we're fine… got a long day ahead with the pruning but everyone has turned up at least.' He looked over his shoulder at the group of men waiting. 'Have you locked your door?'

'Yes, Minnie told me to. I hadn't thought about it.'

'Usually we don't bother but…well, you never know with these seasonal gangs. Better safe than sorry.'

'Oh, and what about the gates?'

'Just use the buzzer on your key ring. They swing open quickly enough and the dogs always follow the car up the drive when you come in. If you're going out they'll follow you right up to the gates and then stop and go back to the villa. Minnie will be keeping them inside today. They're good as gold anyway.'

'Fine, thanks, Gerald. See you at lunch time?'

'Jason and me, we'll be eating out here with the chaps today. Minnie makes us a soup and all sorts. Grace will love it if you're back for lunch though.'

'Bye then.'

Alice walked back to the car and then turned to wave to Jason, who was standing apart from the group of men. He didn't wave back and she thought he looked as though he'd rather be going out than pruning trees. He stared after her and then turned and began to start clipping the nearest tree. Beautifully desirable he might be but chatty-friendly…no, not at all.

Finally, she was outside the gates and driving slowly in the direction of Mougins. The car was easy to drive and she began to relax and enjoy the moment. The heater was warming up and the sky was its usual blue. She sighed with pleasure and, still concentrating hard on the winding road ahead, she took in quick glimpses of the scenery rolling past. The legendary ochre-red earth of Provence, bright in the winter sunshine, stretched away to the thin blue line of the sea on the horizon. Rigid lines of vines, pruned to their winter bareness on one side and pale chalky grey olive groves fell steeply away downhill on the left. Checking her rear view window she was shocked to see a backdrop of snow-capped mountains. This was nothing like driving her mother's old Fiesta through the busy roads of Esher. The white leather seats of the Mini, the small walnut steering wheel… all touches of a disturbing non-reality. She reached out for the radio and turned it on. The small car was suddenly filled with French voices arguing. Alice tried to make out what they were discussing, but she could only understand that it was an intellectual argument about poetry. She switched channels and now pop music took over, French pop music. So, Alice thought to herself, reality check, I am in France, the South of France, and approaching, now entering the mediaeval, hill-top village of Mougins.

    Sitting inside a small café, sipping a freshly squeezed orange juice, Alice decided that reality could definitely be very enjoyable. She had managed to have a conversation with the small, dark-haired woman serving at the bar, relieved to find that four years and her honours degree in French had not been a complete waste of time. They talked briefly about the cold weather and then the woman had asked if she was working at the Villa La Vie en Rose. Alice was surprised at the question and then quickly realised that the white Mini must be well known in the village.

    Oui, je travaille pour Madame Devine.'

    '*Ah, Madame Grace, elle est magnifique, n'est ce pas? Une vraie vedette,* a star!'

    Then another customer had come into the bar and the woman had ended the conversation and turned back to the coffee machine.

Alice bought a Marie Claire magazine from a rack at the side of the café and now sat flicking through it. Reading French was certainly easier than speaking, and she skimmed quickly through the fashion pages and gossip, still thinking of her conversation with the bartender. It was true, Grace Devine was a star. *Une vraie vedette.* Alice looked back at the bar as she would like to have continued talking, but the woman was deep in conversation with the new customer. Alice watched as they chatted, obviously friends and this short friendly break was part of their daily life. And now here she was, Alice Shakespeare, about to enter the scene. Until this moment the English world of Grace Devine had totally enclosed her. A world of great luxury and isolated peace, which Alice appreciated, but now she determined to spend her time off in the real world. She was conscious of time slipping by and the afternoon ahead. Minnie expected her for lunch at one and then… Alice took a deep breath as she thought of it… then her first afternoon of work with Grace. After all, she must remember that she was still on a month's trial. Well, there was no point sitting around worrying about something that she could do nothing about. She paid for her drink and went out into the village square. The Mini was parked, conspicuously white and immaculate, amongst the various battered Citroëns and Peugeots. Alice walked across the square to the stone fountain. Water spluttered into a round stone trough and Alice dipped her fingers into the icy water, imagining the heat of the summer to come. She followed the narrow cobbled streets that spiralled around the heart of the village. The winter quiet of the art galleries spoke of a busy summer tourist season ahead. Aware that she had lost all sense of direction, Alice turned around and hurried to find her way back to the square. After several false turns she finally found her way back to the parked Mini. Anxious now that she would be late for lunch, she drove directly back to the villa.

8   'Everyone has a story.'

'Now, we have time to talk.' Grace settled back on a white leather chaise longue and looked at Alice over the rim of her small white porcelain coffee cup. Cloud and Smoke were spread out at her feet, their elegant bodies outlined against the white marble floor. A large log smouldered in the fireplace… the stage was set. 'First,' Grace continued, 'I shall take a little time to talk about myself… always my favourite subject, and then you can tell me about yourself.'

Alice smiled and moved nervously on the large white sofa.
'I'm afraid there's nothing very interesting in my life… not much to tell.'

'Rubbish!' Grace replied abruptly, 'Everyone has a story. Anyway, to begin, I expect you have been wondering about your duties here.'

'Yes, I certainly have… I hope I can help in any way possible.'

'Hmm, well I'm sure you can. As I told you before, my agent wants me to write my life story. In fact, it's not quite as simple as that,' Grace sighed and sipped the last drop of her coffee and then held out her cup and saucer. Alice jumped up from the sofa and took it from her and placed it on the low glass table. Obviously, Grace was accustomed to her every action being anticipated.   'Thank you, dear, how sweet of you..,
'Grace smiled graciously and continued, 'as I was saying, not just my life story but a screenplay. There is some wild plan in the air to make my life into a movie. What do you think of that?'

The last few words were suddenly delivered forcefully and directly at Alice.

'How interesting,' Alice replied, playing for time as she tried to decide on a diplomatic answer, 'Obviously it would be an intriguing project… but how do you feel about it'

'Hmm, I thought you were a clever one when I first set eyes on you. You have answered my question very neatly with another. Well, the truth is, strictly between you and me, I am rather flattered and… yes, intrigued is a good word. On the other hand, I am not sure I can be bothered with all the work it would involve.' Grace's rich voice trailed off into silence and Alice hastened to reply,

'Would you be required to have a great deal of input?' She asked the question but wondered to herself if there was anything else in Grace's daily life that needed her attention… apart from the daily appointments for treatments. 'I mean, would it be interesting or a boring commitment?' Alice sat forward and waited for Grace to reply.

'Exactly, that's exactly it. I am sure you are thinking that I have nothing more in my life but, do you know,' Grace sat up straight for a moment, 'I worked hard from the age of twelve and now I think I deserve to be idle, bone idle if I want.'

'Absolutely, I am sure you are right. I suppose the question is whether you are truly happy doing nothing. I mean, after a lifetime of hard, continuous work, is it easy to be idle?'

Grace gave one of her long, low laughs, 'My dear girl, I think we shall get on very well indeed… you have completely caught me out. It's true that lolling around in paradise can be excruciatingly boring!'

Alice laughed, 'My mother always told me that if I couldn't make up my mind about something then I should try a compromise for a while until I made a decision.'

'Hmm, how lucky you are to have such a clever mother. My own mother would probably have told me to stop thinking about myself all the time.'

'It does seem as though you do have an interesting life story to tell… you know, you started to tell me about your ballet school. I would be happy, more than happy, to just take some notes.'

'Hmm, I see what you mean. Maybe that would be the sort of compromise your mother would suggest. My wretchedly greedy agent has a contract ready to sign for a full-length feature film… a screenplay writer in the wings ready to go… but what we could do… maybe, is to keep him on the hook and prepare some sort of… what would you call it… autobiographical notes?'

'That sounds possible. It would take a while to get your memories into some sort of timeline, keeping it simple at first, then filling in the detail later… maybe… I mean, of course, it's completely up to you.' Alice finished speaking and looked into the fire, waiting for Grace to reply.

'Hmm, I like your idea. Let's work on that tomorrow. But now, what about yourself?'

'Me… oh, not much to tell really. My Mum's a single Mum, brought me up all on her own… neither of us minded much about that… on the whole we had a great time. Not much spare cash around but always plenty of fun. She worked so hard to give me everything… I had it all… ballet, riding, tennis, piano… and she was very good at doing museums and art galleries and stuff. I had a lovely childhood. I enjoyed school and managed to get to uni…well, you know that… and, now, here I am in my very first job and feeling very fortunate.'

'Goodness, what it is to be so young that your life can be encapsulated in one paragraph! Even so, it could make a film … that's the wonder of cinema. Anyway, what about romance, you're an exceptionally beautiful young woman so there must be a man hanging around?'

Alice found herself blushing under Grace's amused glance. 'Well, there was… at uni I had a relationship with a guy called Simon Stafford from the Geology department… but I ended it when I left Bristol.'

'Hmm, Geology… rocks and things… ah well, he will probably still be around if you change your mind. Rocks do, in my vast experience… stay solidly around…whether one wants them to or not.'

Alice laughed but before she could answer, Grace continued, 'So, you will have seen Monique's printed job brief, you have some idea of the agenda. Are you happy with it?'

'Oh, absolutely, yes, but I wondered if I will be taking over Monique's work?'

Grace laughed, 'Goodness me, no way! Monique, in a sense, doesn't exist. It is just an agency that screens all my phone calls and arranges boring things that have to be managed. The first girl I employed from there happened to be called Monique and it sort of stuck. Of course, the agency has shift workers and I have no idea who they are really. They have a very high reputation in Cannes and in the film world, and they are very discreet. No, the work we will do together will be much more fun. Well, I hope so anyway. You have every morning and weekend free… what do you intend to do with all that time?' The question was fired quickly and directly and before Alice could think, she found herself replying,

'I'm writing a book.' As soon as she said it she regretted it. It was something she had never told anyone, not even her mother and she dreaded having to talk about it more.

'Hmm, what a good idea. Absolutely ideal. Good for you! Now the time has passed most pleasantly and I think most productively so I'll say *au revoir* to you, dear girl. Our time is up for today and you have left me with plenty to think about. Off you go now.'

Alice stood up hastily, relieved at not being questioned about her own book writing and surprised that the time had passed so quickly. She picked up Grace's empty coffee cup and went toward the kitchen door. The dogs followed her and she turned to ask Grace one last question but, to her surprise, she saw that Grace was fast asleep.

She went quietly into the kitchen but found it empty. The villa seemed to be sleeping. She went out into the cold, late afternoon air, still followed by Cloud and Smoke. Half-way down the drive they galloped ahead and Alice saw they were joining the group of men still working in the olive grove Long shadows fell across the terraced hillside and Alice could not think of ever having seen a more beautiful landscape. Nor, could she remember a more interesting afternoon. Her first day of work was over and she knew it had been a success.

9 *'two short ear-splitting whistles'*

It was already Friday afternoon. The week had passed so quickly that Alice had hardly noticed the days slip by. The mornings had been spent in exploring all the small local villages. Venturing to the east of Mougins she had discovered a vast forest and taken Smoke and Cloud for a long walk. That day, on her return to the villa, she had found Jason waiting near the gates, idly turning over the earth beneath an olive tree. As the gates opened he looked up and waved. Alice drew to an abrupt halt. This was the first time he had willingly acknowledged her. He walked over to the car, holding his fork over one shoulder. Alice looked at his perfect muscled torso and narrow hips… had he been planted on this particular piece of Provençal earth just to torment her? As he drew near he ran his fingers back through his hair… did he know how attractive that small gesture was to anyone with blood in their veins? She sat in the car and determined that he would have to start the conversation for once. He leant down to the open window and looked at the dogs, curled up together on the small back seat of the Mini.

'Hi, my beauties, looks like you've had a good run.' So it was the dogs he wanted to talk to? Alice sighed and still remained silent. Two could play the dumb game. His arm was now resting on the window ledge, close enough for Alice to see the pale, blonde hairs on his tanned arms, close enough and rather tempting to stroke. Jason's hand reached in and ruffled Smoke's ears and then patted Cloud. Right, that was enough. Alice pushed open the car door, abruptly moving Jason's golden arm, and let the dogs out. They stood between Jason and Alice for a moment, stretching fully and yawning. It was impossible not to admire them and Alice finally spoke,

'I took them up to that forest just up the road, Valmasque or something… they loved it and ran for miles.'

'How did you know you could get them back?' Jason answered, suddenly looking down at Alice and giving her the full benefit of his blue-eyed gaze. The dogs had now begun to gallop up to the villa and Alice smiled back at Jason then, putting her thumb and finger to her lips, she gave two short, ear-splitting whistles. The dogs both stopped immediately and raced back to Alice's side.

'Awesome! Way impressive… you don't look like the sort of girl who could whistle.'

Alice was about to ask him what a whistling girl should look like but decided to let him off the hook. It was something that he was talking to her. She wondered again how old he was and whether she could actually be attracted to a man with so little conversation… probably not, she thought regretfully although it did seem a shameful waste. 'Well, I'd better get back up to the Villa now, see you later.' Alice jumped back in the Mini and drove on up to her cottage, the dogs galloping alongside. Maybe Grace would tell her something about Jason later, when they were chatting together. So far the subject had not arisen.

'Well, already the last working day of our first week together, I think it has gone really well, Alice. What do you think?'

'I've thoroughly enjoyed every minute of it. My notes on your early school days are stacking up well, last night I put most of it into good date order and I think there are some spaces we could pad out but, I think, it's going well.'

'Well, there's a long way to go yet… I have been alive such a long time… let's hope we can finish writing it up before I pop my socks.' Grace gave another husky laugh as she saw Alice's shocked reaction. 'Don't worry dear, I have a black sense of humour. Anyway, you mustn't spend your own time on my work… how is your own book going?'

It was a question that Alice dreaded. She had regretted telling Grace that she was writing as it was still such an abstract idea in her head. She began to answer vaguely,

'Well, I can't really say yet, I have the characters absolutely ready in my mind but they don't seem to say anything yet.' Alice was surprised at her own words. This was so exactly what was happening. She had enjoyed the hours of background research and the plot was straightforward. She already loved the characters like good friends but… dialogue… how did they speak?

'Hmm, interesting. Do you have it in your iPad thingy? Why don't your read me something?'

'Alice looked at her in alarm, 'Oh no, there's nothing worth reading, really.'

'Well, give me an outline, some sort of synopsis.'

'Err, well… it's a historical novel, I suppose, loosely based on fact, about the life of Madame Pompadour while she was mistress to Louis XV and her political influence… it was a period I studied for my final dissertation. Does it sound boring?'

'Well, yes, the political bit does sound rather dreary but I'm sure you could spice it up. I once had a wonderful part in a film about Marie Antoinette… such wicked costumes… I had a fling with the director… and there was another lovely man… I can't remember his name now… he only had a small part but otherwise he was very well-endowed!' Grace gave one of her wicked laughs, 'Hmm, where were we? Hmm, dialogue, getting the right historic tone…I can imagine how hard it would be to hear their voices, so to speak. I don't know if you're doing anything this evening, but perhaps you'd like to join me in the cinema… we could go through some old movies, historical stuff… maybe some inspiration… if not plagiarism?'

'I love old movies… but where is the cinema… in Mougins?'

'Good God no, I have a screening room under the villa… like a home cinema… do you know what I mean?'

'Well yes, not that I've ever been in one… but it would be great. I've been watching a few movies on my iPad this week but…'

'Sacrilege… you have committed an art crime. Movies are made for the big silver screen, my dear, not some little pocket gadget. I'll show you what I mean after dinner tonight. Oh and one more thing… this Sunday is my open Villa Sunday buffet … I do it once a month for my few remaining local friends, famous and infamous… those who are still alive at least, and some brave young things. I hope you'll join in?'

'Fantastic, I'd love to, thank you very much, Grace, it has been such a great week.'

'Hmm, I've enjoyed it too, now off you trot, I need my rest.'

Alice left the room, now accustomed to Grace's remarkable ability to fall asleep in the next moment.

On Sunday morning, Alice awoke early and immediately felt the tingle of excitement at the thought of the lunch party. Since a small child she had loved parties and her mother had been very good at planning them. Now, she had no idea what a lunch party of ageing stars might be like nor did she have any idea what to wear. Alice jumped out of bed and went over to the long wardrobe and peered inside. Well, there was the faithful grey linen dress ready washed and ironed but she wasn't sure if that would be dressy enough. Maybe the pale turquoise silk shift that she had worn to her best friend's wedding? Alice held it up it in the glancing sunlight and decided it would do… especially as she had no other real choice. She hadn't yet driven down to Cannes or been shopping anywhere. Alice smiled at her own reflection in the mirror… going shopping in Cannes… the thought was so ridiculous. On the spur of the moment, she decided to call her mother. The last time they had spoken she had been in a hurry to get up to the Villa for lunch so she had been rather short. Yes, Sunday morning her mother would be around. She rang her home number, imagining the small hallway and the phone on the wall. But there was no answer. Alice rang her mother's mobile and just when she thought it would go to voicemail, her mother answered.

'Alice, are you alright?' Her mother sounded breathless and anxious.

'Of course I am, Mum, I just wanted a chat. There was no answer at home… oh, gosh, have I woken you? I've just realised it's only seven thirty!'

'Six-thirty here, Alice, I was sound asleep.'

'Ever so sorry, Mum, I didn't think. Shall I ring later?'

'No, of course not, I'm wide awake now, wait a moment and I'll get my dressing gown.'

Alice gripped the phone tight, why hadn't she thought? Of course, her mother would be at nice Mike's house… in bed with him. Alice closed her eyes and tried to think about something, anything else. Of course, that's what her mother had tried to tell her when she had cut their last conversation short. Then her mother was talking again, 'You gave me a fright, Alice, I thought something was wrong.'

Alice felt a sudden shame at her selfishness, 'I really am sorry, Mum, and I completely forgot about the hour difference… and everything, you know, being so different.'

'Nothing is that different that you can't phone me any time of the day or night, Alice. I miss you so much and we need to talk. You shooting off to France has been quite a shock.'

'Sorry again, Mum. I've just been drawn into this magic world over here and I'm not thinking properly. Grace even has her own cinema and we watched old films together… some with her in as well… and she has two of the most beautiful dogs… the whole place is simply amazing… but, how are you, anyway?' Alice gulped and added hurriedly, 'And how is Mike?'

'We're absolutely fine, Alice, very happy and contented. But I have been worrying so much about you. It's so different from when you went off to Bristol university… or even your time in Bordeaux. Anyway, tell me more about how it's all going before you have to dash off again.'

'I wrote you a long, proper pen and ink letter, well, It's more of a diary really. I thought if I wrote a weekly account and you could keep it for me… it would be interesting to read one day. My work with Grace has made me realise how important memories are, Mum. When I have time I'm going to write about all the wonderful times we had when I was little too… I've talked about it a bit with Grace and she told me I am lucky to have such a good mother. And I am.'

Alice ended abruptly, suddenly feeling tears prick her eyes as she thought of all she had shared with her mother. There was a moment's silence before her mother replied,

'Alice, I don't think you've ever said anything nicer to me… don't laugh, but I have tears in my eyes.'

'Me too, Mum!' Then they both laughed at the same time.

'Well, we are a soppy Sunday morning couple, aren't we. Now tell me what you have planned for today, Alice?'

'I'm so excited, Mum… Grace is giving a lunch party… goodness knows who will be there…vintage celebs maybe… I really don't know… and I was just wondering what on earth to wear.'

'Why don't you wear your turquoise silk dress? I should have thought it would be perfect.'

Alice sighed with satisfaction and relief, 'Exactly what I thought, but I'm glad you said the same. You always know best.'

'Goodness, this going away from home has changed you, Alice. I was quite expecting you to say something more like …oh no, Mum, I couldn't possibly wear that…'

'You don't think I am growing up at last, do you?'

'I doubt it… and I'm not even sure I want you to,' Alice's mother laughed and then said hesitantly, 'but there is something grown up that I wanted to talk to you about.'

'What is it, Mum, you're scaring me now.'

'Oh nothing awful, just I'd like to know how you would feel about putting our house on the rental market. Obviously, now I am married to Mike I will be living in his house in Oxshott, where his surgery is and, of course, there is a really nice bedroom for you here…' Her mother seemed to run out of breath and came to a halt.

Alice replied quickly into the hesitant silence on the line, 'Of course, it's a great idea.' She spoke forcefully, but her heart was beating fast as she thought of her little room in Esher.

'Don't just say it because you think you should, Alice. If there is any chance that you might want to live in Esher then, of course, the house is yours.' Another small silence fell between them but this time her mother filled the gap, 'Anyway, it's only an idea… you don't have to make up your mind now. We could talk about it when you have finished your one month trial out there. You might want to come straight home.'

'No Mum, I really don't need to think about it.' Alice answered slowly, realising, as she spoke, the truth in her own words, 'Of course, it would be great to know I can always stay over with you and Mike but I think I really must have grown up because I simply can't imagine living in Esher ever again. Whatever happens here at the Villa la Vie en Rose… and I'm pretty sure I shall be staying on after the end of the month… but anyway, just being here has made me realise how I want to see more of the world.'

'I'm happy for you, Alice. I do miss you so much, but I shall get used to it and really, Mougins should not seem so much further than Bristol. Mike said the other evening that we could get Eurostar or even drive down to see you for our next holiday.'

'That's a great idea, Mum…why not.' Alice tried to imagine how she would cope with having her newly-married mother visiting her newly-found world in Provence… and failed miserably, but she carried on, 'You know my language school… they are always looking for somewhere for students to stay… maybe you could ask there for tenants?'

'Alice, I am so proud of you. You really have been very, very sweet and understanding about my marriage to Mike… and now this about our little house. Thank you, darling.

'Don't be silly, Mum, of course, I'm happy for you and Mike. Tell him again from me that he is the luckiest man on this planet.'

'I will… you sound like you have to go… are you going to help prepare the lunch?'

'Er, yes, I'd better go now… let's talk again very soon and I'll try not to wake you up… lots of love… and to Mike, too.'

'Bye then, darling, look after yourself and I look forward to receiving your letter. Love you.'

The phone line went dead and Alice sat down on her bed and threw herself back feeling completely drained. She looked at the white ceiling for a long while, trying to work out how much of what she had said to her mother was true. Did she mind that her home was disappearing onto the Surrey rental market? Was she happy for her mother and Mike? Would she ever stay in the really nice bedroom at his house? Did she want them to visit her in Mougins? Would she even help prepare lunch? Alice sat up quickly and decided that was one thing she could try to do. She would dress in a t-shirt and jeans and go to help Minnie in the kitchen. Maybe take the dogs for a run and then change later into the turquoise silk. Suddenly filled with renewed energy she ran into the shower and began the day again.

11 *'swift ride through the forest'*

When Alice bounced into the kitchen, full of the good intention to insist on helping Minnie, she found to her surprise that there was another girl already there, busily chopping onions on a board alongside Minnie.

'Hello love!' Minnie looked up briefly and then carried on mixing mayonnaise. 'Do you want a coffee… help yourself, there's some in the pot on the Aga. Have you met Josette? Josette, this is Alice, Grace's new wonder-girl.'

The girl called Josette looked up briefly and smiled, *'Bonjour, Alice!'*

'Bonjour!' Alice answered and then went over to the hot range and poured herself a coffee. 'I wondered if there was anything I could do to help this morning, Minnie?'

Minnie carried on energetically beating the slow trickle of dark green olive oil into the egg yolks. 'Well now, there is … Grace has got this idea into her head for a winter salad party. I was thinking if you took the dogs out, maybe you could pick some winter greenery, maybe sprays of catkins or some wild herbs for the table. I thought I'd just lay them along the cloth… you know, down the middle with the breads. I can't for the life of me explain all that to Josette and she doesn't speak a word of English.'

'Yes, I'd love to do that… are the dogs outside? By the way, I do speak French if you need me to translate anything?'

'Now there's a thought…' Minnie looked at Alice and then at Josette, 'Could you ask her if her mother is better and what time she has to leave tonight?'

Alice spoke rapidly in French, glad to be useful at last. Josette's face lit up as soon as Alice spoke to her in French and they had a short but friendly conversation before the girl returned to her chopping.

'Josette said to tell you that her mother is much better, but she won't be up to help out later. She'll pick up Josette at seven as usual though.'

Minnie nodded and smiled at Josette. 'There you see how easy it all is if you speak English?' The girl looked puzzled and then looked to Alice for an explanation. Alice decided not to translate Minnie's words but said instead to Minnie. 'Does

Josette come up here from Mougins? I could take her home this evening if it helps?'

'Now that would be a good idea. Of course, Gerald could go but he does like his day off and a glass of wine or two on a Sunday. But, if you don't mind, then you tell Josette and she can ring her Mum. She runs the bar in Mougins, but she wasn't well yesterday and had to close.'

'Is it the bar in the square, where they sell magazines?'

'Yes, that's the one. Josette's mother is a widow and runs it all herself. Josette's a good girl and works here when she can, but she's studying as well. She's a good girl even though she speaks French.'

Alice again decided to dodge the language issue or protest that Josette would speak French as she was French… it didn't seem to matter to Minnie. Instead, she arranged with Josette to give her a lift home later and then went out to find the dogs. Outside in the courtyard she gave her two usual piercing whistles and in less than a minute the dogs came tearing round the corner to greet her. They were wearing their soft white leather collars so Alice guessed they had already been out on the estate. A moment later Gerald came round the corner.

'That whistle of yours… certainly calls them in… makes me laugh, you don't look the sort of girl who would whistle like that.'

Alice laughed, 'That's exactly what your nephew, Jason, said to me. I did wonder why?'

'Well, you know, you're the sophisticated sort, aren't you… don't expect you to whistle like a barrow boy.'

'Well, I'm glad I surprised you both then. A boy at school taught me how to whistle and very useful it is too. Sorry, if you were out with the dogs already… did I drag you back?'

'Well, I had thought to take them up to the forest but if you're going I should be glad not to go really. I can put my feet up for a while.'

'Was Jason going with you?'

'No, he's bundling up the olive tree trimmings… Minnie wants some for her barbecue. You'll see him on the way out I expect.'

'Do you think he'd like to come for a walk with me and the dogs?'

For some reason, Gerald looked at Alice uneasily and then looked down at his boots and kicked the gravel around as he answered briefly, 'No, he won't want to go out… no need to ask him.'

Alice sensed she had said something wrong so she quickly opened the Mini doors and the dogs jumped in. Gerald leaned forward and spoke quietly to Alice through the open car door.

'My nephew was in a spot of bother in London so we're keeping a bit of an eye on him for a while. He's a good boy really and just needs a chance… and that's what he's got here, thanks to dear Grace. I hope you understand, Alice.'

'Yes, of course, I do. Don't worry, Gerald, it's fine with me, everyone needs a chance in life. I've just been very lucky myself.'

Gerald patted her on the head and then shut the car door for her and raised an arm in farewell as she backed out of the courtyard.

Once again that morning, Alice found herself wondering how much of what she had just said was true? Certainly everyone deserved a chance or maybe a second chance and yes, she was lucky herself, but as for understanding about Jason… that, she decided was definitely not true in the slightest. By the time she had arrived at this conclusion, she had reached the end of the drive and had just pressed the buzzer to open the gates, when she saw Jason raking the ground under an olive tree. She gave a small friendly toot on the horn and carried on her way. Better, she thought, to seek greenery in mid-winter to decorate the dining table than to try to understand the Jason enigma.

It was a perfect morning for a forest walk. The low winter sun cast long shadows across the leafy earth and turned everything to gold. The air was full of the scent of pine and eucalyptus. Alice watched the dogs as they ran ahead, noses to the ground picking up scents and weaving in and out of trees in endless search, their tails wagging continuously. Alice heard the sound of a horse hooves beating on the soft path and she whistled to the dogs. They came back to her obediently and she held their collars as the horse and rider passed. The man was wearing a riding helmet and so she hardly had time to see his face as he touched his whip to his forehead and gave a quick thanks. She watched as he cantered away, envying him his horse and the swift ride through the forest. She watched him out of sight and then turned back toward the car. She clipped a few long branches of fresh green catkins and then found some branches of bright yellow leaves entwined with ivy. She carried the large bunch back to the car and stacked it neatly in the boot. She brushed off the dogs and then let them jump into the back. Provence didn't seem to have mud in the same way as Surrey, she thought, as she looked doubtfully at the dogs, now curled up on their rug on the white leather seat.

12   *'she could hopefully do something about not being a stranger'*

The long dining room was slowly filling with people. Grace stood at the far end, leaning on Alice's arm and exuding charm. As each guest entered they walked the length of the room to be greeted by Grace, given a small but royal kiss and then introduced to Alice. The room looked even more splendid than usual, lit by the mid-day sunshine filtering through the louvred blinds and the dozens of cream candles. Alice was pleased to see the effect of the greenery she had gathered from the forest set between the large white plates of Minnie's amazing food. She was beginning to lose count of the guests she had been introduced to when Grace said quietly,

'I think that is nearly everyone now, I want to make my way over to the window and introduce you to my very favourite guest. Do you see, sitting on the small sofa near the window, I shall take the seat next to her.' Alice felt Grace lean a little more on her arm as they walked across to the window. Realising that she was probably being used as a human walking stick, she moved slowly and gently. Of course, Grace would be far too proud to lean on a stick or wear sensible shoes. Alice smiled down at Grace, so very small and slight and moving so gracefully on her high heels… there was a lot to admire.

'So, now then. I have great pleasure in introducing you to each other, Madame de Fleurenne this is my Alice Shakespeare.'

The very elderly woman sitting very upright on the sofa looked up and held out her hand.

'Alice, *enchantée*, Grace has already told me about you… how fortunate she has been to find you.'

Alice took the outstretched hand, a hand so thin and frail that it had a dry papery touch. The next thing she noticed was the delicate perfume in the air.

'Enchantée, Madame.' Grace dropped her head and almost curtsied.

'Vous parlez français, ma chère? Grace n'a pas dit…' Before Madame de Fleurenne could say anymore, Grace interrupted impatiently. 'But of course, she speaks French, she spent four years learning the language… a complete waste of

time in my opinion. Now, you know the house rules very well. French is not spoken here. You are only allowed within my walls because you speak such beautiful English… and your boy, too. I see Jean-Michel is with you today but where is Rosie? I was hoping to introduce her to Alice. Two young girls from London.'

'Rosie is not very well or she would love to have come,' replied Madame de Fleurenne, 'we all look forward to your lunches, you know that very well, my dear Grace.'

'Hmm, you all enjoy my Minnie's cooking, I know that. I am so old now that no-one would visit me if I didn't have such a wonderful cook.' Grace sighed dramatically and sat in the white leather chair, next to Madame de Fleurenne and closed her eyes.

'Really Grace, you are just fishing for compliments. You are quite disgraceful…in fact you could well be called Disgrace. There, I have made a joke and that is something I try never to do. Now behave yourself, Grace, and tell me when you are going to come and see me. Why do I always have to make the journey across from Grasse?'

'Oh, I never go out… the world has to come to me. But your perfumery may well tempt me one day in the better weather.' Grace turned to Alice, 'Do you remember I told you about the de Fleurenne parfumerie… you would love it.'

'Well, maybe Alice will visit us soon if we can't persuade you, Grace, then she can meet Rosie.'

The conversation continued and Alice looked around the room, wondering if she should circulate. As though reading her thoughts, Grace said, 'Now run along, Alice, we two old ladies need to wallow in some maudlin nostalgia and talk about our youth… I know you have studied history, but this is your day off.' Suddenly she waved her hand in the air and summoned a man from the other side of the room, 'Bernie Goldman, come here this minute, you arrived impudently late and you haven't yet met Alice.'

A balding, bulky man turned immediately to wave back at Grace and began to thread his way through the other guests and over to Grace. There was something about him that made it no surprise when he spoke in a strong New York accent.

'Grace, darling, you know how I try not to be late. The traffic in Cannes this morning was…

Grace gave him no opportunity to continue, 'Rubbish, Bernie, you should have left town earlier, but now you are finally here, I want you to meet Alice.'

'Ah, Grace has told me about you, Alice, you're her ghost writer.'

Alice shook his warm, slightly damp hand in hers and hesitated before she replied,'Pleased to meet you…'

Again, Grace interrupted, 'Bernie, why do you always exaggerate? Alice is simply helping me jot down an outline of my memoirs… ghostwriter indeed. Alice, you may have guessed by now that Bernie is my agent, my greedy, grabby agent, the man who has been destroying my privacy for the last…well, I refuse to say how many, years.'

'Grace, darling Grace, you are a killer. You know you love me really!' Bernie leant over Grace and kissed her cheek. To Alice's huge amusement, Grace produced a large white handkerchief and carefully dabbed the cheek that Bernie had kissed.

'Now run along Bernie and chat to Alice about me and how wonderful I am, trot along now.' Grace abruptly turned away and began a quiet conversation with Madame de Fleurenne.

'Isn't she absolutely fabulous? Grace Devine, my very favourite star of all time. So, how are you getting on?' Bernie turned his attention to Alice as they drifted toward the table of food.

'Oh, she's simply wonderful to work for… it hardly seems like work. Of course, I've only been here a week but we get on very well.'

'That's great, I can tell she likes you. Grace works completely by instinct… she loves to treat me like dirt and yet there is no-one I have ever met who is more loyal or caring. One time my wife was ill and she arranged for a nurse to come over and some theatre tickets for my kids… and she never once forgot to ask about her… it's little things that make her so special. The team of people that work for her here… well, they're all her friends and I love the way she treats them as equals. Some of the celebs I have to deal with are as rude as Grace pretends to be… but for real and they treat anyone that works for them like dirt. I could tell you some stories that they wouldn't want in the gossip mags and fanzines.' Bernie carried on talking whilst managing to eat large quantities of food. Alice watched with some amazement and then began to nibble some food herself. Just as she had bitten into a slice of quiche, he suddenly asked,

'So, little Alice in Wonderland, ghost-writer or not, when do you think you might have something ready for me to read?'

Alice gulped and choked down her mouthful as quickly as she could, 'Well, I should be able to tell you more in a fortnight or so.'

Bernie smiled at her and then said, 'My, you have a very cool Brit accent, it's cut like crystal glass… have you ever thought about going into the movies?'

'Oh no, never,' Alice replied hurriedly, relieved that he seemed to have moved on from asking her about the work on Grace's memoir. 'I blush deep red if I have to make any sort of speech. I had to speak for part of my university dissertation and I absolutely hated it.'

'Is that so, well, you sure look composed. Alice, will you excuse me a minute, I've just spotted another of my clients…' He raised a hand in the air and disappeared back into the crowd of guests on the other side of the room. Alice watched him, as he moved with the strange, light grace of an over-weight man, and then realised someone was waiting to speak to her. A tall dark handsome stranger, Alice thought to herself, as she shook his hand.'

'*Bonjour*, you must be Alice Shakespeare, you have been talking to my grandmother, Mme de Fleurenne?'

'Why yes, so you're Jean-Michel, she told me you were here and that your wife, Rosie, isn't it…that she isn't very well?'

'Oh, she's just exhausted. These lunches are great fun but sometimes she needs time to herself so I came along with Grand-mère. Visiting Grace is one of the few outings that Grand-mère undertakes nowadays… but we won't stay long. I just wanted to ask you if you would come over one day next week? Rosie would love to meet you and we like to think the parfumerie is interesting. If you have time?'

'I'd love to… I could come any morning… I work for Grace at two-thirty every day.'

'Oh, we're only half an hour away…just this side of Grasse. How about Tuesday morning… about eleven?'

'Thank you, I'd love that.'

'Here's my card, just call if you can't make it. But hope to see you Tuesday.' He gave a quick, flashing smile of perfect white teeth and ducked his head in a small bow, showing his smooth, close-cut dark hair, a strong tanned neck… and then he was gone. Alice took in a deep breath, well, she had a date with the best-looking man in the room and he wasn't even a film star. Even though it was a date to meet his wife. Alice glanced around the room and caught a glimpse of another dark haired man, slightly taller than Jean-Michel, just disappearing out of the door. Unless he had left a glass slipper, Alice thought, it was a lost cause. She helped herself to a small slice of Minnie's treacle and almond glazed meringue and decided on some comfort eating. Anyway, hadn't she determined that men were not on her agenda at the moment? When did she think that idea up? She was munching the last spoonful of delicious sugary almond meringue when there was a quiet voice beside her,

'Alice, Alice Shakespeare?' She turned and came face to face, very comfortably close, to the man she thought had disappeared. He really was tall and dark and definitely handsome, but she could hopefully do something about not being a stranger.

'Yes, I'm Alice.' she answered and realised it was not the most intelligent of openers… but his dark eyes were looking into hers and she felt her heart thumping ridiculously fast under the thin silk of her dress. Surely it was beating loud enough to be heard? She struggled to say something, anything, more interesting or intelligent, 'I'm at quite a disadvantage today, everyone seems to know who I am, but I don't know anyone here.' That was rather a gabbled, confusing line… but his eyes were still on her and her mind was full of things she couldn't possibly say.

Then he spoke again,'We met earlier…'

Alice looked at him in surprise, 'Oh no, I'm sure I would have remembered.' Alice almost sighed aloud as that had sounded so very silly.

'No really, we met this morning in the forest.'
Alice suddenly remembered, 'Oh my goodness, you're the man on the horse, of course!' Now she was speaking in rhyme, could this go any worse?

'My name is Guy, Guy Bond!'

Alice burst out laughing and then they were both laughing together.

'Is your name really Bond?'

'It is indeed, I'm just grateful my parents didn't call me James.'

'So you don't work for MI6 or anything… and are you a Commander?' Alice carried on, relaxed now and still giggling.

'No, I am a complete and utter coward and pacifist… but they say the pen is mightier than the sword… I'm a writer, recently a screenwriter.'

'Really? How amazing… that must be a fun job.'

'It has its moments. Someone has to do it, as they say. I hear you're writing Grace's memoirs… now that has to be an interesting.'

'Well, I answered an ad for a private secretary and to be honest, I wasn't sure what that entailed, but now I'm here and we spent the last week trying to make a start. I'm confident about compiling research, I love research, but I don't know how the actual writing will go… it's early days.'

'Fascinating… and strange, I hate research and love writing. We are obviously destined to meet. Now, what can I get you? Anything more to eat… or coffee?'

Anything or everything would be just wonderful, Alice thought to herself and then answered demurely, 'A small black coffee, please.'

13   *'he will turn up on a white horse… so Disney'*

Alice woke with a start and looked at her phone to check the time. Only seven am. She threw herself back on the bed and relaxed. She looked up at the white ceiling but today it was full of filmic images. She closed her eyes and enjoyed the luxury of feeling in love. The sheer happiness of it. Of course, it was much too soon to be so sure but… but who made the rules of love? Guy Bond, she whispered his name to herself. Guy Bond had entered her new magic world. He was just too good to be true. Alice looked at her phone again and longed to call her mother, but it was too early and, anyway, did she have time? At nine o'clock she was meeting Guy in the Fôret de Valmasque… not only that, he was bringing a horse for her to ride. Now that, she thought to herself with a wriggle of satisfaction, that is a knock-out first French date for a girl fresh out of Esher. There had been an extraordinary sense of shared understanding between them. It was as though now that they had met they both knew they would spend every possible minute together. Over coffee, they had talked about each other's work but it was like a subtext to what their eyes were reading in each other's gaze. Maybe they would still be talking now but Jean-Michel had come over to them and said they were leaving. Grand-mère was tired and Jean-Michel wanted to get back to Rosie. It appeared that Guy had come in the car with them and so… Alice had felt a physical ache as she escorted them out to their car and waved goodbye. The rest of the party had been a blur of meeting new people and helping Josette hand out coffee and then large balloon glasses of cognac… it seemed that a lunch party *chez* Grace stretched well into the early evening. The sun had already sunk behind the distant blue line of the Mediterranean when Bernie, the last guest to leave, had rolled away down the drive in his chauffeur-driven limousine. Alice watched the dogs chase the car down the drive to the gates and then come galloping back to her where she stood on the terrace. The air was cold and clear. Alice took deep breaths, shivering in her thin dress and thought for a moment about the last party, her mother's wedding day. So much seemed to have happened… her world had completely changed in such a short time. Then, the dogs were back, circling around her and she ran with them round to the kitchen door. Minnie and Josette were busy clearing and stacking the dishwasher. Alice had attempted to help but after she had brought through the last tray of glasses, Minnie had said firmly,

'Alice, you go and find Grace, she's resting in the salon and asking to see you.' Alice had found Grace reclining on one of the white sofas by the log fire, the dogs already stretched out on the floor beside her. The lights were low and candles burned on the low table between the sofas. The scene was set again.

'Ah, there you are Alice. What did you think of my party? Every time I think I will never give one again…so completely exhausting… but then a month slips by and it all happens over again. I buy another load of candles at fifty euros a wick… quite scandalous but then, you know, there is nothing so flattering as candlelight on a wintry afternoon. And so it happens again, a repeat performance.' she sighed dramatically and fluttered her small white hand up to her forehead.

'It was a wonderful party, everyone said so. Can I get you anything?'

'Minnie will bring me a pot of tea in a minute, I'm sure. I just wanted to tell you that you mustn't worry about all this ghostwriting nonsense that Bernie kept going on about. He's so full of enthusiasm that it's absolutely tiring. Underneath all his bluster, he really is the very nicest of men. A good family man and a true friend. He has been my agent ever since I was so-called discovered and he has never ever let me down. He's just a bit larger than life. Anyway, there was something else on my mind. Now, what was it? Hmm, Guy Bond.' Grace dropped the name into the air as though by chance. Alice immediately blushed deep red and waited for Grace to continue. 'Yes, Guy Bond, so very handsome that one has to wonder if he can be real. Very dark brown eyes that burn like coals. Personally I have always preferred blue eyes but I can see the attraction. Yes, if I were fifty years younger I would probably have had him.' Grace laughed, 'Don't look so shocked, my dear Alice, you are quite safe with a fifty-year advantage. But seriously, I hardly know him except that he is a good friend of Jean-Michel Fleurenne's. They look like brothers, don't they, both brown-eyed and handsome in a swarthy Mediterranean way? And both half-French, I think, but then they can't help that… and Mme. de Fleurenne, Jean-Michel's grandmother, is an exceptional French woman and my very best friend. I think she told me that the boys met at school in England and then Guy came out here to write a book about perfume. Jean-Michel and Rosie helped him with the research.'

'Yes, Guy told me he often stayed at the Château de Fleurenne. Oh, and Jean-Michel has invited me to visit them on Tuesday morning… is that all right with you?'

'My dear girl, of course, it is… you don't need to ask me. What you do in your free time is completely up to you. Nothing planned for tomorrow morning then?' Grace looked at Alice, her head tilted to one side in question and her bright blue eyes shining with amusement.

Alice blushed again and replied, 'Yes, how did you know? I'm meeting Guy for a ride in the forest at nine o'clock.'

Alice gave one of her wicked laughs and clapped her hands together, 'Even I couldn't have dreamt up anything more romantic. I do hope he will turn up on a white horse… so Disney!' Alice laughed with her and then Minnie brought in a tea tray.

'Ah, my tea, thank you, Minnie. Now off you go, Alice,' Suddenly Grace began to sing in a pure clear voice,

> 'Twinkle, twinkle, little star,
> How I wonder what you are!
> Up above the world so high,
> Like a diamond in the sky.
> Twinkle, twinkle, little bat!
> How I wonder what you're at!
> Up above the world you fly,
> Like a tea tray in the sky…'

Here Grace broke off singing and began to laugh again. Minnie set down the tray and joined in the laughter.

'Come along now, Alice, let's leave Grace to her tea. I can tell she is in one of her wicked, teasing moods.'

'You're so right, Minnie, I'm a wicked woman and have made Alice blush at least twice. Run along now, Alice, but look out for rabbit holes in the forest.'

Back in the kitchen, Alice did indeed feel as though she had made an escape and was still wondering how Grace knew about her date with Guy. She looked around and saw the kitchen had been restored to its usual immaculate white order.

'Goodness, you've cleared everything, I really wanted to help. Where's Josette? I'm giving her a lift, aren't I? She hasn't gone, has she?'

'No, she's just taken the last bag of rubbish out and she said she was going to sweep the back terrace though I told her not to worry. She's already got her coat on… I expect she'd like to get off as soon as you can. You could see if she's outside. Here, put your coat on… it's chilly out there and you in your thin little dress… you'll catch your death.'

'Thanks, Minnie, and thank you for a great party. Everyone raved about the food.'

'Get on with you, I just keep it simple.' Minnie sat down at the kitchen table and began to sip from a large mug of very strong tea. 'Ahh, that's better, that's what I needed a good cuppa. If you see Gerald tell him there's a cup in the pot waiting for him. Off you go then.'

Alice went back out into the night but could see no sign of Josette. She pulled her coat around her and went over to the Mini, then she heard a scuffling noise by the woodshed. She went over cautiously and then stopped in shock. Jason and Josette were wrapped in each others arms, or rather Jason's hand was up Josette's skirt while she was holding her arms around his neck. They were so passionately engrossed that they hadn't heard her footsteps. She turned and went back as quietly as she could and sat in the car. Maybe they had heard the car door because, after just a few minutes, Josette emerged from the woodshed, swinging a broom. As Alice drove her home, they had chatted about everything except Jason.

Now, opening her eyes and looking again at the white ceiling over her bed, Alice smiled as she remembered Josette's flushed cheeks and ruffled hair. It had obviously been a Sunday for romance. But, now, no more time for day-dreaming. Alice jumped out of bed. Today was Monday, another Monday so unlike any other in her life that it was laughable. Alice was so happy that she did, indeed, laugh out loud.

'she felt her pulse quickening'

Alice pulled into the lay-by in the Valmasque forest at exactly nine o'clock. The sun was already warming the day and a light mist hovered between the trees.Guy was waiting for her, astride a handsome chestnut horse and holding a second by a leading rein. The horses glistened in a shaft of sunlight. Alice almost giggled as she made her way across the car park thinking that Grace would find it difficult to stage a more romantic scene.

'*Bonjour*, Alice, you're very punctual.' Guy jumped down from his horse and, holding both horses' reins in one hand, stretched out his other hand to greet her. Suddenly Alice felt her usual shyness swamp over her. Yesterday had been so different in the crowded party atmosphere and their conversation had flowed so easily. Guy, too, looked unsure of what to say next.

'Well, I should have asked you yesterday… err, have you ridden much before? Are you happy to ride one of these two? He stroked the soft nose of one of the horses, 'This one is Castor and an absolute saint. He never puts a foot wrong and knows the forest paths better than I do.' Guy looked at her, his dark eyebrows raised in anxious enquiry. Alice looked admiringly at the handsome horse and stroked its strong neck. Well, she thought to herself, she could hardly stroke Guy although it was very tempting. Standing close to him again she felt her pulse quickening. She answered quickly, 'Don't worry, I rode a lot as a kid, show-jumping and dressage, the lot… and there are forest trails in Surrey near where I lived, so I rode out every weekend for years but then… well, I went to uni and it all stopped, of course. So, I haven't been in the saddle for quite a time. Your horses are very beautiful.'

'They are, aren't they!' Guy smiled at Alice. 'I keep them in a livery stables near Mougins. They are my one and only real luxury. I bought them when I was paid for my first film script… my so-called breakthrough moment… and now I have to work my socks off to pay for their upkeep.'

'Why two horses?' Alice asked and then wished she hadn't, suddenly thinking that one of the horses might be for Guy's girl-friend or partner. With a sinking feeling she looked away from Guy and stroked the horse again.

'Madness, I know, but I bought them from a bankrupt movie star and the horses had always been together. Anyway, I love them both, this one is Pollux. Castor and Pollux, such posh names!' Guy laughed and both horses shook their heads then nuzzled each other.

'Oh my, I think they understood every word of that,' Alice laughed, too and began to relax, 'and they certainly get on well together.

'Shall we go, then?' Guy looked at Alice.

'Fine.'

Guy released the left stirrup then put his shoulder against Castor and cupped his hands together, 'Here you go then, she's over fifteen hands so you'll need a leg up.' Alice reached up and grabbed a handful of mane, took the reins in her left hand and pushed her heel into Guy's hands. She hopped for a moment and then said, 'One, two, three, go!' With a slight push from Guy, she swung easily up into the saddle, released the other stirrup and put her foot into it. She looked down at Guy's dark head as he adjusted the girth. Well, she thought, that must have given him an up-close view of the back side of her jodhpurs. Now he was walking round the front of the horse, giving it another pat and then came round to check her right stirrup.

'Are you quite comfortable, do you want the stirrups a bit shorter?'

'Yes, I think so, I can do it though.'

'No, let me…' He put his hand on her knee and then held her booted foot as he adjusted the stirrup strap. 'Is that better?'

'Fine.' Alice answered with the one word… just from his touch her heart was again thudding loudly in her ears. She gabbled on in confusion, 'Lucky I brought my boots and one pair of jodhpurs from England. I had really hoped to ride here but had no idea where or how… anyway, I just about brought everything from my room at home. I had no idea what to expect here, really.' Certainly in her wildest dreams, back in Esher, she had never… Alice brought herself back to the moment, 'I didn't bring my hard hat though…'

"I've borrowed one from the stable girl. I hope it fits.' He went over to Pollux and unhooked a riding hat hanging from the saddle. 'I hope it's OK, she's petite and delicate like you and it has a good strap.' Guy looked up at her as Alice tried it on, his dark, tanned forehead creased with worry.

'You've thought of everything, thanks, it's fine!' Alice tapped the top of the grey velvet hat and smiled. 'I'm perfectly ready.'

Guy laughed as he mounted his own horse and they began to move forward into the forest. 'You have no idea the number of things I have thought of… and yes, you are perfect!' Then, pressing his knees gently into Pollux's sides, he moved ahead in a fast trot, rising and falling easily in his saddle.

Alice followed on, thinking about what he had said as she adjusted to the long pace of her horse. The narrow trail threaded through the trees and then began to rise uphill. Guy turned to her, his face happy and excited. 'Isn't this a dream scenario? Are you OK?'

'Very OK, thanks… yes, just what I was thinking… it's stunning up here.'

Guy turned again to face forward and called back over his shoulder, 'There's a wider grassy path coming up… do you want to try a slow canter?'

'Absolutely… lead on!' They emerged from the shady path into a wide pasture, Guy urged his horse forward and Alice followed, soon they were cantering across the meadow, the scent of wild herbs filling the air. Alice looked across at Guy and at the very same moment he looked at her and they exchanged smiles. Alice had a rush of happiness, the speed, the open air and sunshine and, possibly most of all, Guy riding beside her. As they reached the other end of the stretch of open land, Guy reined in Pollux and Alice felt Castor slow to the same pace. Trotting and then slowing to a quiet walk, they were once again back in the shade of a pine forest.

'I've a little cabanon about five minutes from here… do you want to stop for a break? We could give the horses some water… it's getting quite hot now.'

'Sure, whatever you say. I thought it wasn't good to give horses water when exercising.'

'Well, that was a point of view at one time. I've done quite a bit of research and read that a horse's stomach takes about three gallons so you can't let them gollop down a five-gallon bucket-full… that would risk colic … also it's good to have the water slightly warm. Provence is such a dry climate… very low humidity, so the horses quickly dehydrate.'

'I thought you didn't like research!' Alice laughed, looking across at Guy's serious, intent face as he spoke.

'Ah well, anything for my horses... that's different. But when I'm writing I like to have all the facts in the back of my mind and then write freely and quite fast. It seems to be the only way I can work... full tilt. I'd like to be able to take it slowly but once I start I don't seem to be able to stop.'

'Are you working on anything at the moment?'

'I've just finished a long screen play. Exhausting stuff. I'm glad to take a week or so off.'

'Do you mind my asking what it was about?'

'Oh, not at all... nothing is secret. It's a sequel to the film already underway. Basically, the first one is a mythical legend transported to modern life in New York.'

'My, that sounds complicated.'

'Yes, but I enjoyed it... even the research wasn't too bad as I managed a trip to Norway to get the atmosphere. I'd never been there before. It's a fabulous country.'

'Full of fables then,' Alice laughed, really beginning to enjoy talking with Guy again as they walked the horses slowly side by side, 'So it was a Norse legend?'

'Yeh, all Valhalla and the White House... crazy stuff! Look over to your left... you can see the roof of my *cabanon* now.'

Alice followed the direction of Guys pointing finger and saw a wooden shingle roof amongst the trees. The horses, still blowing and snorting a little, shook their heads, jangling their tack and walking faster.

'Castor and Pollux certainly know the way to the *cabanon*.'

Guy laughed, 'I know, they look forward to their treats, I keep some hay and a few apples there. By the way, I call them Cassie and Polly... not such a mouthful as Castor and Pollux.'

'Well, that's a relief. I was wondering actually... surely Castor and Pollux were twin brothers, bright stars in the constellation of Gemini? I mean, your horses are mares and although they look alike they can't be twins, surely.'

'You're quite right on all counts, Cassie is Polly's mother. Obviously the bankrupt film star had chosen rather unsuitable but dramatic names... so crazy! Anyway, they've always been together...that's why I ended up buying two horses instead of one.'

Alice laughed aloud, 'What a story! Two not for the price of one, I'm sure.'

'Absolutely, and they cost me a fortune at livery here,' Guy patted Polly's neck, 'But worth every euro! Well, here we are at my humble residence, *bienvenu*!'

'Is it really yours then?'

'Well, I have a long lease on it. It belongs to a conservation organisation…all the land here does, but I was lucky enough to get a twenty-year lease.' Guy jumped down from his horse and came round to hold Cassie's head. As Alice slid down to the ground, Guy put out an arm to steady her and again, just at his touch, she felt a ripple of excitement shoot through her whole body. Then, he took the reins of both horses and led them round to the rear of the cabin. Alice followed, still shocked by her instant reaction to being close to Guy. Had he felt the same desire? She watched as he loosened the girths of both horses. Two buckets of water were waiting ready under the gable of the roof. Guy fastened the reins to a wooden rail then took down a basket from a hook in the eaves. He tossed an apple to Alice.'Do you want to give Polly her treat?'

Alice caught the apple and held it out on her palm for the horse to take. The horse nuzzled and nudged her hand and then, almost like a word of thanks, gave a soft whinny. Alice smiled with delight and looked at Guy. Again, he was looking at her at the same time, but this time there was a difference… suddenly she was sure he was looking at her with as strong a desire as she felt. They went together into the cabin, leaving the horses tied to the railing.

'Now, time for our refreshment. I've put some lemonade in the fridge.' Guy's voice sounded tight with a new tension and Alice felt her heart begin to thud as he moved across the small room and rinsed his hands at a small square sink. Then, he opened the fridge. and poured two tall glasses of lemonade and added ice cubes. He came over to Alice and gave her a glass then chinked his against hers. 'Welcome to my cabin in the woods, Alice.' They looked at each other for a moment and then drank quickly. Alice felt the coldness seep through her body, but nothing could cool her blood pulsing and racing through every vein. Suddenly, Guy placed his glass down on the table and took Alice's glass from her. For one more brief second they looked again into each other's eyes and then they were wrapped in each other arms. Guy held her tight against his body and she reached up and held his head in her hands, raking her fingers through his dark hair. Then they were kissing, their mouths hungry for each other. Guy began to unbutton Alice's shirt and she sighed with pleasure as his hand, cold from the icy glass, circled and caressed her breast. She dropped her hands to his belt and began to pull at the buckle. He was breathing fast and she felt him shudder as her hand made contact with his bare skin. Now, there was no stopping, Guy lifted her in his arms and she wrapped her legs around his waist as he carried her across the room and they fell together onto a low divan. They made love, frantic love and then they made love again, slower and deeper. They knew each other's rhythm as though they had always been lovers.

15   'a glass of milk at bedtime'

'So, tell me, how was your ride this morning with the talented Mr Bond?'

Alice felt an annoying deep blush spread across her cheeks at Grace's direct question. She was still recovering from the emotion of the morning. There had been no time to absorb all the aroused feelings between them. When all she had wanted to do was to fall asleep in Guy's arms, they had realised the morning was nearly over, the horses were waiting and Alice had to get back to the villa. Reluctantly they had dressed, recovering their clothes and boots from where they had fallen across the floor in their mad and frantic rush to make love. Laughing, they had kissed and hurried back to the horses. Alice, her thighs aching, had ridden back to the Mini and left Polly with Guy. Back at the villa, hurriedly showering, she had just been in time to run up to the villa for lunch as usual. But nothing was as usual and Alice knew in her heart that nothing ever would be. She had been with Guy and now she wanted little else.

Alice managed a small smile and replied to Grace,

'Heavenly, the Valmasque forest is superb for riding and Guy has two beautiful chestnut mares, called Castor and Pollux. We had a great time.' Alice felt no need to mention that Guy had a cabin deep in the woods.

'You certainly look rosy-cheeked and bonny. The exercise must be good for you. Now, let's talk about me, my favourite subject!' Grace looked sharply at Alice, her blue eyes bright with humour and waited.

'Right, we left off when your mother had told you that you were leaving your local school and going to the ballet school. How did you feel about that?'

'Hmm, let me think, how did I feel all those years ago?' Grace paused and closed her eyes, laying back on the chaise longue and resting her hand on Cloud's silky head. Smoke immediately sat up and pushed her head toward Grace's hand. Then, as Grace continued talking, both dogs sighed and settled down as though ready to listen to the story. 'I do remember the actual moment. My mother came into my bedroom, she always brought me a glass of milk at bedtime, and she sat on the end of my bed while I drank it. I had been in a talent competition and I won, of course. I remember having to go up for the prize and curtsey to a dreadful woman with a hat… you know the sort of hat that looks as though a bird has given up the will to live and landed on her head… anyway, my mother told me that this woman ran the Fontaine Ballet School and that I had won a scholarship to go there. I was excited but scared, too. I was only eight years old and I remember, after Mother left, I cried myself to sleep.'

'Cried? Why did you cry?'

'Well, I had good friends at my little school at the corner of our road. I was always a very emotional child, as you can probably imagine,' Grace opened her eyes, looked at Alice and laughed, 'and I was scared at the whole idea. I had heard of the school, of course, the bird-hat woman was no other than Madame Fontaine, a fierce French woman, I think I had the idea it would all be very foreign.'

'True enough, I suppose. Did your mother know you were scared?'

'Goodness knows, maybe… but we weren't close really.'

'She sounds nice, though, bringing you a glass of milk every bedtime.'

'Hmm, well that was for the calcium to strengthen my bones. I actually hated milk… never drink it now. But I was a very small child and she was determined that I should grow strong and healthy. What she lacked in emotional love she certainly made up for in caring for my health. Nowadays, she would make a fine dietician or nutritionist.'

Alice was quiet for a moment trying to imagine Grace as a scared little girl, 'It's hard to imagine you scared,' she said suddenly coming out with her thoughts, 'you are such a confident woman. What about your father, was he a kind man?'

'I have no idea! I never met him!' Grace laughed, one of her spectacular low, husky laughs. 'But I am glad I appear confident now. In fact, now you mention it, I think I am… nothing scares me nowadays, not even death, the Grim Reaper! But then I played against him in a film years ago… oh, I had such a fine time making that film!'

Alice stopped taking notes and sighed. How was she ever going to cope with notating all this? But Grace was continuing,

'It was about mid-sixties, when I was asked to co-star in a horror film called Death Defied…or was it Defying Death? I can't remember now. I played the part of a prostitute who cheated Death but was constantly chased by the Grim Reaper. Oh, it was hilarious, I have never had to scream so much in any film… and believe me I have screamed a great deal. The guy playing the reaper was so very sweet… very tall and handsome and very gay. He played the part magnificently, but it was hard to be scared of him, such a sweetie. Then there was his sidekick, now he was gorgeous! Yes, I very nearly married him, I think. Ah well, it's all so long ago. I have a copy of the film in my archive collection. Shall we watch it one evening? It would be so hilarious. Why don't you invite your charming Mr Bond?'

Suddenly, it seemed that Grace had neatly brought the conversation back to where she had started. Again, Alice blushed as she answered,

That would be great, thanks, I'll ask him. When would suit you?'

'My dear girl, any time that suits him, haven't you noticed yet that I never go out? Well, hardly ever, although you may have to accompany me to the Cannes Film Festival, I might have won some sort of award, according to Bernie. I have no idea what it can be for, apart from a medal for still being alive… anyway, that's in May, in the distant future. At my age, it's better to enjoy everything day by day, minute by minute, Carpe Momentum.' Again, Grace laughed and the dogs stirred and looked up at her, both resting their heads on the sofa. 'Ah, my beauties,' Grace stroked both dogs and then lay back again and settled herself amongst the cushions. 'Now where were we?'

Alice took a deep breath as she hurriedly returned to the notes on her laptop. 'Err, you never knew your father, so your mother brought you up on her own?'

'I suppose you could say that, although there were a series of uncles in my life.'

'Uncles?'

'Well, not real uncles, dear girl, not as in brothers to my mother. No, men that I was told to call uncle. My mother's lovers.'

'Ah, I see,' Alice said hurriedly, turning to look down at the keyboard, embarrassed at her own naïveté. She thought for a brief moment about her own mother… how devoted she had been to bringing up Alice… but there was no time for more comparison as Grace was still talking,

'I say lovers, but I don't know why I use that word. There was never any love in the house. There seemed to be no room for it. Just shouting, rowing, endless alcohol and my mother's grim determination that I should work to become famous.' Grace was suddenly silent and empty of her usual laughter.

Alice spoke into the silence, 'Well, that came true, anyway. You did become famous.'

'I suppose so and she did live long enough to know it. She died when I was making my second film. I was in LA and she was in a small flat that I had bought for her in Islington. I heard she had died just as I was going on set. I remember feeling a great relief flood over me and then feeling very sinful. But even now, I still remember the relief. It wasn't just that I didn't need to worry about her anymore, but it was relief for her too. She was very ill, unsurprisingly with cirrhosis of the liver, although she died of a heart attack. I didn't even go back to London for the funeral. I sent the money and arranged everything, but I didn't go back. I doubt there would have been more than a handful of old friends there… all going for a free glass of booze. Sad but true. And then, of course, she would never have wanted me to give up a moment of my work. It seemed fitting in some strange way.'

'I can see that, it sounds to me as though she would have wanted it that way. I think you did the right thing, the thing that she would have wanted… to carry on with your work.'

'You're a very sweet girl, Alice. Now, tell me, how is your own book going?' Grace sat up straight and looked at Alice eagerly, the sadness draining from her face and a new light of interest filling it once more, 'Can you read me anything yet?'

Alice shook her head and stroked the dogs, 'Sorry, Grace, no progress at all. I haven't even looked at my files.'

'Aha, now I know, your talented Mr Bond is filling your mind, am I right?'

Alice nodded and looked up at Grace, smiling, 'Fraid so, I'm a lost cause.'

'Hmm, well, if you ask me, which you haven't, it is better to live real life than spend too long writing about a fictitious one. '*We are such stuff as dreams are made on'*…Now,

I shall ask just one more question and then leave you to your blushes. What are your plans for this evening?'

Alice hesitated to reply, 'Well, actually, I've just told Minnie I shall be out for dinner tonight, I hope you don't mind?'

'Mind? Why should I mind? I am delighted. I promised no more questions, but I can make a wild guess and say that you are having dinner with Guy Bond… probably in Cannes?'

'How did you guess? By the way, that was Prospero in the Tempest, wasn't it? I love that quote so much… it was a crime, an art crime you would say, when they used it for a stupid advertisement on the telly.'

'Yes, I saw that ad, some silly girl falling out of a cloud. Well, it's the words that will be remembered forever. The advertisers soon forgotten or not even noticed. Don't you think, the bard would be laughing up there on his own cloud somewhere? Now off with you, the joys of an evening on the glittering Riviera are spread out ahead of you, go girl!'

'running his hand lightly down her back'

Grace was so right, Alice decided as she drove down from Mougins toward the coast. A bright arc of lights outlined the coast, like a necklace of bright jewels. The moon was high and full and there were so many stars in the sky that they seemed to touch each other. Yes, the Riviera really was spread out before her, glittering and tempting. Alice drove carefully, trying to control the excitement that filled her. To be meeting Guy would have been enough, but to be meeting him on the famous Croisette promenade was almost too much. Mougins was nearer to Cannes than she had realised so very soon she was cruising slowly along the coast road, looking out for the restaurant that Guy had booked. She passed the grand building of the Carlton, Guy had said it was nearly next door and then she saw it, *Le Poisson Bleu*, between the palm trees and with a parking space right outside. Alice indicated quickly and pulled over. That had to be a lucky omen, she had been worried about parking. Guy had wanted to pick her up from the Villa but she had wanted the independence of driving. Now, pleased to have parked so easily, she was glad to have the Mini. She would be able to leave when she wanted, although truly, she wasn't quite sure when that would be. Alice checked her reflection in the driving mirror and smoothed her hair, there was nothing she could do about the flush of excitement tinting her cheeks pink. Then she saw Guy, coming out of the restaurant to meet her. Her heart missed a beat as she saw his long easy stride and wide smile. He held out his arms to welcome her and she jumped out of the car and ran to him. They embraced and kissed and went into the restaurant with their arms still around each other.

'I was here ridiculously early,' Guy said as soon as they were seated. 'I think the waiters were beginning to think I had been stood up.'

'But I'm not late…we said eight o'clock, didn't we?'

'Yes, I know, I just couldn't wait to see you and I must have been here nearly an hour. Do you see what you have done to me? Now, before you answer that, what will you drink?'

'I'd love some sort of fruit drink, I'm driving so…'

'So you intend to stay cold sober and get me drunk so that you can have your wicked way with me, is that the plot?'

Alice laughed, 'Well, you're the screenwriter, now be sensible, the waiter is waiting.'

'Isn't that what waiters are supposed to do?'

'You know very well what I mean, if you've already been here an hour they must be wondering if you will ever order anything.'

'True,' Guy turned to the waiter, '*deux cocktails de la maison, sans alcool, s'il vous plaît.*'

'*Oui, Monsieur Bond, deux Affections, peutêtre… fraises et citron?*'

'*Oui, ca marche! Merci, Pierre.*'

The waiter disappeared with a happy smile.

'So they know you here then?'

'Oh yes, I often come here… my apartment is just round the corner.'

Alice was quiet for a moment wondering who he had been with last time he had sat in the restaurant, maybe at the very same table. Of course, surrounded by film stars it was ridiculous to think that he would ever eat alone. Before she could think anymore the waiter returned with two tall glasses of pink cocktails and a little plate of canapés. Guy picked up a glass and passed it to Alice and then took his own and held it up to her. 'To our future, Alice, to our future together.' Alice raised her glass and clinked it against his, looking at the bubbles rising to the surface between the slices of lemon and strawberries in the bright pink liquid. His words seemed chosen to disperse her fears. Had he guessed what she had been thinking? She looked into his eyes and suddenly felt a return rush of excitement. This was meant to be.

The dinner was leisurely and long, they talked, as new lovers do, of their childhood. Alice was surprised to learn that Guy's mother was French and that he had spent his early years in Paris.

'No wonder you speak such perfect French. I've spent four years at uni trying to perfect your language. You make me feel it was a waste of time. Still, I enjoyed it and I was fascinated by   everything French… language, history, fashion, literature, films…'

'Men?' Guy interrupted, 'French men?'

'Well, to be honest, I have always had a weakness for a Frenchman speaking English with a French accent. So sexy!'

'I can do that… *pas de problème*… I 'ave not ze difficulty wiv speakin' like dis?

Alice laughed at Guy's exaggerated French accent and his shoulder-shrugging. 'You don't need to do a thing, You are quite perfect just as you are, believe me.'

''ow can I be sure, 'ow will you prove it to me, *mon petit chou*?'

'Oh do stop, Guy, your mock accent is not the slightest bit sexy… anyway, I have always wondered how being called a little cabbage could possibly be a turn on.'

'Really? I think it might be *chou* as in a round puff of pastry, like a profiterole… or maybe it is cabbage? The French do love their food…

'Well being called either is not a bit appealing.'

'OK, I'll give up and return to my usual natural charm and flat middle English voice.'

'Your voice is quite posh, actually. So after Paris, where did you live next?'

'Well, my mother divorced my father and remarried an English man. He had a huge old pile in Wiltshire but I was parcelled off to public school so I hardly lived there. I boarded at school and holidays were supposed to be spent with my father. He had remarried, too, and gone to New York… usually I ended up with my French grandparents.'

'Sounds a bit lonely and sad.' Alice looked at Guy to see how he was reacting to talking about his childhood.

'Not really, I spent all my time writing and riding. Luckily for me the girl next door in the old château was mad about horses and very spoilt. There was quite a stable of horses and I could ride whenever I wanted. I learnt just about everything I know about horses from helping the stableman there. Then I could mess around on the river that ran through my grandparent's garden … and they had a vineyard. I had quite a good time. School was OK, too, once I had made my mark.'

'Made your mark? What does that mean?'

'Oh, the usual struggle against the archetypal resident bully boy and general teasing about my Frenchness. They called me Frenchie right from the beginning. Anyway, I used to charge them to do their French prep and I was soon in all the first teams for sport. That was it really… prowess on the sports field can get you into any gang of privileged thickos. If ever I have children they will never be sent away to boarding school, that's for sure.' Suddenly he looked at Alice and smiled, 'Do you want children one day?'

Alice sat back in her chair, surprised at the change in direction of the conversation. 'Of course, I want children... one day,' She answered without thinking but at the same time, knowing it to be true, 'but I haven't thought about it seriously yet.'

'No, nor me, really. I just have this sort of vision of a sunny house filled with laughing children...'

'And puppy dogs and the smell of bread baking! Really, Guy, you are such a romantic.'

'Guilty as charged. Well, anyone can have a dream.'

'True enough, and if you want something enough, my Mum always says, you can make it happen.'

'That's a good thought. I'd like to meet your mother, she sounds so good and kind.'

'Yes, I guess she is... Grace told me, just the other day, that I was lucky to have such a good mother. I suppose I have always taken her for granted.'

'Easily done. Now she's married, you said. How's that going?'

'Oh, I think she's really happy. I haven't seen her since she went away on honeymoon but we speak sometimes on the phone. Of course, it's very different now.'

'It must be strange for you. This doctor, Mike... is he nice?'

Alice laughed aloud, 'Yes, nice is exactly what he is and I shall have to try harder to be nice to him. I think I gave him a hard time up to the wedding but now I think I feel better about it all.' Alice sipped her coffee slowly and thought about what she had just said. Again, her own words rang true in her ears and she realised that, probably because Guy had come into her own life, she was happy to accept Mike into her mother's life and even her own. She smiled at the thought and Guy took her hand across the table and squeezed it gently.

'I'm glad we had this talk... it's good to find out more about each other. There are three words I want to say so much to you but...'

'I think I know exactly what you mean and I agree. We hardly know each other yet.

'I'm glad you said yet, I hope we have the rest of our lives to find out more, no, everything about each other. Shall we go?'

'Yes, let's go.'

'Shall we walk along the Croisette to get some air after all our talk?'

'That would be great! You have no idea how excited I am just to be in Cannes.'

'Don't you believe it, I haven't been part of it all for long enough yet to not get a thrill every time I look out of my window.'

Guy paid the bill and they went out of the warmth of the restaurant and into the cold air blowing in from the sea. Guy put his arm around Alice as they walked across to the marina and along the pontoons running between the moored yachts. The moonlight was as bright as day and the lights sparkled on the water, the wind jangled and whistled through the rigging of the harboured yachts. It was cold and Alice shivered in her light coat.

'The nights are cold in January, do you want my coat?' Guy slipped off his long overcoat and wrapped it round Alice, at the same time, running his hand lightly down her back.

'You'll freeze without your coat,' Alice protested but pulled the soft coat around her, 'My, is this what quality cashmere feels like? It's so soft and lightweight.'

'Well, one has to keep up appearances in show-biz!' Guy laughed, 'But if you want to save me from pneumonia we could run back to my apartment. It's just over there.' Guy pointed back across the road to the outline of baroque buildings that faced the sea front. 'You see that dome, well, my place is just behind. Would you like a coffee or a night-cap? The night is still young.'

'Guy, will you give up trying to tempt me? There's no need, I'm dying to see your flat. Let's go!'

They ran across the road and were soon standing outside a large, dark green door in a narrow street just behind the promenade.

'This is it? It's better inside than out, I promise.' Guy unlocked the door and took Alice's hand to lead her through a dark and dusty hallway. He turned on the stair light and Alice looked around at the dilapidated hall and staircase. She followed Guy up the creaking bare wood staircase and stopped behind him as he found another key and opened another dark, green door. He reached in and turned on another light and then moved aside for Alice to enter before him. Alice gasped with surprise at the sudden change. The door led straight into a wide open living space, subtly lit with up-lights and table lamps, warm and vaguely perfumed with lavender. Alice walked across to the tall windows on the far side and looked out… through a narrow gap in the buildings opposite she could see the bright promenade lights reflected in the sea. She turned to Guy,

'It's so lovely!' She spun in a circle, taking in the whole feeling of the place. Then she saw the huge black and white photos on the long wall opposite the window. 'Wow, Cassie and Polly, what a great photo…and it's so huge! Larger than life! Fantastic!'

'I'm glad you like it. I took the photo when they were running loose in a field near the stables. A friend of mine made the blow-up… I never get tired of looking at it…but I've never enjoyed looking at it as much as I am right now.'

Alice turned from looking at the photo and saw that Guy was looking at her. He was smiling with a certain look in his eyes that she was already beginning to recognise. Her stomach fluttered and her knees definitely trembled in the most ridiculous way. She took a deep breath and walked slowly toward Guy, unbuttoning her coat as she went. He took a step toward her and she held up her hand. 'Stay right where you are Guy Bond. I'm going to have a look around the flat.' She threw her coat onto the floor and stepped out of her high-heeled shoes. She walked slowly round the large room, enjoying Guy's eyes following her every move. She opened a tall cream painted panelled door and peeped into the next room. Yes, a large bedroom. She turned back to Guy who was still standing as though frozen on the spot in the middle of the living room. She slowly slipped her dress off her shoulders and beckoned to him, 'Shall we go in here?' Guy ran across the room and swept her off her feet, burying his face in her neck and kissing her repeatedly, he carried her over to the bed. 'You are a naughty girl, Alice, a very naughty girl and a wicked tease, too.'

Alice laughed and kissed him hard on the mouth. 'Your face was such a picture!'

'OK, bad girl, you asked for it!' Guy ran his hands round her waist and began to tickle her.

'How did you know I was ticklish?' Alice screamed and giggled, squirming to get away from him but he held her close and ran his hand up her skirt. Soon they were wrapped in each other's arm, laughter and teasing replaced with fierce passion and desire.

17 'she remembered the long night'

Alice woke later than she had ever woken in her life before. She looked at her phone and saw it was nine thirty… and there was a message from Guy. She flicked it open and saw,

'i love you - 3 words i wanted to say all the time last night - i love you x sleep well'

Alice stretched and smiled and looked at the time of the message. Five am, so he must have sent the message as soon as she was inside the gates. She ran her fingers through her hair as she remembered how Guy had insisted on following her in his car up to the villa. That was after half an hour of persuading him that she would be driving back in the Mini. She wasn't used to this level of gentlemanly behaviour but she decided she rather liked it, in an amused way. She read the message again and then quickly tapped a reply. It only needed four words. Then she remembered her invitation to Château Fleurenne. She couldn't believe she had slept so late, she had a lifetime habit of waking at seven am… but then she had never made love in the way that she had last night. Alice felt her whole body ache and throb with pleasure as she remembered the long night. Wide awake now, she sprang out of bed and into the shower, turning the temperature up and letting the steam and hot jets of water pour through her hair and over her body. Slowly she massaged the shampoo through her hair and, as the foam poured over her, she began to feel her tired muscles slowly relax. Half an hour later she was walking up the path to the Villa, accompanied by the two bounding dogs. As she rounded the corner into the kitchen courtyard she found Jason cleaning the Mini. He looked up as she approached and smiled shyly,

'I heard you were going to visit over at the Fleurenne's so I thought I'd give the Mini a wash-over. Be ready in a jiff.'

'Thanks, Jason, that's really kind.' Alice smiled to herself as she remembered the last time she had seen Jason… Jason wrapped around Josette. 'Would you like a lift down to the village if you have time to get away?' Jason's looked up quickly and then shook his blonde head vehemently, 'No, no thanks… no, you're alright, thanks. I don't go to the village… and I have work to get on with here.'

It seemed a strange answer and said in an anxious voice. Yet, again, Alice was puzzled by Jason and his mysterious attitude . Now she had seen him with Josette it seemed even stranger that he wouldn't want to go down to the village.

'OK, if you're sure. I don't suppose your uncle would mind if you went down for a coffee, I could ask him if you like?'

'No, I'm fine, thanks. It's not that…' Alice thought for a moment that Jason was going to explain just why he never went out but then, suddenly he threw down the cloth he had been drying the car with and walked off. Alice watched him walk away, realising that she was no longer stirred by his muscular back view… somehow, now that she was with Guy, somehow… Jason had slipped into the role of a friend. As his handsome hulk disappeared round the corner of the garage, Alice frowned and wondered if he was a friend who needed help.

The dogs chased the Mini down to the gates and then peeled off and raced back up to the villa. Alice looked in her mirror as the gates closed behind her and saw that Jason was standing between the two dogs, looking after her. The black iron rails made an image of Jason behind bars. The Villa La Vie en Rose might be a luxury property but was it more like a prison for Jason?

Driving through the sunlit hills towards Grasse, Alice soon forgot the mystery surrounding Jason and enjoyed the scenery. She had tapped in the address of the Château Fleurenne and she had been surprised to see it come up as a place of interest. The Musée de Parfumerie Fleurenne. The route was in the opposite direction to Mougins and Cannes and so it was the first time she had travelled inland. The other surprise on the sat-nav information screen was that it was only fourteen kilometres and should take less than half an hour. Alice sighed with pleasure and drove slowly, taking in the olive groves that stretched above her on the right, ancient trees settled onto the thin steps of land… then, on her left the rough red earth covered in wild herbs, rolling down to the wide open panorama of the sparkling Mediterranean. Alice was so thrilled with the landscape that she jumped when the sat-nav suddenly spoke,

'*Dans cinq cents metres tournez à droite.*'

Five hundred metres? She looked at the small screen and saw the red arrow pointing to the right, then she slowed and looked at the road ahead, sure enough there was a large sign pointing to Château Fleurenne and advertising the museum.

Alice pulled into the lay-by, she was too early. She turned off the engine and sat for a moment, reading the large sign board. *'Visitez la parfumerie -Horaires Ouverture: mai a novembre, du mardi a dimanche - 10h00 à 17h00.* So the museum was officially closed at the moment, Alice thought, wondering if she would be given a private visit. Just then a car swept by and hooted, pulling to a stop inside the Château gateway. Jean-Michel jumped out the car and came back to where Alice was parked.

'What are you doing in the lay-by? Come on up?' He smiled, the flashing smile that Alice remembered from the party. How many good-looking guys were there in Provence and was she destined to meet them all?

'I was early, the journey took no time at all.'

'Oh, you shouldn't have waited, come on follow me up to the Château.' With a wave and another smile he went back to his car, a battered Peugeot estate and pulled ahead. Alice followed, feeling suddenly nervous as the Château came into sight, majestic, peaceful and all in the pinkest stone she had ever seen, every window with chalky grey shutters… the effect was stunning. Jean-Michel swung his car round to the left and then parked in a cobbled courtyard. Again, he jumped out of the car and came over to open the door of the Mini.

'I hope you don't mind coming in the back way, as a matter of fact we hardly ever open the front doors until we open to the general public… coach loads of them! Come in, come in! Rosie is looking forward to meeting you.'

Alice followed him, trying not to show how nervous she felt.

'Is it your family Château, I mean, have you always lived here?'

'Well, yes, on and off. My grandmother is the real owner and she has always lived here. I tried to escape several times but when I married Rosie we came to live here full time. She loves it as much as Grand-Mère does… so I gave in!' Another flash of a smile and then he was ushering her into a large kitchen. Alice stopped on the threshold, there, sitting at the large table and chatting to an auburn haired girl was Guy Bond. He stood up as she slowly entered the room. 'Surprise! You see you cannot escape me. My spies told me you would be here this morning and so here I am! Rosie lets me have breakfast here now and again as she worries I don't eat enough on my own. Rosie this is Alice Shakespeare'

The auburn-haired girl stood up and came to meet Alice, holding out her hand, 'Pleased to meet you, Alice, what a marvellous name, any relation? I'm Rosie de Fleurenne as you must have guessed. Take no notice of Guy he's incorrigible. I don't worry about him at all as he is a born survivor and just makes up ridiculous stories… luckily he's found people will pay him for his idiotic fables.'

Alice shook her hand and then sat in the chair that Guy held out for her. She still felt shy and was pleased that Guy was there to help the conversation flow. It certainly seemed to be one of his strong points. Now he was talking again,

'Is your grandmother around this morning, Jean-Mi? I was hoping she would let Alice concoct a perfume in her lab.'

'My Grand-Mère never appears before noon… that's probably how she stays so young. Anyway, Rosie has practically taken over the Parfumerie now. Grand-Mère trusts her implicitly to carry on the tradition. I am just a grease monkey around the place.'

Rosie ruffled Jean-Michel's smooth dark hair and laughed, 'Grease monkey? Wherever did you get that idea? You're not nearly as useful as that… you are just a beautiful play-boy.'

'How I envy you, Jean-Michel,' Guy said wistfully, 'I should love to be a play boy.'

Jean-Michel laughed, 'You may have the film star looks but you are a workaholic, Guy. You don't have the necessary qualifications for doing nothing. No, you'd never make a play-boy.'

Rosie looked at Alice, 'Really you mustn't believe Jean-Mi, he actually works very hard but he likes the whole idea of being a play boy.'

Alice laughed and looked from one to the other, still feeling like an outsider at the table. Then she decided she should enter the conversation, 'I was brought up with the saying *'Choose a job you love, and you will never have to work a day in your life'*. I've certainly managed that with my first job here with Grace.'

'Was that your mother's advice, Alice?' Guy turned to Rosie and Jean-Michel, 'Alice seems to have an enviable mother, unlike my own absentee one.'

'Mine too,' Rosie nodded, 'she absconded, in a beautiful hippie way, quite early on… I should love to have had a mother who advised me or was even like a friend. But Jean-Mi had the worst luck as far as parents go…'

'Well, I was saved by my Grand-Mère when my parents were killed in a plane crash. But I was quite grown up when they died. I remember them as a beautiful couple, in love with each other but quite removed from me. I'm sure they both loved me in some sort of remote way. I was sent to school in England when I was very young… that's where I first met Guy. He looked after me like a brother and saved me from the bully boys. Both born in France we had a lot in common. Now we are often mistaken for brothers… but he is definitely the working model.' Jean-Michel stretched lazily, 'I so long to do nothing today, Rosie, what do you think?'

'I think you would be bored in less than half an hour,' Rosie smiled and this time smoothed his hair gently, 'let's go down to the museum and show Alice around.'

They all stood up and Guy put his arm round Alice's shoulders as they made their way outside. She was quiet, lost in her thoughts and going back over their conversation round the kitchen table. It seemed strange to discover that her life with her single mother in a small, semi-detached house in Esher should be so envied by the rich and privileged young people now around her.

18   *'the bluebells and the sweet violets hiding amongst the tall ferns'*

Alice looked at the small bottle of golden liquid standing on her dressing table. The little square label simply read 21750. She carefully took out the small cork and dabbed a little of the perfume on the inside of her wrist. The air was immediately filled with the delicate aroma of bluebells and violets. Alice reached for her phone and dialled her mother's number.

'Hi Mum, how are you?'

'I'm fine, Alice, are you alright?' Alice heard an overtone of anxiety in her mother's familiar voice.

'I'm absolutely fine, Mum. I just thought you'd like to know I'm having a sort of Alice in Wonderland moment. It's not too early is it? It's gone nine your time.'

'Of course not, anyway, I told you before, you can phone me any time day or night. It's just when I see your number come up I feel some sort of small panic. You're so far away. I know I'm being silly… now what's all this about Alice in Wonderland then?'

Well, to start at the sort of beginning, yesterday I was invited to a nearby Château that has a perfume museum. It's an amazing place and I was taught how to design a perfume, well, the bare essentials and then, guess what… I actually mixed my own perfume recipe.'

'Fantastic, Alice, well done…Mike and I've been studying a map for the area and see you are very near Grasse, the French centre for perfume… how lucky you are.'

I know! You have to see this place to believe it. The perfume laboratory is amazing, all huge old copper vats and steaming pipes… more like an antique factory. Then there are rows of antique mahogany desks, like church pulpits, with tiers and tiers of little phials of essences. I was sat at one of these and helped to create my very own perfume. Jean-Michel… he's a good friend of Guy Bond… anyway, his grandmother first asked me my favourite perfume and I remembered walking through the woods near home in spring time… do you remember the bluebells and the violets hiding amongst the tall ferns… that sort of woodland smell, slightly earthy… anyway, Jean-Michel's grandmother… they all call her Grand-Mère …'

'Alice, slow down, you are completely losing me… and where does Alice in Wonderland come into it?'

'Sorry, Mum, there's just so much to explain. I was just looking at my little bottle of perfume and thinking about how we used to watch the Disney film, you know, that bit where Alice decides to drink the bottle labelled 'drink me'. I was always so scared I used to hide behind the sofa and you had to tell me when to look.'

Alice heard her mother's laugh and felt a rush of love for her, quickly followed by a wave of homesickness. Then her mother was talking again,

'Well, you just remember all the trouble that Alice fell into and look out for yourself. I do worry about you out there.'

'No need, Mum, I'm having the best of times. Anyway, the next few pages of my diary will tell you all the details of the week past. Did you get my first episode?'

'Yes, darling and it made wonderful reading. You have a real talent for recording detail and making it amusing. I look forward to the next episode then. Are you sure it will give all, I mean absolutely all the detail, Alice?' There was now a hint, maybe an insinuating quality of amused laughter, in her mother's voice.

'I'm ringing off now Mum before you ask any more questions.'

'I thought you might,' Alice's mother laughed out loud, 'Just look out for mad hatters and white rabbits etcetera… especially the etcetera.'

'Will do, Mum, will do. Love you lots.'

Alice closed her phone, feeling another pang of homesickness at the disconnection. There were so many things she should have asked her mother… had she even asked how she was and she certainly hadn't remembered to ask after Mike? Alice sighed and looked again at the perfume. Life in Provence could certainly make one very selfish, she decided, as with a shiver of pleasure she thought of the day ahead. In fact, it was time to get showered and into her jodhpurs as today, at ten, Guy was bringing the horses up to the villa. They were going to follow some of the uphill trails in the hinterland and Guy was bringing a picnic. Alice had already told Minnie of her plans and when Grace had overheard she had asked Guy to dinner that night. Guy would have time to take the horses back to the livery stables and said he needed to catch up on some work before he returned to the Villa La Vie en Rose. Alice gave a smile of satisfaction at the day's neat plan.

At ten o'clock Alice walked down toward the gates, accompanied as usual by Smoke and Cloud. She watched in amusement as they raced ahead of her, Smoke always slightly ahead, sometimes turning to circle round Cloud and then tear ahead again. Then she saw they had seen Jason, working in the olive grove and she wandered over to him,

'Morning, Jason, did you swim this morning?'

'Hi, yeh, I swim every morning.'

'Isn't it cold?'

'Nah, not really, the water's heated, so once you get in it's great.'

'Really, I didn't realise.'

'Haven't you seen the steam in the mornings?' Jason looked at her for once and she thought again how strikingly good-looking he was. Not just the deep, blue eyes but the perfect symmetry of his features, under the pale blonde hair. The dogs were roaming off again and Alice gave a short sharp whistle and they immediately circled back to her.

'That's some whistle!' Jason laughed and Alice realised she had never seen him laugh before. His eyes creased in the most enchanting way and his teeth were faultless. Why was this perfect specimen of young manhood hiding away in a remote olive grove? Afraid to break the moment, she asked none of the questions teeming through her mind. It was so good to see him relax enough to laugh. 'Maybe I'll brave up to join you one morning?'

'If you swim as well as you whistle then I'll give you a race.'

With another disarming smile, he suddenly turned away as though he had said enough, maybe more than enough. Smoke and Cloud looked first at Jason and then to Alice as though unsure which to follow. Jason slapped his hand against his thigh and both dogs rushed after him. Alice laughed, 'They're still your dogs, Jason! I'm just a newcomer. He carried on walking but raised his hand in the air as though to answer her. Alice walked back to the path and was just in time to open the gates to Guy. He was driving a Landrover, towing a small horse box. Once through the gates, he pulled to a slow halt and opened his window.

> *'Bonjour, mon petit chou chou! Ca va aujourd'hui?'*
> *'Bonjour, oui, très bien merci, mon loup, et toi?'*

'Did it take you four years to learn to call your loved one a wolf? Anyway, shall I park here or do you want to hop in and we can drive on up a few kilometres?'

'Je n'en ai aucune idée, ma crotte!'

'Did I tell you that I have a weakness for English girls speaking French with an English accent? Hop in then, can't keep the horses waiting or I'd let you lead me astray… again. *Ma crotte,* indeed!'

Alice laughed and pulled herself up into the passenger seat of the Land-rover. She leaned across and gave Guy a light kiss on his cheek. He turned to her, his dark eyes burning and then turned to reverse out of the driveway. Alice buzzed the gates closed and saw Smoke and Cloud standing back and looking wistfully after her.

'Poor dogs, I think they thought they were going to the forest with me.' She caught a glimpse of Jason standing quite still under an olive tree, watching. Then the dogs turned back and joined him as Jason turned back to his work. She thought of telling Guy about Jason and the mystery surrounding him but then, the Landrover was pulling away uphill and once again, overcome with selfish enjoyment, she gave herself up to the morning ride ahead.

19 *'The photo was provocative...'*

'So, how was your ride in the hills this morning, Alice?' Grace had moved from her usual place on the sofa and was sitting at a long desk near the window. She turned to Alice as she spoke and arched her eyebrows.

'It was perfectly lovely. Quite a cold wind but the sun was warm. We rode a long way uphill and the views are amazing. We had picnic lunch and then coffee at a little bar by a river… it seemed miles from anywhere.'

'I look forward to meeting Guy again this evening. I know him as a friend of Jean-Michel but we have never cacaspoken much. Is he good company?'

'Yes, he is. Funny you should ask that of all questions because that is particularly why I like him. We talk and talk about a thousand things and he is a good listener too.'

'Good, that's quite a rare thing in a man, especially a good-looker like Guy. Believe me I am very experienced in good-lookers. Although you shouldn't take advice from me really as I always made the worst of choices. Some of the men I didn't marry, I should have and vice versa. Very much vice versa. Now, I'm sitting here because I have been looking through my photo albums. I wondered if you would like to go through a few to get some idea of my life… this one is all in the sixties and should be good for a laugh. Oh my, the clothes we wore!'

Alice went across and looked over Grace's shoulder at the open album. There was a young Grace, surrounded by young men, lying on a sun-lounger, palm trees and the edge of a blue swimming pool in the background. 'You were so beautiful!' Alice spoke without thinking and hastily added, 'Well, of course, you still are…'

'Oh please, spare me the tactful after-thought, Alice. You know I can't stand humbug. Of course, I was more beautiful then than now. My beauty was really my downfall.'

'What do you mean?'

'Will you carry the album over to the coffee table. I think I'll sit on the sofa now.' Alice took the album carefully and held Grace's arm as she rose from sitting at the desk. The dogs stood up and stretched lazily and went over to the sofa and slumped down.   'Smoke and Cloud know when I've had enough. They must be the laziest dogs ever, always quite happy to stretch out at my feet.'

'Well, they get plenty of exercise out in the olive grove. They were out all morning with Jason. Actually, I was wondering, Grace, whether they would be happy following the horses next time I ride out?'

Hmm, I'm not sure, they've never been with horses, but I don't see why not. Maybe next time Guy brings his horses over you could try just riding round the estate first. They might behave very badly, they are such jealous creatures and I wouldn't want them to frighten the horses. See what Jason thinks, he knows them so well.'

'Thanks, that's a good idea. Jason loves the dogs, doesn't he?' Alice was tempted to ask Grace more about Jason, but something stopped her. It was as though Jason was always a taboo subject for some reason. 'Another thing I wanted to ask, Grace, I hope you don't mind, but I was wondering if it is all right for me to have visitors at the cottage?' Alice looked down at the album to hide her blushing confusion.

Grace gave one of her low, husky, laughs, 'My dear girl, you are quite hilarious. I'm not Mother Superior running a convent here. Of course, you can have guests to stay… maybe Guy Bond?' Again she laughed and the dogs looked up and wagged their tails as though sharing the joke.

'Thanks, Grace, I just thought I should ask. I know this is a very special and private place so…'

'I shouldn't have laughed at you, my dear. You have been very well brought up and you are very sensitive and correct. This is indeed a haven of peace, but I am sure you won't be having too many raving parties in the cottage.'

'No, no, of course not…' Alice said quickly, 'I don't know anyone here yet anyway… except the de Fleurennes and Guy Bond.'

'Maybe he will be your first guest then… now, in case I start to laugh at you again, let's turn the page and have another look at my favourite subject…me, in my prime, in the sixties.'

Alice turned the page and there was another Grace, this time a large colour photo with her signature in the corner. Her hair was piled high in a honeycomb of curls and her pale peach dress revealed a deep cleavage in her swelling breasts and the suspicion of nipples pushing through the thin material. She wore a pink pearl necklace and ear-rings and her make-up was immaculate, every long eyelash standing out against her delicate pale skin, her lips, slightly parted, shone with glossy pink lipstick, her eyebrows arched in the way that Alice recognised. The photo was provocative, teasing and at the same time… Alice searched for the word… was it mocking?

'Absolutely stunning. You were magnificent.'

'Hmm, I know, of course, that is a promotion photo but there was not much touching up and no sophisticated air-brushing and photo-shopping like today. I still remember the day it was taken. Now, he was another good-looker, the photographer, at the top of his profession… hmm, such a great body and gentle hands, a sensitive, arty soul. Probably one I should have married… anyway, I didn't and back then I was just beginning to understand the power of my looks and beginning to exploit them.'

'How do you mean? There is something in your expression that I can't quite identify. I've seen the same look on your face here in this room. You arch your eyebrows and… I don't know, what is it?'

Grace laughed, 'I'm afraid it's simply suppressed laughter. Not the nicest sort of laughter maybe. More derision? I think it is when I am laughing at you. Back then I was beginning to laugh at the whole mad world, and particularly at the foolishness of men.'

'Were you a sixties feminist?' Alice asked in surprise.

'Oh no, I don't think so. I never wanted equality, but then I have always thought men far inferior to women… so why would I want equality?'

Alice laughed, 'It doesn't look as though you were the type to burn your bra, either.'

'Good god, no! Bras were my stock in trade. You have no idea how much I paid for a bra to fit me. My breasts were legendary by then.' Grace sighed, 'And when I think how my mother used to bind them flat with crepe bandages. Can you believe it?'

'What? What do you mean?'

'Well, when I was in the ballet school, I was always very small for my age. By thirteen, I was the smallest in the ballet corps, except for my tits. Oh goodness, they were growing like melons, it was a surprise I didn't fall over.' Grace laughed again, 'There I was, always cast as a fairy or a nymph, with tits beginning to bounce up and down. Hopeless! Anyway, I had the luck of a part as a fairy in Midsummer Night's Dream. I was chosen as Pease-Blossom. My mother was beside herself with joy as it was to be staged at Sadler's Wells. My costume was a flimsy wisp of a dress with wings attached to my wrists. All went well in rehearsals, my mother's wheeze of binding my breasts flat went quite well… but oh my, on opening night…' Grace was laughing even more now and the dogs stood up and wagged their tails as though waiting for the punch line, 'I tip-toed across the stage to Titania, curtsied, stood up and turned full front to the audience and flapped my wings… out popped my tits, right out of the top of my bodice.' Grace threw her head back and gave in to her laughter, the dogs jumped up on the sofa and began to try to lick her face. 'Down dogs, down! Oh, Alice, it was too dreadful, I had to run off the stage. My mother was in the wings, in a fury of rage… she slapped me hard on the face… as though I had meant to do it? I remember her face now, twisted with rage.' Grace helpless with laughter, stroked the dogs and pushed them away from her at the same time.

Alice closed the album and stood up, taking the dogs by their white collars and getting them to lie down on the floor again. Then, she began to laugh too, Grace's laughter was so infectious that it was a while before either of them spoke. Then Alice sat down and said, 'But how awful for you, whatever happened next?'

'Well, it was in all the London newspapers the next morning. Some bright reporter had taken a photo and it was splashed everywhere. Some wonderful headlines attached involving Titania being upstaged by titty fairy etcetera. Anyway, it was the end of my ballet career.'

'Were you very disappointed? And what about your mother? Was she still angry?'

'I wasn't disappointed at ending my ballet dancing. I had begun to really hate it and all the painful practice. My mother was very soon consoled when I had an offer from a film company. Yes, the night my breasts popped out my star was born. I went from top-heavy fairy straight to top starlet. That was the beginning of it all.' Grace's face suddenly became serious and reflective.

'But you were still so young?'

'I certainly was… but I grew up very quickly, too quickly of course. Now, my laughter has quite worn me out so off you trot now. I need my rest if I am to be at my best to meet your young man at dinner tonight. I'll ask Minnie to find a film for us to watch afterwards. Maybe we can dig out one of my earliest. Off you go now and would you take these two silly dogs with you? They need a run as much as I need a snooze.

'awoke at the first light of dawn'

The screen flickered and then the famous lion roared,
'Ah, that's Leo, my favourite… did you notice he roared twice? That was him actually roaring… his mane is smaller than Tanner's, his predecessor because he was only young. A film star in his own right. I was on set with him in some epic, I can't now remember the title, but I remember how beautifully behaved Leo was during the whole boring business. Such a softie, once, when he was on set in a series called The Pet Set, goodness me, you two still weren't born…' Grace laughed as she looked across at Alice and Guy who were sitting beside her, 'yes, it would have been the seventies, anyway, I remember a very touching scene where Leo let a blind teenage girl stroke him. None of your digital imaging, it was the real thing, well, I don't know if the girl was really blind, but I think so, and certainly Leo was real enough. Anyway, look here come the titles, starring Grace Devine… hmm, yes, this is the one where my co-star was a complete alcoholic…'

Alice and Guy were sitting in the pale, grey velvet reclining seats of Grace's screening room. Guy had his arm around Alice and they were both turned toward Grace, listening raptly to her vivid memories of cinema history. The flickering light from the projector lit her face and Alice thought how beautiful she was and how, in this half light she seemed hardly changed from the young woman in the photo. Grace turned to Alice,

'Don't look at me, Alice, watch the movie.'

Alice hastily turned back to the screen and Guy gave her shoulder a little squeeze. Now the credits were rolling and music filled the small cinema. Alice sat back in the luxurious seat and felt the thrill of excitement that she had always felt since a child… the show was about to begin.

The film was no disappointment though it had been surprising. Alice had expected Grace to be beautiful and to act well, even to dance, but she had no idea that she would sing.

'Was that actually you singing?' Alice asked as soon as the film ended.

'Why, of course, and my co-star, as long as he was well-oiled with Bourbon, he was a great baritone. I think he had wanted to be an opera singer but, well, you can see how good-looking he was… that did it. Talent spotted just like me. Ended up drinking himself to an early death. And, of course, cinema was moving in a new direction.'

'In what way?' Guy leaned forward to ask Grace.

'Well, Ursula had come out of the waves in Dr. No… that sparked off a number of secret agent films.' Grace gave a low laugh, 'How tempted your parents must have been to call you James, James Bond. Kind of them not to, I suppose.'

'Yes, bad enough being called Bond… it still rings bells, but my mother is French and Guy is a family name, pronounced *Guy*, of course to her.'

'Your mother is French, well, I suppose you can't help that.' There was an awkward silence and Alice intervened,

'Like being called Shakespeare, it's such an iconic name I always feel I have to make an excuse not to be related in any way to the great bard.People are always so disappointed..'

'True, but again, hardly your fault.' Grace continued. 'Sorry, Guy, you have to excuse my rudeness…or put it down to an idiosyncrasy of old age. I know I deserve to end up with Tourette syndrome. I live in France and it is the most beautiful country in the world, but I was once married to a Frenchman who managed to put me off the whole race. But that's another story. Where was I? Oh yes, the sixties cinema…well, fortunately for me there was quite a spate of horror movies and gothic mythical stuff going on then, too. Possibly the fore-runners to the film you have just been working on, Guy. Now let's go back to the salon and sit by the fire.' Grace held out her hand, more like a princess waiting to be kissed than an elderly woman needing help to rise from the low cinema seat. Guy moved forward quickly and Grace glided forward on his arm, her white chiffon dress floating around her. Alice followed, amused and admiring. If anyone had grown old gracefully then Grace certainly lived up to her name.

Back in the salon, Grace once more reclined on the sofa. Alice watched as Guy sat on the floor with the dogs, sprawled at Grace's feet. He had a natural animal elegance and self-confidence in every move he made. Was it his privileged upbringing that made him so at home in any environment? Alice envied him his self-assurance and regretted her own natural shyness. There was no vanity in Guy, just complete belief in himself and his ability. It was little surprise that he was successful in his career. He was talking now, to Grace as he stroked Cloud.

'I loved all the old Hammer horror movies when I was a teenager. Jean-Michel and I used to watch them on video at school.'

'Ah, of course, you were at school with Jean-Michel. He must be older than you though?'

'Yes, he was a few years above me but both being French, sorry about that Grace but, as you said, we couldn't help that, we were *les bons amis!*'

'I really must try not to be so rude and, of course, I am sure that French is a lovely language if you are…' she hesitated and gave one of her wicked laughs, '… if you are unfortunate enough to be born French and don't have the opportunity to learn another language. But, where were we? Hmm, Hammer horror… excellent and dreadful, don't you think? Now tell me about your latest screenplay.'

Guy stretched out and began to stroke Smoke but Cloud immediately nudged his elbow and begged attention. 'You two dogs are just like my horses, both jealous and spoilt rotten. *Mais, vous êtes les chiennes les plus belles de monde!*' Both dogs nuzzled Guy and tried to sit on his lap. He looked up at Grace, laughing, 'Sorry, Grace but I have to tell you that your beautiful dogs both speak perfect French.' Grace laughed her low, wicked laugh and reached out and tapped Guy on the head in rebuke. Guy fondled both dogs one last time and then went to sit on the sofa next to Alice. 'Well, my screenplay is being worked through right now, on set in LA. I think it's going quite well and I am already commissioned to write a sequel, set in Delphi and Paris. Greek gods this time round, Zeus and his gang. It's all going well, so far, but I live in dread of getting a call from Hollywood. I have to go over for re-writing when the proverbial stuff inevitably hits the fan. I can't stand the great sprawling place.'

'Hmm, I quite agree. It's completely soulless and yet full of people who talk about their souls, their innermost self and other rubbish.'

'Very true, my director is one of them. He has to mystically feel his way through the script. I'm sure you have met directors like that in your career.'

'Hmm, and how I remember the re-writes… staying up all night to re-learn lines. But I think it must be very different being the star. I enjoyed the power of walking off the set whenever things became too sparky or free-spirited. Then, of course, I was usually sleeping with the director at the time… that helped.'

Alice and Guy laughed and then Alice said, 'Guy, you haven't really answered Grace's question… and I want to know, too. All you have told me is that the film on set now is a mythical Norse legend played out in New York? Is that right?'

'Exactly right… and you have managed to encapsulate the whole thing in a few words. It only took me a year to write. Perhaps you could help me sort out the ancient Greeks?'

Alice laughed, 'Well, I'm just going by what you told me. I'm sure Vikings or Greeks would be hideously difficult to bring to life…not to mention weaving in the modern day.'

'Not really, once the plot is in my head I turn to dialogue to tell the whole story. It's fatal to write a story and then try to turn it into a film. Well, it wouldn't work for me, anyway. I sort of hear my characters talking me through.'

'Hmm, how interesting, Guy,' Grace looked across at Alice and Guy, her blue eyes bright and piercing, 'How would you both feel about working together on a biopic of my lurid life?'

There was a silence in the room apart from the sound of the crackling log fire, then Alice spoke first, 'Wow, that's quite a thought, Grace. I mean, I don't know if…'

'For goodness sake, girl, don't start on your self-doubting. You are a very clever young woman, organised, compassionate and empathetic. Quite capable of compiling and sorting out my old life. As for Guy, he has a proven track record in a different genre so it would be a challenge… but maybe something he would not be interested in taking on.' Grace raised her eyebrows and looked at Guy.

'On the contrary, it's a fascinating idea. I'll have to think it through, of course, but I think it's a project that I would be proud to take on.'

'Hmmm, good… then let's all think about it for a few days. I have my wily agent, Bernie Goldman, coming over next week and he has already put the idea forward. The opportunity seems to be there for the taking. Now, it is time you young things went off and do things that young things do so well. I shall retire to bed and try for some beauty sleep… I need all I can get to make me even presentable in the cold light of tomorrow morning. Off you go now!'

Alice and Guy hurried down the path to Alice's cottage. The night air was cold after the heat of the villa and Guy held Alice close to him,

'Never have the stars shone so brightly, Alice, stop for a moment and look up… there's a shooting star, look!'

'I saw it! I've never seen a shooting star before… in fact, I've never seen the stars so bright, they look close enough to touch. This must be what star-gazing is all about.' Alice snuggled into the warmth of Guy's body as she stared up at the vast night sky.

'I love the stars, do you see the Milky Way?' Guy reached up and pointed his hand in a wide arc, 'and the Great Bear. I learnt to recognise them when I was a boy. Sometimes, lonely at school, I used to feel the stars were my friends, keeping me safe, somehow.'

'I don't know,' Alice answered doubtfully, 'I think it just makes me realise how insignificant I am down on earth… the magnificence of it all above, so high above me.'

'Not insignificant to me, Alice. You have brought more light into my life than all the stars above.' He kissed her then, gently, 'And, not to change the subject, you do have a heavenly body.' He held her now close against him and kissed her more passionately. Alice pulled away from him and took his hand and began to run on down the path.Reaching the cottage door, Alice quickly unlocked it and then they were inside, warmth enclosing them as they kissed again and the rest of the world, even the stars, were lost to them.

Alice awoke at the first light of dawn and lay quite still, flat on her back, remembering the night of love. There was a familiar pattern forming as they began to understand each other. She opened her eyes and turned to look at Guy. In the half-light she saw his dark hair against the white of the pillow and then he opened his eyes and looked at her and smiled. He stretched out his hand and laid it on her breast and began to slowly stroke it in light circular movements. Alice arched her back in pleasure and, when he gently tugged at her nipple, she turned toward him and then sat astride him, slowly lowering herself over him. He reached up and held both her breasts as she moved up and down on top of him, her long hair falling forward and brushing his chest. Finally with a primeval cry she fell onto him and he held her tightly to him. 'Don't ever leave me, Alice.' She heard his words and then fell into a deep, dreamless sleep.

21   'Madame Pompadour would have to remain forever silent'

When Alice awoke she found that Guy had gone. She looked around sleepily, realised it was past ten in the morning, and then saw a small sprig of olive leaves and a note on the bedside table.

'My lovely Alice, *mon petit chou chou*, You are so beautiful when you are asleep and bewitching when you are awake. I am creeping away as I have an appointment this morning and if I wake you to tell you… well, then I should never be able to leave. I'll call you later and until then keep you close in my heart. All my love, Guy.'

Alice read the short note twice and then smiled and kissed the paper. It was ridiculously romantic, of course, but then Guy was a writer. She sat up in bed, suddenly remembering Grace's suggestion about writing a screenplay of her life. It was an exciting idea and, in her heart, she knew she was capable of the work. Grace had reminded her of that and so quickly dispelled any self-doubts that Alice had about her own abilities. Of course, she could do it and working with Grace was such a pleasure. How would it be to work with Guy? Was there a risk of mixing their newly found love with the emotive business of writing? Alice went over to the desk in her bedroom and picked up the file of her own work that she had brought from England. The book that she had begun to research after her finals at university. It was a thick file and well organised with cited references and a long alphabetical bibliography. to all the relevant books about the court of Louis XV and his various courtesans. She sighed and closed the file with a firm tap. She knew with complete certainty that she would never be able to bring the historical characters to life. Guy was right when he spoke about dialogue bringing the story into existence. Alice shook her head and, with a distinct sense of relief, she placed the file into her empty suitcase. Madame Pompadour would have to remain forever silent and would now be replaced by the real life Grace Devine. Alice hugged herself in delight at the thought. She switched on her favourite, loudest music and danced wildly around the room, punching the air. How much better a character to write about could there be in the whole world than Grace Devine?

Half an hour later she was sitting at the large table in Minnie's kitchen.

'I've a hot *pain au chocolat* in the oven, how would that go down with a large milky coffee?' Minnie stood, hands on her hips, looking at Alice with a small smile. 'You need feeding up… there's nothing of you!'

'How can you say that, Minnie? I eat so well here… in fact, I don't think I've ever eaten so much in my life.' Alice rubbed her hands together, still cold from the walk uphill from her cottage. 'But that does sound like the best breakfast offer. Yes, please.'

'They're only small so you better have two.' Minnie placed a plate with the two flaky chocolate pastries and a wide cup of white frothy coffee in front of Alice, 'There you go. Are you in for lunch today?'

'Er, yes please, Minnie.' Alice was waiting for Guy to phone her, but it was already gone twelve. She checked her phone again, but there were no missed messages. 'I'm so late eating breakfast I shouldn't really need lunch.'

'Course you will, by one o'clock you'll be starving again. This cold weather you need to eat more. I'm glad you popped in as I wanted to tell you how pleased we are, Gerald and me. Pleased for Grace. Your coming here has livened her up.'

Alice looked at Minnie in surprise, 'Really? She seems very lively to me all the time anyway, I mean, she's such great company and so full of fun.'

'That she is… but only when she has an audience. She's enjoying showing off to you and now to your young man, too. He seems a good bloke… a bit swarthy.'

Alice tried not to laugh aloud, 'Yes, his hair is very dark and he does have a permanent tan. He spends a lot of time in Los Angeles, I think.' Alice smiled now, pleased to talk about Guy.

'Well, he seems a nice lad and he likes the dogs, that's good enough for me. Did he meet Jason?'

Alice was surprised at the question, 'Er, no, I don't think he did, no, I'm sure not. You and Gerald weren't at dinner with us, nor Jason, and then we watched a film until quite late. Why do you ask?'

'Well, I'd like to answer that, Alice, really I would, but the truth is I can't. I'd just like to ask you not to talk about Jason with anyone outside of here.'

Alice frowned, 'I just don't understand. Is he running away from something? Is he a criminal? I can't be party to hiding a criminal, can I, Minnie?'

Minnie sat down at the table beside Alice, suddenly looking tired and drawn. 'Don't worry, Alice, maybe I shouldn't have said so much. Jason's not a criminal. I'll have a word with Gerald and see what he says about explaining things more. Until then I should be so glad if you just give the lad a chance and stay out of it all. Stay quiet, like.'

'Of course I can, don't worry Minnie. I'm quite sure you know best how to help Jason. I'll just mind my own business. I like him anyway, what I know about him. He does seem like a good guy.

''And you're a good girl, Alice. There must have been some lucky star in the sky above the Villa the day you came here to us. Now, I must get on… I'm making a tasty herb omelette for lunch with a green salad. How does that sound?'

'Sounds fantastic.' Alice sipped her coffee and thought back through the conversation. There was no understanding it. She checked her phone again and sighed, no message yet. 'I think I'll take the dogs for a run around.' At her words, the dogs jumped up from their place by the Aga and began to circle excitedly around Alice.

'I swear they understand everything that goes on!' Alice laughed as she fastened the dogs white leather collars and thinking to herself that she wished she did. Half way down the olive grove her phone buzzed. Alice hastily pulled it from her pocket and saw it was a text message. She had hoped Guy would ring.

'sorry not to contact before - have difficult video conference still online now - call you this evening x'

Alice quickly tapped back in the word 'fine' and then hesitated before adding more. Should she say she loved him? He had added a kiss. She hesitated for a moment longer and then just added 'speak later x' and pressed send. She walked on downhill, watching the dogs as they galloped ahead and feeling distinctly unsettled. What had she been expecting? Of course, Guy had to work, she knew she was being ridiculous but… then, Alice whistled to the dogs and walked back uphill. If she hurried there would be time to call her mother before lunch. It would be good to talk with her. Maybe she would tell her about Guy Bond and the way he had stormed into her new life in Provence. The dogs had caught up with her and giving them each a quick stroke and a dog biscuit from the supply in her pocket she said,

'Come on then, race you back to the cottage!'

The dogs had become quite used to visiting Alice in her cottage and now they lay sprawled at the feet as she dialled her mother's number.

'I'm so glad you rang, Alice. I've had such a morning.'

'What's the matter, Mum? Are you alright?'

'Yes, yes, I'm fine but can you guess who came calling this morning? Simon Stafford.'

'Simon? Oh my god, Mum, what did he want?'

'Well, what do you think he wanted? He wanted to speak to you, of course. He had been to our old house and the new tenants gave him Mike's address here.'

'Oh, goodness, sorry Mum… I had no idea… I mean, he knew it was all over between us.'

'Well, he doesn't want it to be, I can assure you. I made him a coffee and he sat in the kitchen like a lost dog. It was awful.'

Alice looked down at Smoke and Cloud at her mother's words. She sighed, Simon Stafford was nothing like a lost dog.

'Oh no, I am sorry… but I thought he had a job to go to in Birmingham or somewhere. He definitely had an offer of research in a university somewhere.'

'Oh yes, he is working in Birmingham but he is lonely and miserable. Really, you know me, I can usually find a way to cheer someone up but he seemed determined to be sad. I thought he'd never go. He is a nice guy, though. I don't really understand why you broke it off, Alice. He obviously loves you.'

Alice looked around the room as her mother continued. The bed was still unmade and Guy's note lay on the bedside table. She hesitated but somehow it didn't seem the right moment to take her mother into her confidence. Better to leave it a while before she told her about meeting Guy. 'Anyway, Mum, I'm sorry he troubled you but there is no possibility of my going back to Simon. It's over. I know he seems very nice…' The word stuck in her throat… nice, like her new step-father, she thought, 'but do you know what, Mum? Nice is not enough.' She heard her mother sigh on the other end of the phone.

'Well, it's completely your decision, Alice, of course, but don't roam around seeking the impossibly romantic hero. That only happens in fiction.'

'OK, Mum, I know what you mean. But, thinking about it, I'm not even sure he was completely nice either. He was very possessive and sort of bossy. I can't really explain it, but somehow we always had to do things his way. Anyway, it is most definitely over. Sorry, Mum, I have to go now as I'm having lunch at the Villa and then it will be time to start work. Can we speak again soon? I have lots more to tell you, but I am still writing my diary. I'll send the next episode at the end of the week.'

'Of course, darling, I'd better go, too. Mike has a half day surgery today so we're going out to lunch in Guildford.'

'I'm so glad you're having a good time, Mum. It's about time, isn't it? All you've ever done is made sure I enjoyed everything. It really is your turn. Give my love to Mike.'

'That's sweet of you, Alice. You have no idea how happy you make me feel saying that. Speak soon then and look out for mad hatters while you roam around your wonderland. Love you lots!'

The phone went dead and Alice smiled at her own reflection in the dressing table mirror. 'I did it!' she said aloud, 'I sent my love to Mike.' She raised a thumb to her own reflection, congratulating herself and thinking that it was quite a change for her to be able to cheer her mother up. A change for the better. As for Simon Stafford, well, it was hard luck but she was sure he would soon find someone else… a really nice girl who enjoyed everything being arranged for her, just so.

'You're in high spirits today, Alice. Now, why is that?' Grace looked across the lunch table at Alice, her eyebrows raised. Her voice was serious, but her blue eyes were laughing mercilessly.

'How could anyone not be on such a beautiful sunny day in Provence?' Alice answered, keeping her composure whilst knowing that her usual lunch companions were well aware that Guy had stayed the night in her cottage. Alice knew that Grace could be a relentless tease and she was determined not to be ruffled. Blushing and being dreadfully shy had to become a thing of the past if she was to withstand the jibes. She had work to do and although she already regarded Grace as a friend there could be no more teasing. Alice was filled with a new confidence and she knew very well why that was. It was having Guy in her life. Until he had called her just before lunch she had been full of doubts. His voice, full of love, had quickly reassured her. He had not waited until the evening to call her but taken time away from his meeting. It was obvious he was as anxious as she was to be together again. Although it had been a hurried call, it was all Alice had needed to feel up in the clouds with love. They had arranged to meet in Mougins at seven that evening. Every beat of Alice's heart was ticking away the seconds until then. Now looking back at Grace she smiled and said quietly,

'The truth is Grace, I'm in love.' Then, Alice looked round the table at Minnie and Gerald and finally to Jason, she allowed a long silence to fall and then added. 'I know it sounds ridiculous… but I am in love with Provence and being here with you all. Thank you for making me so welcome, thank you all.'

Grace gave a high-pitched ripple of laughter, nothing like her usual husky laugh… then she clapped her hands. 'Alice, you are a wonder! You have come quietly into our lives and won all our hearts. I salute you. Your words were perfectly timed and caught us all on the wrong foot. Maybe you should be an actress?' Grace raised her glass, 'To Alice who brings her wonders to our land, here at the Villa la Vie en Rose. She really is a star performer!'

Alice smiled and raised her glass in return, 'And right now I am concentrating on not blushing. I have a lot to learn and I think this is the best place in the world to learn.'

There was general laughter round the table and Alice was pleased to see that Jason joined in. Maybe it was good for him to realise that there were other shy people in the world around him.

'Well, I can't even remember how it feels to blush,' Grace said, 'and I can't help thinking it is a form of conceit. If you are blushing then you are thinking about yourself. You should rise above it.'

'Oh, I don't think it's just that easy,' Alice said and caught a sympathetic glance from Jason, 'you may be right about thinking about oneself but it's not in a conceited way. No, more a feeling of not being good enough or something…' Alice stopped, unable to explain how she felt and, into the silence, Jason joined the conversation for the first time.

'I know exactly what Alice means, although it's OK for her, it just makes her look prettier. But it's bad for a boy to blush. I wish I didn't. At school, I never put my hand up to answer questions… I knew the answer all right… just as surely I knew I would blush.'

There was another short silence as they took in his sudden outburst. Then Grace spoke,

'It's true, Jason, it does look cute on Alice… but you know, it hardly notices under your tan. Now, don't blush, but you are a very handsome young man… I am something of an expert in that field… and you can rest assured that if anyone is looking at you it is only with admiration or… something stronger. Maybe we should give you more practice in blushing… and then you would get fed up with it.'

'Well, I've had plenty of practice this dinner time! I never thought about my tan hiding it though.' Jason rubbed his cheeks as he spoke and then gave a wide and perfect grin. 'Thanks, Grace, I'll remember that.'

'I think I used to blush, too,' said Minnie, 'but it's one of those things you grow out of. Now, who's for more salad… I've made a different dressing with our olive oil and a touch of honey?'

The lunch continued with general conversation about the morning.

'Jason and me, we've finished collecting all them olive tree prunings.' Gerald said, 'You ought to go for a walk this afternoon, Grace, the sun will be lovely in the olive grove and Jason has made a winding path all the way down.'

Grace smiled at Gerald, 'You both work so hard. It looks so well trimmed.' She looked down at her newly manicured nails, 'But I couldn't possibly go for a walk today. I don't want to spoil my nail varnish.'

Gerald laughed out loud, 'Grace you are a caution and lazy with it. I'm not suggesting you walk on your hands, am I now?'

'Anyway, Madame Clare told me this morning retrograde Mercury supports an alignment by conjoining Mars and squaring Neptune…and that I should be very careful this week.'

'That Madame Hot Air-Clare, it's just a load of balderdash, I can't understand you, Grace, listening to it all… moon and stars.' Minnie sounded unusually cross and she stood up from the table, wiped her hands on her apron and began to clear the empty plates.

'I know, I know… you tell me repeatedly, Minnie… and you Gerald, don't you start. I like my mornings with Madame Clare, she's a good friend.'

Minnie snorted and walked out with the plates. Jason followed her, carrying more washing up and Alice stood up to follow him.

'Don't you desert me, too, Alice. Do sit down. Minnie will be back in a moment with the pudding and she will have quite forgotten about Madame Clare.'

Gerald laughed, 'That's true, my Minnie can't stay cross longer than two minutes maximum.'

'So, Madame Clare is your astrologer?' Alice asked, sitting down again, 'I have to say it sounds fascinating to me.'

'There, you see?' Grace glared at Gerald, 'The girl has an open mind. Next week, Alice, you must try and find time to join me… Madame Clare comes every Wednesday at eleven, after my manicurist. In fact, why don't you come earlier and have your nails done?'

'Really? That would be great! I've never had a manicure.'

Grace took Alice's hand and inspected her nails, 'Hmm, I can see that. Never mind, Marie will do her best. Now, here comes Minnie with pudding and I can tell by the look on her face that she has quite forgiven me.'

The sweet smell of chocolate filled the room as Minnie proudly laid a large and shiny chocolate and orange tart on the table. Everyone gave a sigh of pleasure and the meal continued amicably. Alice resumed her silent countdown to her date in Mougins that evening.

23 *'water trickling over every muscle of his body'*

Alice drove slowly back from Mougins. The evening had not gone as she had hoped or imagined. Had it been their first argument? The archetypal lover's tiff? Why hadn't Guy understood that she couldn't possibly just fly off to Greece with him?

'But it will only take a week and we could have such a great time… there's snow on Mount Parnassus right now… the ski resort is really near Delphi… I know this little hotel…'

'Stop, Guy, do stop. Do you think I don't want to come with you? But I can't possibly let Grace down. I've only worked for her a week or so … it just wouldn't be right.'

'Let me ask her on your behalf then, if you won't… I bet she won't mind at all.'

'No, Guy, my mind is made up and I am not giving up on my new job just like that.'

'But you wouldn't be giving it up… it would only be a week or maybe ten days.'

'There you go… you don't really know how long your research will take in Greece, do you. No, I can't possibly come with you and that's that.'

There had been an awkward silence between them as they sat at dinner in the small restaurant in Mougins. The red candles burned bright, the food was excellent, the red wine soft and smooth but the mood had changed. Alice spoke first,

'I'm sorry, Guy, I hope you do understand?'

'Of course, it's completely up to you. I'm just disappointed I suppose. Don't worry about it any more. I'll be back soon.'

'When are you going then?' Alice asked, her heart missing a beat.

'Well, I may as well fly tomorrow. I'll go down to Nice and just take the first flight to Athens. Delphi is only a few hours from there.'

'Right, yes, of course.' Alice tried to talk casually, but she felt near to tears. Had she made the wrong decision? Maybe Grace wouldn't have minded. She took a deep breath and blinked back her tears. 'Well, I hope it all goes well and that you'll be back soon, then.'

Guy took her hand in his and kissed it gently, 'Of course I will, Alice. Without you there I shall have a miserable lonely time but I'll get through the work quicker, that's for sure!'

They both tried to laugh and then continued with their meal. Talking of everything apart from Greece, their work and the days ahead that would drive them apart.

Later, sad and alone, Alice drove back to the villa and the gates swung open as she approached. The sky was pitch dark and cloudy and no lights shone from the villa. It was late, well after midnight. Alice parked by her cottage and was standing by the door, looking for her key when she heard footsteps behind her. She turned quickly and gave a gasp of relief as she saw Jason standing there.

'Crikey, Jason, you scared the life out of me.'

'Sorry, Alice. Really sorry. I heard the Mini and I thought I'd just check you were OK.'

'I'm fine. Just looking for my key. Where are Smoke and Cloud?'

'I left them up at the villa. I didn't want them to start barking and wake everyone. Anyway, have you got your key?'

'Yes,' Alice held the key up, 'found it at last… it was right at the bottom of my bag. It's so dark tonight.'

'Yeh, forecast is for rain tomorrow. You haven't had rain here yet, have you? It rains like the end of the world … usually four days and then out comes the sun again.'

'Really? It's been sunny ever since I arrived. Have you been at the Villa long?'

Jason shuffled his feet in the gravel by the front door of the cottage, 'Yeh, nearly three months now.'

'You like it then?'

'Oh yeh… anyway, I'll be getting back to the villa. Good night, Alice.'

'Night, Jason, thanks for looking out for me.'

Alice watched as Jason walked back up to the villa. The night was so dark that his tall, bulky figure was soon lost to sight. Alice went into the cottage, pleased to be in the warm. She threw her bag down on the sofa and went through to the bedroom. She looked at the large double bed… it seemed bigger and emptier than ever before. She had known Guy for such a short time, but he had quickly become part of her life here. How would she get through the next week or maybe longer? Would it have been better never to have met him than to feel so deeply unsettled now? She turned on some music and decided to take a hot shower. Tomorrow would be another day and she would just have to get on with it. Wrapped in a large towel she decided she really could not allow Guy to disturb her so much. She was so lucky to have landed this job, working with Grace and being so well looked after by Minnie and Gerald. Even Jason had become a good friend. Maybe he had secrets that could not be revealed but he was a kind and gentle young man. Maybe she would brave up to swimming with him tomorrow morning. So many 'maybes'… Alice's head was swimming as she lay down to sleep. The music still played quietly in the background and Alice began to think again about her dinner with Guy. She stared into the dark, her eyes stretched wide as she tried to decide if she had done the right thing. Was this to be a sleepless night? But in less than a minute Alice drifted into a deep and dreamless sleep.

When she awoke she heard the soft patter of rain on the large windows. She pulled the duvet overhead as she remembered the evening before. Would Guy already be on his way to the airport? She reached out and checked her phone. No messages, but she was surprised to see that it was nearly nine o'clock. She groaned as she remembered she had thought about swimming in the pool outside her window. She wrapped the duvet around herself and went over to the window. She peered through the slatted shutter and saw Jason pounding through the water. With a quiet whistle that was almost a deep sigh, Alice dropped the duvet and ran to the wardrobe and pulled out her black swimsuit. Somehow it seemed warmer than a bikini. Knowing she was being ridiculous, she grabbed the large towelling robe from the shower room and ran outside before she could think about it. The air was not as cold as she had thought it would be, but the rain was falling fast. The sky was grey and large clouds scudded across the wide landscape. Alice ran quickly round to the back of the cottage and stood by the pool, watching Jason as he ploughed through the water. Smoke and Cloud raced round the pool to greet her and Jason must have heard their excited barking as his head came up, glistening with water, and he raised a hand in greeting.

'Morning, Alice… I never thought you'd really swim.' He laughed and trod water, his broad shoulders running with water and his eyes, as turquoise blue as the pool, were laughing at her. Alice waved back, once again shaken by his breathtaking good looks. He was a superman, absolute perfection… but he wasn't Guy Bond.

Alice quickly threw off her robe and dived into the water, surfacing close to Jason. 'Oh my god, it's so warm! I thought it was going to be freezing. It's wonderful!'

'I know, do you see the steam just above the water level. That shows how hot it is. I took the temperature earlier… it's nearly 28 degrees in the water this morning and just about 5 degrees outside. You'll find your head gets cold if you stop too long though.'

'True, my shoulders feel cold, too. I'd better swim… and what was that about a race?' Alice laughed at Jason, feeling exhilarated by the cold air and the rain falling over them in the luxuriously warm water. 'Will you give me a start?'

'A start? You must be having me on… I can swim three lengths in the time it will take you to swim two.'

'Oh yeh? OK, you're on. You start at that end and then we'll see who finishes first back here.'

'Done!' Jason slapped the water with his hand and swam to the far end of the pool while Alice swam to the other end. 'Are you ready, then?'

'Ready when you are… prepare to be beaten hollow!'

'On the count of three… one, two, three!'

They both pushed off strongly from the side and were soon thrashing through the water. Alice was aware of Jason passing her in the other direction She pushed herself to move faster, kicking strongly and pulling with her arms as hard as she could. She made a good tumble turn at the end and moved faster through the water again, feeling confident that she was well ahead. Then she realised that Jason was close behind her and gaining. Only a few metres to the end of the pool and she strained every muscle to keep in the lead. Finally, her hand reached out for the pool edge and she stopped and turned to see that Jason had just beaten her to it. 'She laughed, trying to catch her breath, 'Dammit, you beat me to it. You're so fast!'

Jason was laughing, too, his head thrown back and his large Adam's apple pulsing in his throat. 'I very nearly didn't though, Alice, you're a great little swimmer. You move through the water like a tadpole. Well done! You might beat me next time. You weren't even warmed up.'

'No, I don't think I'll ever beat you. I bet you could swim faster if you really tried.'

'Well, might be true. I had to put a spurt on at the end. I seriously underestimated you. And don't forget my arm is much longer than yours so when I reached out…well…'

'That's a very kind winner's comment, Jason. Now, I'm finished. If I don't get out now I'll never face up to the cold.'

'Hold on then,' Jason pulled himself easily out of the pool and went over to get Alice's robe. 'Here you go!' He reached out a hand to Alice and pulled her up from the water. She took the robe from him and wrapped it close around her.

'Thanks, Jason, you really do look after me. Don't get cold yourself.' Jason was standing on the edge of the pool, the water trickling over every muscle of his body. Alice sighed as she looked at him. It would just be so convenient to fall in love with this beautiful man. Then she remembered seeing him in a clinch with Josette… and then, she remembered Guy. Had that really been the order of her thoughts? 'I'm off!' she said quickly and ran back into the cottage before her thoughts could lead her astray.

'there is a little shoe-maker in Nice'

'So you swam this morning while it was still raining?' Grace looked at Alice as she sipped her coffee.

'Yes, I've been thinking about it for days but I really needed to clear my head this morning. So…'

'Anything to do with this news?' Grace held up a small, blue sheet of hand-written paper She raised her eyebrows and gave Alice a piercing blue-eyed stare from under lowered eyelids.

'What's that?'

'A very elegant letter from your Guy Bond to advise me that he had to go to Greece for a week.'

Alice felt her cheeks begin to flush so she spoke hurriedly, trying to sound calm. 'Yes, he has to do some research for his next screenplay.'

'Hmm, ah well, that's a shame… just when you were getting to know him. He also says that he is very interested in working on the script for my biopic.'

'Does he? That's good.' Alice felt her spirits rise a little. Surely if he wanted to work with Grace then he would soon be back at the France? Back in life at the Villa la Vie en Rose, back to her.

'Did he ask you to go with him?' Grace was now looking hard at Alice and now she could do nothing to stop the colour rising to her cheeks as she replied,

'Yes, he did mention it last night…'

'And you said no because you had just started working for me… have I guessed correctly?'

Alice looked down and began to stroke Cloud who was lying at her feet. Now she was struggling to hold back tears as she remembered the look of disappointment on Guy's face as she had refused to go with him. 'Yes, well, something like that… I mean, we do have work to do here and you have been so very kind to me from day one.'

Grace interrupted, 'What a sweet girl you are, Alice. One day I should like to meet your mother and compliment her on the way she has brought you up… such a strong sense of moral duty. Of course, I have no idea how that works out in life in general… I never had any morals or conscience… I suppose I picked up some way of living my life as I grew older. But as a young woman, when I think I how heartless I was… ruthless, even.'

'Well, that's certainly hard to believe sitting here now.' Alice had recovered from her confusion and listened with interest to how Grace described herself as a young woman. She pulled out her laptop and opened her file. 'Shall we have a look at where we left off?'

'Yes, but before we start I just want to drop a few more pearls of wisdom… joking, of course, because you should probably take no notice of me at all… in fact I probably know more about pearls than wisdom… but I was just thinking that Guy should have understood your loyalty to your new work here. Men should not be allowed to think that their work is more important than a woman's … never follow that path, my dear. And, lastly, I promise this will be the end of my attempt at life advice… but, you know, if you and Guy Bond can't pick up where you left off in a week or so then…then, I'm afraid it really wasn't the right thing after all. Now then, let's talk about me again. Where was I… had I just left the ballet school?'

Alice was still trying to absorb all that Grace had said when she realised they were back at work. She scrolled quickly through the last file and found her notes.

'Yes, your boobs had just fallen out of your fairy dress!' They both laughed and Alice sat back on the sofa. A huge sense of relief flooded over her. Of course, Guy would be back and, one way or another, they would see each other again. Grace appeared to be such a capricious woman but, in fact, she was probably as sensible and grounded as Alice's own mother. 'So, I made a note here that your mother was at first angry and then very pleased when you were offered a part in a film.'

'Ah yes, good girl, that reminds me now. Hmm, my first film role. Quite a disaster.'

'A disaster movie?'

'Goodness no… a dreadful musical. And, of course, because of my figure I was cast as a young woman… no child parts for me. I was launched straight into a world of sexual promiscuity and lechery.' Grace shuddered, 'You just can't imagine how unprotected a young actress was in those days.'

'What about your mother? Did she stay with you… look after you.'

'Alice, you are sweetly naive and maybe it is a shame to disillusion you… and you obviously have such a good mother yourself… but, I'm sorry to say that my mother was more like a pimp… or a madam in a brothel. No, that time of my life was very hard.'

Silence fell between them for a moment. Alice tapped at her keyboard and then stopped, not sure how to continue. Grace suddenly clapped her hands, the large diamond ring on her finger glittering in the firelight. The dogs jumped up and looked at her expectantly. 'Yes, my beauties, time to change the subject. Alice, why don't you let them out for a run? The sun has come back to us now. And would you ask Minnie if we could have some tea. We'll have it a bit earlier than usual, shall we?'

Alice flipped her laptop closed and stood up, 'Good idea, I'll ask Minnie and take the dogs for a quick run myself.'

'Thank you, Alice. Tea will be waiting here for you… about half an hour?'

Alice nodded and went quickly out of the room, followed closely by Smoke and Cloud. She looked back at Grace as she closed the door. Grace was lying back on the white leather sofa, one hand to her forehead as she gazed into the fire.

Walking through the olive groves, Alice thought back through her disturbing conversation with Grace. The dogs ran ahead, noses to the ground as they zig-zagged back and forth between the huge trunks of the olive trees. The sun glinted through the branches, lighting up the freshly rain-washed world. Alice found a certain peace in the beauty of nature and she wondered if Grace ever made the effort to be outside in the fresh air. She strolled down to the gates and her mind turned to Guy. Was he now wandering a hillside in Greece, was he alone? She pushed the thought away and whistled to the dogs. They immediately circled back to her and she ran with them all the way back up the hill to the villa.

When she went back into the salon she found Minnie sitting with Grace, pouring tea.

'Here you are dear, nothing like a cup of tea on a cold, wintry afternoon and how about a nice piece of carrot cake?'

'Thanks, Minnie, how could anyone resist your carrot cake. The icing is to die for… what's that special flavour in it?

'Well, I mix the icing sugar with orange juice… maybe that's the trick. Just simple. Anyway, I was just saying to Grace that you two spend too long sitting around. Why don't you go out sometimes?'

Alice looked at Minnie and then to Grace, 'That's funny, I was just thinking the same thing. It may be winter but it's so beautiful out there and the sun is warming up again.' Alice stopped as she could see that Grace was pulling a face of disapproval. 'Of course, it's up to you, Grace. I mean, it's lovely sitting here by the fireside, too.'

'Hmm, well I was thinking it was about time I treated you, Alice. And while your talented Mr Bond is roaming around the Greek ruins maybe we should make the most of some extra time together. I always think comfort eating and retail therapy are hard to beat when one is a bit down in the dumps.'

Alice finished the last crumbs of the carrot cake and nodded, 'Mmm, well, this cake certainly takes care of the comfort eating.'

'Exactly, wonderful cake as usual, Minnie,' Grace nodded in agreement and held out her empty plate. Alice jumped up and took it from her and laid it back on the tray as Grace continued, 'My idea of retail therapy is probably not how you imagine it.'

'Well, to be honest, I can't really imagine you trawling through Primark or Prisunic!' Alice laughed and sat back on the sofa, exchanging an amused look with Minnie.

'Quite right, Alice, no, but there is a little shoemaker in Nice… '

'A little shoemaker… that sounds like something out of a fairytale.' Alice interrupted.

'No, no… he's a very real shoe-maker. He trained in London with Anello and Davide… he has made all my shoes for years now.' Grace stretched out her dainty foot and looked admiringly at her white kid high-heeled shoe. 'Yes, I think we could make a visit to him.'

'Really?' Alice looked at Grace in surprise. 'So he makes all your shoes to measure?'

'Why, of course, how else would they fit?' Grace now circled her foot, the white enamelled buckle shining as she turned her ankle round. 'I particularly like these… but they are getting rather shabby. Yes, I think we could pay a visit to Gino. What size do you take, Alice?'

'Well, really I'm a size five and a half but they don't often make half sizes so I wear a six.'

'There you are, you see, and then they don't fit properly at all. My goodness, six… that is large… twice the size I take in fact.'

Minnie interrupted, 'Six isn't that big for young girls now. Really, Grace, you're just dreadful, you know quite well that most people just buy their shoes in an ordinary shoe shop. I love my trainers… air-wears, they call them. Once I found them I would never wear anything else.'

Grace sighed impatiently, 'Yes, well, Minnie, that's all very well but you don't care a fig about how you look. Beautiful shoes for me… and for any young girl like Alice, are of the utmost importance. I'm sorry if you thought I was being rude, Alice, I seem to care less and less what I say nowadays. In fact, I thought those flat black patent pumps you wore on Sunday… I thought they were very…' Grace seemed to be struggling to find the right word, 'very chic.'

'Really! Did you notice them? I bought them in a sale at Hobbs in Kingston. They're a six and a bit big for me so I put a sock in them.'

'Oh my, a six and sock… oh dear, this just gets worse and worse. My dear girl, we'll get Gino to measure your feet too.' Grace sighed and looked from her own small foot in the soft white leather high-arched shoe and then to Alice's in her flat suede loafer. 'That's if he can make shoes as big as you need… yes, I'll get Monique to make an appointment and Gerald can run us down there. Now off you go both of you, all this talk about shopping has quite exhausted me.'

'cruising along the famous Promenade des Anglais'

Alice slipped her feet into her best black patent pumps and looked at them doubtfully. What would Gino, the bespoke shoe-maker, think of the shoes? Now that she thought about it, they did gape a little round the back of her heel. She took them off and took out the tartan foam inner sole that she usually wore with them, Then, she slipped them on again and walked across the bedroom. The effect was worse… the shoes now hardly stayed on her feet. Pushing the inner soles back into the shoes she was back where she had started. She sighed as she thought how thrilled she had been when she bought them… the most expensive shoes she had ever owned. Anyway, it was time to go. Grace was not a person to be kept waiting. There was an almost childlike impatience in Grace's sudden whims. The appointment had been made at short notice by Monique, or whoever it actually was that worked in the admin agency. At first, a day in the following week had been offered and Grace had thrown a petulant mood, threatening not to go at all. The appointment had suddenly been arranged for today at eleven o'clock. Alice smiled as she ran up the hill to the villa. The sun was shining again, the sky bluer than ever. She had swum again with Jason and now her body felt so good that she could have turned a cartwheel. The thought of Guy, now so far away in Greece, was pushed to the back of her mind. She was excited to be going to Nice with Grace in the old Bentley. Yes, Grace's idea of retail therapy was certainly most effective.

An hour later the huge Bentley was cruising along the famous Promenade des Anglais. Grace opened her eyes for the first time since leaving the villa.

'It is so good that it is called the English Prom, don't you think, Alice? I always imagine the first brave English tourists walking along under the lines of fresh new palm trees. Long-skirted women with pretty parasols and dandy men in boaters…it must have been lovely…' she sighed, 'now, of course, it's all traffic. Look, Alice, there's the Negresco.'

Alice craned her neck to look forward and saw the large pink dome of the hotel on their left. Grace leaned forward and tapped Gerald on the shoulder and without a word he manoeuvred a u-turn in the double lane of traffic and pulled into the kerb right in front of the Negresco steps. The sudden halt caused quite a commotion, cars hooted and two young men in an open-top red Ferrari called out and waved their arms angrily. Gerald took no notice at all, but turned off the engine.

'Long time since you've been here, Grace.' he said, turning round to look at her and Alice.

'Never mind that, Gerald, I just thought Alice might enjoy a coffee here. We won't be long.'

Gerald got out of the car and opened the back door for Grace. She stepped out carefully and stood a moment, waiting for Alice to slide across the seat and join her.

'Take my arm, Alice, I don't want to fall flat on my face up these dreadful steps.' Alice stepped forward and at the same time a doorman, dressed in remarkable blue and red livery with a tall black hat and red feathered cockade, came down the steps to greet them.

'Madame Devine... such a pleasure... it has been too long since you have honoured us.' He bowed and stepped to the side as Alice and Grace made their way slowly up the staircase.

'Thank you, Philippe, it's good to see you, and you are looking very well. How is your son, André?'

'Ah, Madame, you remember, *si gentille, merci, mon fils,* André is now at the university in Toulouse.'

'My goodness, and I remember when he was born. How proud you must be, Philippe, congratulations indeed. How time flies by...is Madame Augier's cat, Carmen, still sleeping in the bar?' Without waiting for an answer, Grace moved forward. Alice was very aware that Grace, small and birdlike, was clinging tightly to her arm as she walked through the vast marble-floored lobby. Another footman came toward them, dressed in the same blue and red uniform.

'*Bienvenu,* Madame Devine, this is a great honour. Will you be taking luncheon?'

'No, no, just coffee... we'll take a table in your ridiculous brasserie. I am sure my young friend here, Alice Shakespeare, will be interested to see it.'

The footman gave a small bow of recognition to Alice and then walked slowly in front of them. It was difficult not to be impressed by the welcome that Grace had been given and Alice, once again, thought how lucky she was to be working for her. That is, if sitting in the Negresco brasserie with a view of the Mediterranean with a cup of cappuccino could seriously be called work. Alice made a mental note to call her mother later to tell her all about it.

'I wonder what possessed them to put a carousel in the brasserie? It's been here as long as I can recall… a faded fairground… rather sad in a way. The whole hotel is very quirky… one of the things I do like about it. In my hey-days it was fun… now it is is rather jaded, don't you think? I don't know if Madame Augier is still in command… she used to run the place. Quite an extraordinary woman. My goodness, she had her work cut out in the old days…there was always some crazy scenario… I remember Richard Burton staying here with Liz, he was sitting in the bar, chatting with the barman and showing him this amazing emerald necklace and ear-rings that he had just bought… anyway, I think Liz suddenly phoned him from their suite and he went rushing off… left the jewellery on the bar stool!' Grace laughed, her spectacular low husky laugh and Alice noticed a table of four people turn to look at them.

'Oh Grace, you do have some great stories to tell,' Alice laughed too, 'Did you often stay here then?'

'Yes, quite often if I was on the Côte d'Azur I would stay here… I always preferred it to the Carlton in Cannes… I like the Italian influence in Nice. And I always stay in hotels that are owner owned… you know, not a chain. In fact, Bernie was telling me the other day that a young couple have taken over a hotel in La Ciotat, down the coast toward Marseille. I used to stay there years ago, too. Wonderful small hotel, right on the beach and very private. Maybe we'll go there one day. I'm glad you suggested this outing, Alice.'

Alice looked at Grace in surprise and was about to contradict her, to tell her that it had been completely Grace's own idea when she noticed that the table of four that had been looking at them had now become a small crowd… all looking in their direction.

'Drink up, Alice, time to move on now. The vultures are gathering with pens and cameras.' Sure enough a young man was approaching, smiling and holding out a pen and paper.

'Grace Devine? It is, isn't it… I have been a fan of yours for years. Would you sign your autograph for me?'

Grace smiled and took the pen and quickly scribbled her signature. Then several cameras flashed and the crowd advanced. Grace stood up and Alice took her arm quickly, wondering what to do next. Then the uniformed footman appeared from nowhere and ushered the small crowd of people back. The doorman appeared next and escorted them to a glass door that led off the brasserie. They made their way to it and out into the bright sunshine of the busy promenade. Alice was relieved to see Gerald waiting in the Bentley parked right outside.

'So now you begin to understand why I don't go out often.' Grace said with a sigh, as she sat back in the Bentley and closed her eyes wearily. Gerald drove slowly away from the Promenade and began to thread his way through the narrow back streets of the old town behind the harbour.

'You certainly are a star celebrity, Grace. I suppose it must be tiresome.'

'Well, of course, I am proud that anyone should still be interested in me… especially if they are true fans, but you know, the press can be very cruel.'

'In what way?'

'Oh, it can be hurtful. A random photo can make an article…journalists like to find any angle, anything that sells and makes them money. Poor Brigitte, for example, photos of her ageing badly and placed against one of her in her prime. It can be cruel.'

'Well, you have nothing to worry about. I can't imagine anyone being able to take a photo of you that wouldn't be totally glamorous.'

'Hmm, well thank you, Alice, that may not be true but it's a nice thought. Now, here we are at Gino's little atelier. At least we shall have privacy here… he knows me well.'

'It's beginning to seem that you are very well known everywhere, Grace.'

'You just wouldn't believe it, Mum!' Alice was back in her cottage and keeping her mental promise to tell her mother all about her day in Nice. She knew it was ten o'clock at night in England but it was the first chance she had to telephone. 'I'm only just back in my cottage… we had this huge day out.'

'Isn't Grace rather elderly for long days out?' Alice's mother asked, 'You're not wearing her out, are you? You have to remember her age, Alice.'

'I thought the same, Mum, but I promise you she just got younger as the day wore on. First, Gerald dropped us at the Negresco for coffee… it was incredible, the staff all knew her and bowed and scraped in attendance and then she was practically mobbed by reporters…flash cameras the lot. She pretended to hate it, but that seemed to be the start of her rejuvenation.'

'Don't tell me you were chauffeur driven in that vintage Bentley, the one you wrote about in your diary?'

'Absolutely, it has to be the very best way to cruise along the Promenade des Anglais. Oh, Mum, you would have laughed, even though Grace has lived in France for years she is so rude about the French… she likes the Promenade because the English built it…so hilarious. She doesn't have a single bit of conscience and she can be so rude.'

'Well, it's a good job you do think it's hilarious, maybe some people wouldn't?'

'Oh, but you can't help loving her and it's all a sort of act. She was really nice to the doorman and remembered his son's name and everything. No, she's great. Anyway, then we went on to her shoemaker and… do you believe… I had my feet measured. Honestly, Mum, it was quite an experience. This little guy called Gino measured every centimetre of both my feet and made notes in a little leather book. Then we looked at swatches of leather and drawings in a huge book…sort of designs of shoe shapes and heels… absolutely the opposite to anything technical. All hand drawings in pencil…it was amazing.'

'So, did you order shoes?'

'Yes, Grace insisted I should have a pair of flat pumps… you know, like my black Hobbs. Oh and you should have seen Gino's face when he looked at my shoes…it was too funny for words… he sort of winced and screwed up his face and then carefully laid them down on the floor as though they were toxic. Grace was laughing all the time… she has this really low, sort of guttural laugh…very infectious, you know what I mean.'

'I'm beginning to imagine, you describe her so well in your diaries, you will keep sending them, won't you?'

'Of course, lately I've been a bit behind, so much has been happening.'

'Last time we spoke I had the distinct impression you had met someone… you remember, when we talked about Simon?'

'Oh well, that's all on the back burner at the moment. Anyway, Mum, I haven't finished telling you about today.'

'Goodness, can there be more?'

'Oh yes! After we left Gino's… by the way, Grace ordered five pairs of her usual very soft leather high heels and then, a breakthrough, she ordered a pair of flat pumps like mine. White, of course, she only ever wears white. Oh yes, and it was so funny she said she might wear them to the red carpet do in Cannes just because the management apparently tried to ban flat shoes. She is such a born rebel. Anyway, after that she was hungry… I was starving as usual… and she told Gerald to drive us round the harbour to this Italian restaurant high above the bay. The view was amazing, the whole Baie des Anges spread out below us in the winter sunshine. All the staff there knew her and treated her like royalty. It seemed she hadn't been there for ages, but they all loved her. We had the most delicious antipasto and then ravioli and salad. Even I couldn't manage dessert although the waiter brought a tiny sliver of tiramisu with our coffee. It was just heaven.'

'Surely Grace was tired by then?'

'Well yes, but when we were back in the Bentley she asked Gerald if he felt like driving up the coast a bit further to show me around a bit.'

'But Gerald is quite old himself, isn't he?' Alice's mother sounded slightly anxious.

'No, I shouldn't think he's more than fifty… I don't know really, but he has worked for Grace since he was a young man and usually he works hard in the garden and the olive grove. Anyway, he was more than pleased to get a chance to tour around… the Bentley is his passion.'

'So where did you go?'

'First we went uphill in Nice to Cimiez, past Matisse's house and a lovely park and then out of town and right along the Grande Corniche to Eze. It was stunning scenery. I had no idea the South of France was so beautiful. Gerald showed me so many places that I could visit in my time off… and Grace was fast asleep the whole time.'

'Well, I suppose the back seat of a Bentley must be very comfortable.'

'Well, she must have slept for over an hour and when she woke up we were just making our way back along the coast in the direction of Mougins. The minute she woke she tapped Gerald on the shoulder and said she thought that Cap d'Antibes would be good for tea!'

'So, after not going out for months she was definitely on a jaunt.'

'Absolutely, and Cap d'Antibes was superb. We went to a hotel right on the tip of the peninsula. Yet again, Grace was received like visiting royalty and we had tea in this restaurant hanging out over the sea… you can see right across to St Tropez and the beautiful blue hills in the distance. The sun was just going down and…'

'Oh, you will have to stop, Alice…it is all sounding just too lovely to be true. And here I am in boring Oxshott!' Alice's mother laughed, but there was no real ring of jealousy in her voice. 'I am so thrilled for you, Alice.'

'I do seem to have landed in a bed of roses, don't I? I hope you will come out for a holiday soon… and Mike, of course. Are you both well?' Alice hastily added the last few words, feeling guilty that she had been going on so long about her own wonderful day.

'Oh yes, we're both fine. Mike won't be able to leave his practice for a while yet but, as soon as we can, we shall drive down to visit you. As it is we have lovely days out when he has some free time. We went to Brighton yesterday, it was very cold, but we managed a walk on the beach and then the famous fish and chips. Doesn't quite compare with your day, I know!'

'Well, it does sound really nice, actually. I'm glad it's all going well. Marriage, I mean.'

'I know, after all this time on my own with you I never really thought I would marry… but then I met Mike. Yes, we are really happy. But I do miss you, Alice, of course. Maybe you will get some time off and come back for a few days?'

'Yes, maybe. But it won't be for a while, I have a lot of work here even though it all sounds like fun.'

'Of course, I do understand, Alice. Anyway, it's good to catch up on the phone.'

'Sorry, it was late again, Mum, but when we eventually got back to the villa I found that Minnie had made soup and we all ate in the kitchen and chatted.' Alice yawned and heard her mother do the same. 'Gosh, Mum, we still yawn at the same time together!'

'You never did guess, did you? When you were little and staying up too late, I used to pretend to yawn and that would start you off. Then, a few minutes of a story read to you in my most boring voice and you would be sounder!'

'Mum, you trickster! I never guessed at all… anyway, it still works well… I feel ready to drop off right now!'

'Me too, darling, sleep tight.'

'Will do, Mum, mind the bugs et cetera, night night.'

Alice looked at the phone for a minute and thought about her mother. The years they had spent together, sharing everything. She did miss her but, she admitted to herself now, if she did have any time off from this most un-joblike job, it would be very unlikely that she would spend it in Mike's nice house in Oxshott… or days out in Brighton.

27   *'Curiouser and curiouser.'*

The early swim with Jason had now become a regular routine. They would both swim several lengths at their own rhythm and then end with a race. This had been the third day that she had failed to win and Alice was beginning to suspect that Jason was pacing himself to end just a fingertip ahead of her. The guy was much too nice and definitely too handsome for words. Alice had showered and was blow-drying her long hair, looking in the mirror as she thought about Jason. Maybe she would ask him later if he would like to go for a coffee in Mougins. He might get the chance to see Josette and, if not, Alice might get the chance to chat and find out more about him. She knew she should be leaving the matter alone, but she had a curious nature. After all, she thought, smiling at herself in the mirror and brushing her shining hair, my name is Alice.
'Curiouser and curiouser! cried Alice (she was so much surprised, that for the moment she quite forgot how to speak good English).' she said the words aloud and was lost in the recollection of her mother reading Alice in Wonderland to her as a child. Perhaps she would give her mother another ring now? She looked round for her mobile and at that moment it buzzed. She saw it on the bedside table and ran to answer it. She snatched it up, hoping it would be Guy. So far he had sent short text messages each day but they had not spoken. Her hair fell over her face as she reached for the phone and quickly pressed the green arrow before the ringing ended.

'Hello, hello.' There was silence on the line, had she missed him? 'Hello, I can't hear you?'

Then a man's voice answered,'Hi Alice, so good to hear your voice.' It was not Guy but Simon, she knew immediately, the voice so familiar after the years they had spent together at university. So familiar that she could hear the anxiety in his voice as he continued, 'How are you, Alice?'

'I'm fine, Simon, just fine. How are you?' Alice strained to keep her voice in a normal register, trying to sound friendly. The last time they had spoken it had been anything but... he had been angry at her decision to break up their relationship and said things he probably now regretted.

'I'm fine, too. I had a few days off so I flew down to Nice... I'd love to see you, Alice.'

Alice's heart sank, maybe he was phoning from nearby right now. 'You know that wouldn't be a good idea, Simon.'

'Oh, I should have said before, I'm here with my girlfriend. I just wanted you to meet her.'

'Oh, oh I see… err, right. I'm so glad you have found someone, Simon. I knew you would… yes, well, maybe we could meet for a coffee. Where are you?' Alice regretted her reply as soon as she had made it. She should leave them to their new lovers' holiday in the South of France. What was it she had been thinking earlier about being incurably curious? She had to admit she was interested in meeting Simon's new love. Would the girl be like herself or completely the opposite?

'I drove past where you are living last night… the Villa la Vie en Rose. Shall I come up there? I'm… we're in Cannes right now.'

Alice stared into the mirror, her eyes wide, 'Oh no, don't come here, I'll meet you in Cannes. There's a cafe on the Croisette called Le 75, it's on the beach, but it's open in the winter. I could see you there at eleven-ish, if you like?' Alice's reflection in the mirror now closed its eyes and sighed in exasperation at herself.

Less than an hour later she was parking in front of the restaurant she had been to with Guy. It was closed and shuttered now and she felt sad just looking at it. There had been another text that morning, short and not particularly sweet. Just to tell her that his work was going well and that Delphi was absolutely amazing. Now she walked across the busy road and over to the beach café. She walked through to the tables laid out on the decking over the sand and immediately saw Simon. He was alone, sitting with his back to the sea and waiting for her. He stood up quickly as she arrived and came to meet her. Alice quickly dodged his welcoming open arms and sat down at the table. A table with one coffee cup on it, now half full.

'You don't have a new girl-friend, do you, Simon?' Alice's first words fell between them, accusing and quiet.

'No, I just had to see you, Alice. I knew you wouldn't come if you thought I was on my own.' Simon sat down beside her and hung his head.

'It was a stupid trick, Simon, and you know it. It's only made me remember how annoying you can be.'

'I'm sorry, Al, really I am.'

'Can't you even remember how I hate being called Al? Simon, don't you get it? We're just not right for each other.'

'But we had a good time at uni, didn't we? What's changed?'

'It wore itself out… our good times ended, little by little and then, for me, bang, it was finished, over, dead.' Alice spoke forcefully, angry that he should have tricked her into meeting him. The waiter came over and she ordered a cappuccino for herself. Simon just sat there, his head hanging down as he ignored the splendid view across the shining bay. Alice felt so furious that she couldn't even look at him. 'I'm going to drink my coffee and go. That's it, Simon. You must either enjoy a few days in this beautiful part of the world on your own or go home, go back to your work in Birmingham. You really mustn't come up to the Villa where I am working… they have guard dogs and security… you will get in trouble.' Alice gratefully sipped the coffee that the waiter had brought as she tried not to think about how she had exaggerated over the security arrangements at the Villa. But at least Simon had looked up and he did look alarmed,

'Security? What is this job, then?'

'I'm working, researching for a biography of a famous film star.' Alice left it at that, she did not want to give details about the wonderful time she was having with Grace Devine and her entourage. 'Anyway, I must get back and you must get on with your life.'

'You look like a film star yourself, Alice. You look different… not just tanned but somehow more sophisticated… and your hair is so beautiful.' He stretched out a hand as though to touch her hair and Alice sprang up from her seat. She had a flash memory, a sudden image of Simon stroking her hair after they had made love. He was looking at her now just as she remembered, loving but in some way possessive. Yes, that was the word, possessive. She thought briefly of how she had tried to explain to her mother how the relationship had been so wrong. She drew away from the table and stood facing him defiantly, now very aware of why she had ended their affair. 'It's over, Simon, completely over. I'm going and you had better not follow me.'

She walked away from him and into the interior of the café, hastily leaving a few euro coins on the counter, determined that Simon would not pay even pay for her coffee. Then she ran across the road and back to the Mini. She slipped quickly inside and started up the engine, glad of the familiarity and security of the little car. As she pulled away from the kerb she glanced across to the café and saw Simon looking around. He looked as lost and forlorn as a big child, standing outlined against the shining sea and blue sky. He didn't look in her direction and she drove quickly away. Simon would have to find someone else to adore… and maybe possess. But it would not be Alice.

'I've had another letter from your talented Mr Bond.' Grace waved a page of blue notepaper in the air above her head, her diamond ring glinting, as usual, in the shaft of sunlight. Did Grace even arrange the sunbeams to stage her performances? Alice suppressed a desire to lean forward and snatch the letter from Grace.

'How is he getting on in Greece?' Alice asked, her voice casual and distracted as she looked fixedly down at the keyboard of her laptop.

They were sitting, as usual, on the white sofas by the log fire, just beginning an afternoon session. Alice tapped her keyboard, waiting for Grace to continue, determined not to give away the frantic beating of her heart as she longed for news of Guy.

'Hmm, you can read it if you want… it's a good letter… typical public schoolboy stuff, correct and grammatical… but unusually good hand-writing for a man. Here, see for yourself!' Grace tossed the letter to Alice and it fell on the floor by Smoke. The two dogs both jumped up and Cloud snatched the letter and raced round the room followed by Smoke… and then Alice. Grace laughed her usual laugh, enjoying the ridiculous scene. Alice stopped and gave a piercing whistle and both dogs immediately came over to her. They both looked up at her, their strange blue eyes waiting for a command. The letter was now hanging crookedly out of the side of Cloud's mouth.

'Sit!' Alice said firmly, holding her hand out flat in front of the dogs. Both dogs half sat at the identical moment, their obedience slightly spoiled by their furiously wagging tails. Alice gently took the letter from Cloud, 'Good dogs, good girls!' The dogs jumped up again and continued to chase each other round the room, skittering and sliding on the white marble floor.

'Oh my, you'd better let them out, Alice, this is worse than a scene from Disney. Tom and Jerry have nothing on my dogs.'

Alice called the dogs through to the kitchen and let them out the back door. She returned to the salon, smoothing out the creased piece of heavy writing paper. The blue ink was smudged in parts, but she could just make out the words. Sitting back on the sofa again, she smiled at Grace,

'So it seems he can't wait to get back to France and already has in mind a scenario start point. That's exciting, isn't it? Are you pleased, Grace?'

'Not half as pleased as you look now, my dear. I thought you looked a bit woebegone when you came through the door. Now you look as though your personal sun has come out to shine.'

'Actually I had quite a difficult morning…' Alice sighed and then found herself telling Grace all about her meeting with Simon.

'Hmm, what a rotten trick… something I don't like about that. Seems to me that your rock is more like a weight round your neck. Your feeling that he was possessive… that was new, was it?'

'Well, I suppose so… although it suddenly just added up to why I had broken it off with him. He did seem to look after me… and I sort of liked that but then… I don't know… it was all a bit too much.'

'Well, like me, you never had a father to care for you. I remember the feeling of wanting someone to fuss over me. For years, I made that mistake, going from one mock father figure to another.'

'Oh, I don't think Simon was a father figure, he just seemed sort of dependable… and I thought it was boring in the end… but now I see him differently. I don't really understand myself.' Alice laughed and looked back at the creased letter. 'It is a good letter, isn't it?'

'I think Guy Bond may well be the type to allow you your own life and career. You've had a bit of a false start, but I'm sure he will respect you for not leaving your work. That's so important. Keep your own identity safe. It amuses me all this talk about identity theft nowadays. Believe me, there are more ways of losing your self than by someone stealing your credit card or your bank details.' Grace looked sadly into the fire and then out the window. Her face brightened, 'Look at those dogs racing round the olive trees… have you ever seen anything more beautiful.'

Minnie came in, then, with a tea tray.'Here you go, girls, tea and today's cake is walnut and honey. That'll keep you going.'

'Hmm, thank you, Minnie, your usual perfect timing. We were running down a bit.'

'Maybe you're tired after your long day out yesterday, Grace. I don't know, you don't go out for weeks and then you stay out all hours.' Minnie fussed around Grace, pouring her tea and then plumping up the cushions.

'Stop fussing, Minnie, although you know I love it. Strangely enough I woke this morning feeling rather refreshed by my outing into the cruel world. Yes, I definitely feel a year younger today than I did a week ago.'

'Go along with you, talking rubbish now, you're as old as you are and that's a fact.'

'Well, it's a fact I can well do without. I am enjoying stealing some of Alice's youth… I have been warning her about identity theft… but I am worse, I am vicariously enjoying the sights of the Riviera through her young eyes.'

'Well, I have no idea what this vicary stuff is all about but, I must say, you do look lovely today, Grace.'

'That's better, Minnie, that's what I need to hear, now trot along, in fact, why don't you go and put your feet up and have a snooze, you're getting on now, you know. Alice and I are very behind with our work.'

'I'll put my feet up at bedtime and not before, you know that very well, Grace. Cheek of it… anyway, plenty of time to sleep when you're dead and six foot under, that's what Gerald and I always says.' Not waiting for a response, Minnie bustled from the room, muttering to herself.

'Hmm, how I enjoy my spats with Minnie. It's so easy to wind her up.' Grace laughed and then, as she often did, suddenly changed the subject.

'So, as it seems your Mr Bond won't be back for a few days, why don't we have another jaunt? How about St Tropez? Have you been there?'

Alice looked up quickly, and put her teacup back on the tray. 'No, never, the nearest I have ever been was on that amazing terrace on Cap d'Antibes.'

'Yes, I saw you looking across to it shimmering in the distance. Of course, all young people want to go to St Trop. It's rather trashy now but in the sixties I had a great time there. Anyone who was anyone in the film world would hang out there… pretending it was just a simple Provençal fishing village. That was where I first went topless on a beach. Oh my god, what a scandal. The monokini. Even the bottom half was hardly there... I was sun-bathing on the Pampellone beach. Such a riot... the gendarmes were out, even a helicopter surveying the beaches... great publicity, of course, more titillating news. But it was just fun, really... and women were beginning to rebel... feminists were around then saying why could men go topless and not women.' Grace laughed, 'I can only think they didn't have breasts like mine or they would know the effect they could have on men. I mean, I can admire a man's muscular chest as much as any woman... but it doesn't drive me wild or lead to fights. By the way, Alice, talking of muscular hunks... I was thinking about Jason.'

Alice sat up straight, once again jerked to attention by the sudden change of conversation. 'Jason, what about him?'

'Well, you may not have noticed, but I think he is in love with our little Josette. The young daughter of the woman who runs the cafe in Mougins.'

'Actually, I did see them kissing once, it was after your Sunday party and she had been up here to help.'

'Hmm, I thought so, well, I'm glad you know about them. I don't think Minnie and Gerald know though. Best to keep it to ourselves for a while. But I was wondering if you happened to go into Cannes, one morning, perhaps you could ask Jason to go with you... a little outing... maybe stop at Mougins for a coffee on the way down to the coast?'

'Oh, of course, but I did ask him once and he seemed worried about going out. To be honest, Grace, I just don't understand the situation at all, I mean, he never ever goes out of the villa grounds.'

'Yes, well, he has his good reasons but I'll have a word with him later. Ask him tomorrow and see if you can persuade him. Better not ask anything more though.'

'No, of course not, it's absolutely his business, I see that.' Alice nodded but felt that she had been so near to finding out more about Jason, but the moment had passed. At least she could ask him to go out tomorrow and maybe he would meet up with Josette at the café. It would be a start. She returned to the notes on the laptop. 'So you went topless in St Tropez in the sixties, really Grace you are quite the rebel.'

Grace clapped her hands in delight, 'I think maybe you're right. I do have a natural inclination not to go with the flow. Anyway, if we go down to St Trop on Saturday, I shall hide out at my old haunt, the Byblos, and you can go to the market on the quayside like a regular tourist. What do you think?'

'I think it sounds great and I am one very lucky girl.'

'Well, Alice, you're a very sweet girl, too and when your Mr Bond returns you must be very careful that he is good enough for you. Remember that.'

Alice looked at Grace in surprise and then said slowly, 'Yes, Grace, I understand. I won't rush madly into anything and lose myself. I will remember, I promise.'

'Hmm, don't promise, my dear, a promise never made can never be broken and young love can be a mad thing. I never make promises or keep secrets… both are equally impossible as far as I can see.' Grace raised her arms theatrically above her head and projected her voice, resonant and clear, '*Love looks not with the eyes, but with the mind, And therefore is winged Cupid painted blind.*'

'A Midsummer's Night's Dream!' Alice said and clapped her hands in applause.

'just keep my head down for a while'

The next day began again with a swim. The water was wonderfully warm, but the fresh air was very cold. Alice had still not beaten Jason and she suspected that soon he would let her win. Their routine continued. At the end of their race, Jason would pull himself out of the pool, fetch Alice's robe, pull her out of the pool, hold the robe while she slipped it on and then quickly dive back into the pool. Today though, he stood awkwardly on the edge of the pool, dripping water and wrapping his arms around himself and jumping up and down. Alice guessed what he wanted to say and spoke first,

'Jason, I'm going down to Cannes later, maybe have a coffee in Mougins on the way…about ten, if you want a lift?'

Jason looked at her with a wide smile, 'Thanks, Alice, Grace said I could pick up some newspapers and magazines she wants from the café in the square in Mougins and she has some jewellery she wants collected from a repair guy in Cannes. Gerald usually goes so he will tell us the address… if you're sure?'

'Why not? It's another lovely day. See you at the Mini at ten then.' Alice smiled and ran quickly into her cottage, deciding to make it seem as normal as possible and not that it was the first time she had ever known Jason to leave the villa. Half an hour later, drying her hair again in front of her bedroom mirror she thought about Jason. Maybe he had some phobia? Despite his muscular strength, perhaps he was scared of the outside world and had panic attacks… some nervous disorder. Well, if he was ready to face his fears she was certainly happy to help… if she could. Maybe she should mind her own business? The vision of a panic-stricken Jason in the confines of the little white Mini was rather alarming… but… Alice's shook her head and smiled at her own reflection, her long blonde hair swinging back and forth in the sunlight and spoke aloud to herself,

'*If everybody minded their own business, the world would go around a great deal faster than it does*'. She frowned and pulled a face at herself as she couldn't decide if it was a quote from Alice in Wonderland or Through the Looking-glass. Ah well, she thought, pulling her hair back into a band, Alice was only a very young girl and really very silly.

'I shall just enjoy a morning out in the sunshine.' She spoke the words aloud to give herself courage.

Jason was waiting by the Mini when Alice walked round to the back courtyard by the kitchen. Smoke and Cloud were standing either side of him. If I took a photo, Alice thought, it could be a full page in Vogue. Jason was wearing black jeans and a hooded jacket over a plain t-shirt… but it wasn't the clothes, it was the way he wore them with such a careless neglect of his own strong attraction.

'Hi Jason, you're on time, let's go then.' Jason got into the car, folding his long legs and with his head touching the soft roof. 'Goodness, I may have to open the roof so you can sit up straight.'

'No, I'm fine, Alice,' He tried to make himself smaller in the seat and looked anxious. 'Please don't open the hood.'

'No, it's too cold, anyway,' Alice answered quickly, wondering if his agoraphobia… or whatever phobia it was… might be triggered by the open air. 'It's not far anyway, we'll stop at Mougins first.' She drove slowly down the winding drive to the gates. Jason gave a long exhale of breath as the gates opened and they passed through. Alice glanced quickly sideways at him but there was a small smile on his face now and he seemed more relaxed, his fine profile as serene as a Greek statue. She switched on the radio and a strident French voice filled the small space in the car.

'I'm learning French.' Jason's words seemed to surprise himself. 'No need to tell Minnie or Gerald, and I know Grace thinks everyone should speak English… but that's a bit crazy, isn't it?'

'Of course it is… it's a great idea to learn French… especially if you intend living here. Are you learning from a book or what?'

'I'm taking this online course… it's really good and you can work at your own pace. You speak French, don't you. Josette told me.'

Alice smiled, at last he had mentioned Josette. 'Yes, I gave her a lift the other evening. Are you going out with her?' As soon as the words left her lips she realised it was a bad choice. 'I mean, are you an item?'

'I think so, I don't get to see her much… only if she comes up to help Minnie. She's learning English, too.'

'Good idea… anyway, here we are… maybe you'll get a chance to try out your language skills this morning.' Alice smiled at Jason and he laughed,

'Yeh, something like that… by the way, Grace gave me this envelope to give to you… I think it's the address of the jeweller in Cannes or something.' He was looking across to the café as Alice parked in the square.

'You go on over, Jason. See if you can find Josette, *cherchez la femme!* I'm going to walk round the village a bit and then have a coffee. If I don't see you before, we'll meet back at the Mini in an hour, OK?'

'Great, thanks, Alice, see you.' Jason pulled his hood over his blonde hair and jumped out of the car. He stretched and then walked quickly over to the café. Alice watched him, wondering why he had pulled up his hood on such a sunny day? Maybe it was part of some therapy, shielding himself from the outside world. She knew lots of guys that wore hoods at university, so maybe it was just youth fashion and she was imagining all this about Jason. There was something though, definitely something hidden and mysterious about him. Even more *curiouser and curiouser*, Alice thought to herself as she walked round the square and over to the fountain. She stood for a long moment, looking into the rippling water and thinking about Jason and Josette. Then, she thought about Guy. Try as she might she could not get him out of her mind. Grace had been so kind, filling Alice's week with outings and treats, as though she understood that Alice was waiting. Not just waiting but yearning for Guy to return. When would he be back in France again and would they be able to retrieve the magic of their first few days and nights together? Alice felt her body shudder and ache with longing. She quickly dashed her hand into the icy water of the fountain, causing droplets of water to splash and sparkle in the sunshine. Then, drying her hand on her jeans, she ran over to the café.

She sat at a table near the bar and waited. There was no sign of Jason and no-one behind the counter. Then, Josette's mother came through from the room behind the bar and smiled at Alice.

'*Bonjour, ça va? Il fait beau, n'est ce pas? Je m'appelle Michelle.*'

'*Bonjour, oui, très beau. Ca va, merci. Je m'appelle Alice, je connais votre fille, Josette.*'

The woman came round from behind the counter and sat beside Alice and they began a conversation. Alice was pleased to speak French and soon they were both sipping large cups of *café au lait* and getting on very well. They soon moved on from the formalities of the weather to the more interesting subject of Jason and Josette. Alice was relieved to find that Michelle approved of Jason and she had noticed how hard he worked in the olive grove at the Villa. She made no mention of Jason's strange reluctance to go out, so Alice kept off the subject. Then it was time to meet Jason so she paid and left Michelle to her work. Jason was standing under a tree in the square, his hood up and holding a large bundle of magazines. As soon as she approached the car he joined her and got in the Mini the moment she unlocked it.

'Did you find Josette?' Alice asked as they drove away from the village and down toward the coast.

'Yeh, thanks, Alice. It was great to see her. She's coming up to the Villa tomorrow so I'll see her again then. Well, I think that's what we arranged… *samedi…* that is Saturday, isn't it?'

'Yes, Saturday, tomorrow.' Alice carried on driving in silence, wondering how much Josette and Jason needed their languages to communicate. She smiled at the thought and then said, 'I've looked up that jeweller's address. Can you tap it in the sat-nav… we're near Cannes now.'

Jason took the address from her and quickly tapped in the address and the small screen lit up,

'Continuez a suivre cette route pendant neuf cents metres et puis tournez à droite.'

'Did you get that, Jason?'

'Yeh, I think so… was it follow this road for another nine kilometres and then turn left?'

'Well, something like that… but nine hundred metres and turn right… here we go now!' They both laughed and Alice wondered again how he made out with Josette. Then the sat-nav announced their arrival.

'Après cinquante metres vous êtes arrivés à votre destination'

Alice looked at the small jeweller's shop in the narrow one-way street. The dark windows were covered with security grills.

'I suppose it is open…do you want to wait in the car while I pick up the jewellery or will you go?'

Jason suddenly laughed out loud, more than she had ever heard him laugh before. Was it some new form of his neurosis? She looked at him anxiously and he turned to her, his handsome face creased with helpless laughter.

'I'll pick up the stuff, Grace has given me the receipt. Just a ring she is having cleaned and repaired. Anyway, you're on the yellow band so you'd better watch out.' He straightened his face and looked at her seriously, 'One day I'll tell you what I was laughing about Alice, you'll understand then.'

He pulled up his hood, jumped out of the car, straightened his long back and went into the jewellery shop. Alice sat waiting in the car, hoping that he would tell his story very soon. She was getting very tired of all this intrigue.

Jason had only been in the jeweller's a few moments and so they were soon driving on down the narrow back street. Jason passed Alice a small brown paper package,

'Will you look after Grace's ring, Alice?'

'Yes, put it in the pocket of my bag and zip it up. That's fine. It's still early… shall we have another stop? I don't have to get back to the Villa until two… how about you?'

'Grace gave me the whole day off. She seemed to think I deserved it, though to be honest, working for her is more like being on holiday.'

'I know, I feel just the same. She's so kind, isn't she?' Alice drove on, doubling back through the one-way system to get back to the coast road.

'More than you could possibly know.' Jason said quietly, pulling up his hood again as they cruised along the palm-fringed Croisette. 'Yes, OK, let's find a cafe near the front, why not?' There was something in the way he spoke that made Alice feel it was against Jason's better instincts but, well, she was getting very tired of his hidden agenda.

'Look, that's the Palais des Festival,' she drove slowly past the huge building, 'You know, where the stars all go to the Cannes Film Festival.'

'Wow, I've seen it on TV, it's even bigger than I imagined. It's really ugly, isn't it and looks all wrong blocking out the view of the sea. Still, I suppose it is famous.'

'I thought we'd go to a bar I saw near the marina if I can find a parking space.'

'There's a car park sign up there, is that any good?'

'Yes, I think it would be the easiest.' Alice swung into the car park and took the ticket from the automatic machine at the barrier.

'I thought we'd try that café over there with the green awning.' Alice didn't add that she was avoiding the café where she had met Simon and the restaurant near to Guy's flat. No point dwelling on the past and, after all, there were plenty of cafés to choose from. As they crossed the road together, Jason pulled a baseball cap out from his pocket and pulled it down low over his forehead. More disguise and cover-up, Alice sighed and decided not to comment. Jason was most probably the same age as herself, but then it did seem to take boys such a long time to become men.

They sat in the winter sunshine, enjoying the sweet orange juice and watching the exotic people passing by. Alice was about to point out a woman with no less than five giant poodles, tottering by on platform shoes when suddenly Jason stood up. Alice looked up at him and saw his face pale under his tan.

'I'll see you at the car, Alice.' He muttered the words briefly and left the café by the side door. Alice looked after him in bewilderment… would she ever understand this man? She drained her glass and put the money on the table and left the café, feeling slightly cross that the morning's small moment of pleasure had been unaccountably cut short. She went back to the Mini in the car park and found, to her further annoyance, there was no sign of Jason. Alice blew out her cheeks in impatience and sat in the driver's seat wondering what to do next. She started up the engine and made her way slowly to the exit. Just as she was pushing her ticket into the machine, Jason emerged from nowhere and jumped into the passenger seat. The barrier lifted and Alice drove through, waiting for some explanation from Jason. Of course, he remained silent.

'We'll go back to the villa then?' Alice said, her voice tight with suppressed temper.

Still there was no reply. Jason sat turned in his seat, looking backwards.

'Are you expecting someone to follow us?' Alice felt a moment of panic as she glanced at his face and saw it was still pale and …well, terrified… was the first word that came to her mind. She accelerated out of the Cannes traffic and took the road up to Mougins. 'Listen to me, Jason. I would be a fool not to realise that something is up. I'm going to drive straight past

Mougins and up towards Valbonne. I was riding up there the other day and I know a small mountain bar away from everything. Then I want a full explanation and another cold drink. Do you understand?'

Jason nodded and turned around to face forward. 'Sorry, Al.'

'OK, and don't call me, Al.'

They drove on in silence, more awkward than companionable, and soon they reached the riverside bar where Alice had been with Guy. It was a good retreat, well off the beaten track, which seemed to be a good idea in the circumstances. Alice determined not to think about sitting in the same place with Guy, laughing and chatting and admiring the view. No, right now, all she wanted was to finally get to the bottom of the Jason mystery. Alice parked and without even looking at the place where Guy had tied up the horses and then kissed her, leaning against the wall over-looking the mountain river, nor… Alice strode into the bar and sat at the first table by the door.

'You order two fruit juices, Jason, I'm fed up with doing everything.' Jason looked at her and then, head hung low he made his way to the bar and mumbled to the barman. By the time he returned to their table, Alice had begun to feel ashamed of herself… nobody could help being shy. The drinks arrived and they both picked up their glasses and sipped. Again there was silence between them but this time, Alice decided not to let it hang on for a moment longer.

'OK, Jason, it's quite simple, I want you tell me what's going on… so you'd better start right now or I'm leaving you here with a long walk back to the villa.'

Jason looked shocked and then gave one of his rare smiles. 'You are scary, Alice, do you know that… but you're right, I need to tell you everything.'

Alice waited impatiently as the silence descended again. She fidgeted in her seat and was about to say something more, when, slowly and quietly, Jason finally began to speak.

'It all started my last year at school. Somehow I had managed to get into the local grammar, well, it was called an academy, and I was doing well, taking four A levels… even acting in the school's Shakespeare festival.' He turned to Alice for a moment and gave a flicker of a smile, 'I know you'll find that hard to believe… and I was dreaming about going to university… I loved it all… and hated everything at home. My Mum's a single Mum, always broke… mainly because she spends too much on gin.' Jason looked up at Alice for a second and she saw he was smiling again as though he still loved his Mum even though she was so hopeless in the role. 'I don't have any brothers or sisters, well, not that I know of anyway, so I tried hard to look after Mum when I got home from school. But, well, it was hard and so I ended up going out most evenings… only to the local park… I had a skateboard and I got into a gang of friends. Well, I thought they were friends. I know it was dumb but I got involved with them and we used to lark around… usual stuff, tipping over waste bins and a bit of tagging…'

'Tagging? What's that?' Alice interrupted.

'Oh, you'd call it graffiti… but it wasn't exactly Banksy stuff. Anyway, somehow it all got more serious… they did drugs all the time, but I never did. I hated the idea of it and anyway I never had any dosh. I worked at the local Co-op, shelf-stacking, to earn enough to get driving lessons and passed my test. Never had a car, of course, and then, yeh, then… one of the gang said he'd let me drive his car as he'd lost his license. That went on for a while, I loved that car, it was a souped up Golf GT…' Jason looked at Alice again and she saw the wistful look of any boy talking about a favourite toy. She nodded but said nothing, waiting for him to continue. 'Anyway, one night we were cruising along the Mile End Road and Jeb, that's the guy with the car, he said he wanted me to pick him up the next night right on the dot of midnight. We were driving up toward the roundabout and he pointed to a small alley. Told me I was to park there and wait for him and not to be late. I won't tell you what he said would happen to me and my mother if I was late… but it wasn't nice. I laid awake all night trying to decide what to do. Next day was worse, the minutes seemed to fly by and suddenly it was night time. I went out to the car and drove around a bit. None of the gang were around, I went to all the usual bars and hang out corners… nothing. Then, it was nearly midnight and all I could think to do was to drive up the Mile and park where he'd said. I was there on time and nothing happened. The alley was pitch dark and I was about to drive off when suddenly alarm bells were ringing, effing deafening. The passenger door flew open and Jeb and two mates piled into the car. Before the doors were even closed, Jeb was shouting, screaming at me. Drive, drive… and called me all sorts of names you would never have heard. So I did. We shot out of the alley, I slew it round the roundabout, nearly losing it in a back wheel skid, then straightened up and made for the Commercial Road. Then they were all laughing like idiots and Jeb was giving me directions. We ended up in a garage in a back street off the Romford Road. We all piled out of the car, I was shaking so much I could hardly walk. Next thing I know they had all scarpered and I was left standing there with the keys in my hand. I pulled myself together a bit and walked to the main road and caught a bus home. It was unreal. Sitting on the bus, a few people on their way home, maybe going on night shift… everything normal.' Jason ended abruptly and took a long draught from his glass of juice.

'So, what was it… a robbery and you were the get-away driver?' Alice tried to think it through.

'Yeh, that's about it. That's why I laughed when I found myself outside a jeweller's in Cannes this morning. To think how Grace trusts me, I mean, it's something, isn't it? Anyway, nothing was normal from then on.'

'So what then' Alice couldn't think of what else to say, but it didn't seem as though his story had ended.

'Then, the next day, the police came round to the supermarket where I was quietly stacking Weetabix and took me in.'

'They arrested you?'

'Well, of course. I was the fall guy, what the Americans call the patsy. I kept telling them I knew nothing about any of it but they didn't believe me… and why would they? In the end, it was them that told me that it had been a jewellery raid. Some stash of drugs, too, that the dealer kept there. The diamonds were rough diamonds that were kept in a store there ready for work at Hatton Garden. I knew nothing about any of it. I still don't, really. There was one copper who did seem to believe me, but I was kept in a cell overnight and he told me to think about things.'

'What did that mean?'

'Exactly what I wondered all night but it became obvious in the morning all right. I was given a cup of tea and a bacon sandwich and quietly told that if I gave them the names of the others then I would get off lightly.'

'Oh my god, what did you do? I mean, they weren't really good friends, were they? You must have hated them for dragging you into it all.'

'Oh yeh, I hated them all right but it wasn't so easy. I knew if I grassed them up then their families would take it out on me… and my Mum, big time.'

'Oh, I see…' Alice said slowly, although she really had no idea what his world could really be like.

'Anyway, the good cop, if that was what he was playing, the one who brought me breakfast, he told me I could probably get protection if I informed on the gang. I think they knew Jeb and his family and they just wanted proof. Once again I was the fall guy.'

'So what did you do?'

'I gave him Jeb's full name and address and the other two. I told them everything I knew.'

'Oh my god, weren't you scared?'

'Scared witless would be putting it mildly. They kept me inside for my own protection and two days later they told me there'd been an arrest and Jeb and his lovely mates were being held. The cops were so pleased with themselves, laughing and drinking beer. I could hear them going on … finally, good cop came in and said I could go… just like that.'

'Go, but… but how could you?'

'Exactly! I looked at him and he said I should just keep my head down for a while. I asked him if I needed to be a witness or anything … at a trial or anything and he just laughed. He handed me my belongings, my wallet and some small change, no car key, and showed me to the back door of the nick.'

'What did you do… I mean, hadn't they promised you protection?'

'Yeh, well promises aren't always what they're made out to be, are they? Not in my world. Anyway, I remember standing outside on the pavement, pouring rain, not even sure what day it was and feeling completely lost. I didn't even dare go home. I got on a bus and just sat there trying to think what to do. Maybe I have some sort of lucky star because the bus took me through Stratford and to Wanstead. Then, I remembered my Mum had a friend living in Wanstead. I'd been to tea there when I was a boy, but my Mum had fallen out with her long since. Anyway, I got out when I saw this big green, edged with trees because I sort of remembered it. I wandered around awhile and then I saw a shop that my auntie had taken me to for ice-cream… from there it wasn't difficult to find her road and I remembered the house because it had this fantastic monkey tree in the front garden. It took me a while to knock on the door but it was still raining so hard and I was so scared that, eventually, I did. In fact, it wasn't a knocker but one of those silly ding-dong bells they have in the suburbs. Auntie Hilda, that's what I called her when I was a boy… she wasn't my real aunt…she came to the door and, believe it or not, she recognised me immediately.' Jason ran his hands back through his short, tow-coloured hair and looked at Alice with his cornflower blue eyes. She smiled back at him and decided she couldn't be bothered to tell him that she was not at all surprised that Auntie Hilda had recognised him at once.

'Then what?'

'Then she took me in, she was so kind. I was soaking wet and kind of crying, I think. Anyway, she ran me a bath and then we had a pot of tea and I told her everything that had happened. She told me then about Gerald, her brother who was working out here. She phoned him up and just a few days later I was here. Grace has been fantastic. She knows the whole sorry story but for some reason she doesn't seem to care about it at all. Can you believe she trusted me to pick up her jewellery today? She's a definite one-off is Grace. You've worked with her for a while… you must have seen she sort of has her own take on everything.' Jason slumped back in the café chair and suddenly looked exhausted or defeated.

'OK, I get it so far… but why the sudden rush from the café on the Croisette?"

'I saw Jeb's brother.'

His few words fell between them like stones into a deep well.

'eat a Tarte Tropézienne'

They were all sitting at the large table in the kitchen. Grace sat at the head, elegant in a white, linen trouser suit, her small hands clasped in front of her. Alice had never seen Grace in the kitchen before and there was a serious air between them all. Gerald and Minnie sat side by side, their usual cheerfulness lost, their faces dark with worry. Jason sat at the foot of the table, his face a picture of youthful misery. Grace unclasped her hands and smiled at them all. She looked very small in the high-ceilinged kitchen, small but very determined. When she spoke she had an upbeat confident tone in her voice. Alice momentarily wondered if it was to be another star performance.

'Right everybody, sit up and pay attention. First, there is no point in moping, you all look like misery and that won't get us anywhere. So, drink your coffee and pull yourselves together.' They all picked up their cups like obedient robots as she continued, 'First, Jason, can you be absolutely one hundred per cent certain that this guy was Jeb's brother?'

Jason quickly put his cup down on the table, 'Oh yes, Grace, absolutely certain. It was definitely Brad, Jeb's older brother.'

'Were you near to him? How can you be so sure?'

'No, not really near, he came in the main door and we were sitting near the side window... but it was Brad all right, he always wears black and...,'

Grace interrupted, 'But Jason, that's my point exactly, so many young men wear black... you may have been mistaken. It seems a ridiculous coincidence that the first time you go out from the villa, that you should see this Brad.'

'I know, it does sound crazy... but it was Brad, I know it was.'

'You don't think that you have been dreading seeing a member of the gang for so long now that the first time you did venture out you... well, you saw someone who looked like Brad and...'

Now, Jason interrupted Grace, 'Not possible, Grace, Brad has this tattoo, and before you say that lots of young men have tattoos, this is across his forehead.'

'On his forehead!' Grace suddenly seemed lost for words and they all looked at Jason as he continued,

'Yeh, just the one word, HATE, in capital letters with sort of daggers on each side.'

There was silence round the table and then Gerald spoke.

'I telephoned my sister Hilda last night and I asked her a few questions. Finally, it turned out that she remembered a young man had been round looking for Jason. He told her he was a school friend of Jason's and wondered where he was. Well, Hilda is the trusting sort, she had him in for a cup of tea and chatted. She told him that all she knew was that Jason was working in France, near where they hold all the film festivals.' That was a week ago.'

There was another silence and Jason put his head in his hands as Grace spoke,

'Well, that cuts the coincidence down somewhat though it does seem very unlucky that he should be in the same café at the same…'

Jason suddenly stood up, 'But that's it, isn't it? The story of my life… always unlucky and always in the wrong place at the wrong time. Anyway, I'll leave here this morning…'

'Don't be so dramatic, Jason, I am the only person in this house allowed to make dramatic or even melodramatic scenes. Now sit down and finish your breakfast. I made a phone call this morning, too. I have a security man at the gates and patrolling the grounds… he's already here. You will stay inside the Villa this morning Jason. I should be very pleased if you would clean out the cinema… Minnie will tell you what to do. Minnie, you always have plenty to do in the kitchen. Gerald, I should like you to bring the Bentley round as planned for my trip with Alice to St Tropez for lunch. One tattooed Brad is not going to make me change my plans. Now, off you all trot.' Grace clapped her hands and stood up. The performance was over and it was as though she was applauding herself.

As the Bentley pulled slowly out of the gateway, a uniformed security guard raised his hand in a salute. Grace gave a royal wave and then turned to Alice.

'He looks large enough, don't you think? Quite a hulk… but not quite a hunk with that dreadful nose. Did you know that noses look bigger on screen than in real life. That guy's nose would never do… of course, there have been actors who made their name through their noses… like me with my breasts. Gerard Depardieu, for instance, what a nose and a very fine actor… although he is French and a dreadful tearaway. He wrote in his autobiography that Putin liked his hooligan side… can you imagine? I believe he has Russian citizenship now… although I think he still has a vineyard in France. So strange, isn't it how one hooligan can be so different from another… maybe just one chance step in the wrong or right direction. Do you remember out first conversation when you came for your interview?'

Alice, who had just been wondering how Grace had taken in so much about the security guard's face in the moment it had taken to drive past, realised now she had to catch up with the flow of the conversation,

'Yes, of course, *Giddy Fortune's furious wheel…* it was that moment that I knew I really wanted to work for you. My fingers were definitely crossed from then on.'

'Oh, you needn't have worried. I was delighted to have found you. How do you get on with Jason?'

Yet another of Grace's quick changes in conversation. Alice was becoming accustomed to it now and she answered quickly.

'Oh, we get on really well. I mean, at first, all any woman would be able to think of would be his outstanding looks… such a superhero. But I was soon past that stage and now I feel I can treat him like a friend, maybe even a younger brother. Not that I ever had a brother or even know how old he is, actually.'

'He's exactly your age. Yes, I can understand all that. He is so very handsome but, despite his education in the hard knocks school, he is rather young and naive. Very charming in its way, of course, but then along came your talented Mr Bond. Have you heard from him recently?'

This was a change in subject that Grace had not expected and she hesitated,

'Err, well, yes… he sends a one-line text every day.'

Hmm, how boring… now in my day, it would have been flowers, even jewellery. But I suppose that was another world and you're not that sort of girl.'

Alice smiled to herself as she wondered whether Grace had intended to be insulting or not. Then she remembered,

'By the way, Grace, Jason was very pleased that you had trusted him to pick up your jewellery. After he told me his story, of course, I understood why… and, oh, I've just realised why he laughed aloud when I parked outside the jewellers. I asked him if he wanted to wait in the car… it must have reminded him of waiting for the gang…oh dear, I didn't realise! But he laughed at the idea, more than I had ever seen him laugh before. We were having such a good morning out… he had met up with Josette and he was telling me about his French lessons…'

'French lessons?' Grace interrupted, 'Jason is learning French?'

'Oh dear, he didn't want you or Minnie and Gerald to know, I shouldn't have said.'

Grace laughed then, her usual low laugh that filled the car. Alice saw that Gerald caught it and smiled in the mirror at them. It was impossible to think that Gerald was more silent than ever, but there had been something in the set of his shoulders that spoke of the worry and tension in him. Now his smile seemed to relax him a little and he spoke kindly,

'Don't you worry, Alice, We all knew about his French lessons, we just didn't ask the lad about it.'

'Quite right, Gerald, give the lad a chance,' Grace gave another chuckle, 'He must think I'm a dragon.'

'Oh no,' Alice spoke quickly, 'He thinks you're simply wonderful… well, 'fantastic and a definite one-off' were his actual words yesterday.'

'Did he? Well, I suppose I am, really, aren't I? Now we're approaching the Byblos. Pass me that mirror from the back seat, Alice.'

Alice looked at the walnut panel in the back of the seat in front of her. She carefully turned the small brass knob and the panel flapped forward revealing everything a movie star might expect to find on her dressing table.

'Do hurry up, Alice, pass me the mirror.'

Alice quickly took out the silver-handled mirror and passed it to Grace. She caught a quick flashing reflection of the Bentley's grey velvet roof, a flash of the deep blue sea and then her own face, looking startled or surprised. Then Grace snatched the mirror from her,

'My goodness girl, you are in a dream today… the sooner that Guy Bond gets back to France the better. You look as though you're auditioning for a part in Alice Through the Looking-Glass. Now take the mirror and put it away quickly. We've arrived and I'm ready. Considering the morning I've had

I think I look marvellous… fantastic , in fact. Now, you stay in the car, Gerald will see me into the hotel and I shall take coffee. He will then take you down to the market and drop you off and return in an hour to pick you up again. That should give you time to wander through the market and eat a *Tarte Tropézienne.* That will be twelve thirty and time to join me back here for lunch. Watch your handbag in the market.'

31   *'without time to think of Guy or where he might be'*

Alice wandered idly through the Saturday morning market, one arm over her shoulder bag. She smiled as she remembered Grace's last sharp words. Her morning timetable had been arranged for her and warning given. It was as though Alice was a school child on an outing and Grace her bossy headmistress. And yet, there was such kindness behind it all. She stopped to admire a long stall spread with bowls of shiny olives and spices. The stall-holder immediately held out a little bowl of dark black olives for her to sample. She shook her head and explained that she wasn't buying, but the stall-holder just threw back his head and laughed, immediately speaking English.

'*Oh là là*, mademoiselle, It is not necessary for a beautiful young woman to buy an olive in St. Tropez! *C'est pas necessaire de tout! Vous êtes en Provence, c'est pas Paris? Allez-y*, 'elp yourself.'

Alice took one small olive and popped it in her mouth, the full taste of Provence was immediately with her, the soft olive oil, the sweet garlic and the subtle mix of herbs. She smiled gratefully and the stall-holder held out a paper napkin. She wiped her fingers and thanked him, thinking about the simple grace of the Provençal lifestyle. Then she saw that the next stall was crowded with young people waiting to be tattooed. She pushed her way through the throng, holding her handbag, looking anxiously for a man with HATE on his forehead. She gave a sigh of relief on reaching a quieter part of the market, glad that the menacing Brad had not been in the crowd. Maybe life was not all grace and fragrant olives in Provence. Then she saw that she had moved away from the food stalls and had reached rows of stalls selling bright Provençal tablecloths and mats. She looked through the piles of fabric on the first stall and impulsively decided to buy two table mats and napkins for her mother and Mike. They would be easy to post and it would be good to send them a present. She chose a pale green set, decorated with a border of black olives and dark green leaves. She thought then of the delicate, silver grey leaves of the olive grove at the Villa. She knew her mother would be thrilled to see it all, but, with so much turmoil now at the villa, a visit would have to wait. She paid the young, dark-haired woman running the stall and then looked around. She saw a stall selling the *Tarte Tropèzienne* that Grace had mentioned and went over. The stall was laid out with large, creamy yellow sponge cakes. Alice bought the smallest slice on offer and bit into it. The cake was so light that it melted in her mouth, the delicious filling, a custardy cream, so rich that she couldn't even finish the slice. She moved away from the stall and quickly dumped the rest into a bin, feeling guilty at the decadence. The whole market was a scene reeling with bright colours and strong perfumes and she had a fleeting moment of loneliness as she stood in the midst of it all. She took a quick photo of the market and sent it to her mother. Then she looked at the time. Still half an hour before she was to meet back with Gerald on the quayside. She was about to leave the market when she saw a stall selling bikinis. She wandered over and began to look through them. The back of the stall had a large poster of Brigitte Bardot in her famous gingham bikini. The young man behind the counter caught her eye and laughed,

'Voilà! Le bikini de B.B., la minette, le sex kitten des années soixante... la nostalgie! Vous êtes un autre 'star', mademoiselle, si belle!'

Alice looked through a pile of check bikinis, embarrassed by the attention of the young man. Fortunately, just when she was about to give up, a young woman came through from the back of the stall.

'Don't take any notice of Miguel, he's always flirting. But, he's right, the B.B. bikini would certainly suit you. You do have the right figure which is more than I can say for some of our customers.'

Alice looked up in surprise, 'You're English?'

The girl laughed, 'Guilty! Hi, my name's Suzie, all the way from Bristol.'

'I was at uni in Bristol.'

'Oh, I was just born there... I dropped out of fashion college in London when I met Miguel. I was down here on holiday and never went back.'

'Really, that's a brave move.'

'Not really, I love it here. It's like my dream come true. I'm mad about sixties vintage fashion and I design all the gear on this stall plus we have a little boutique we open in the summer months. Miguel's father is in the rag trade and he set us up. As you can tell, Miguel is great at the selling point! Anyway, must get on, do you want the blue or the pink?'

'Oh, the blue, I think.'

The girl slipped the bikini into a neat paper carrier and tied it with a blue ribbon. 'There you go, see you again some time, I expect. Believe me, this is a hard place to leave.'

'I'm sure you're right! I'm working in Mougins at the moment so I'll probably come to the market again.'

'Ooh, posh up there in the hills, isn't it? Bit mixed down here on the old Côte d'Az. Watch out for yourself then, see-ya!'

Alice walked quickly back to the Place des Lices, realising she now only had five minutes before she met Gerald. As soon as she was out of the market area she saw the huge, grey Bentley parked on the kerb side at the edge of the port. She ran over and jumped in, trying to ignore the wolf whistles and shouts from a group of young men sitting on the harbour wall.

'Thanks, Gerald, not late, am I?'

'No, I'm always a bit early. Didn't want you hanging around here.'

'Thanks, I could get seriously used to being met with a grey Bentley!'

Gerald laughed and Alice sat back, thinking how another morning had slipped past without time to think of Guy or where he might be.

Gerald dropped Alice at the Byblos entrance and she wandered through the hotel looking for Grace. Finally, she was surprised to find her talking animatedly to a tall, grey-haired man in the hotel cocktail lounge.

'There you are, at last, Alice.' Grace's voice rang out across the marbled floor and caused some guests to turn and stare. Alice walked quickly over to join Grace, embarrassed by the attention. 'Don't start blushing, my dear, I want to introduce you to Mr. Marsden. This is Alice Shakespeare, Alice this is my new friend, William Marsden.'

The elderly man stood up and shook hands with Alice and then gallantly held the back of the chair as Alice sat down. The man was so tanned and good-looking that Alice wondered whether she should recognise him as a star of the past… and his name had a familiar ring to it. 'Pleased to meet you, Mr. Marsden. I'm sorry if I'm late, Grace, but I thought we said one o'clock.'

Grace waved a hand in the air, 'Maybe we did… anyway, I have had a delightful morning, chatting with William, the king of boxes.'

William Marsden laughed, 'King of boxes meets fascinating movie star at the infamous Byblos. I can see the headlines now!' His face was even more handsome when he laughed and Alice could see that Grace was very taken with the man.

'Alice, don't look so blank... Marsden... you must know the name, you see it stamped on nearly every cardboard box in the entire world. Anyway, now he has invested in a hotel down the coast from here. Do you remember, Alice, I said I had heard that there was a small independent hotel being renovated... that it sounded interesting?'

'Yes, I do, in La Ciotat... and, of course, I have heard of Marsden boxes, I just didn't make the connection.'

Grace turned to William, clapping her hands, 'There, what did I tell you, Alice remembers everything. The girl is a wonder.'

'I'm sure she is... but right now she should catch up with us and have a cocktail. Alice, what can I order for you?'

'I'd love a non-alcoholic fruit cocktail, please.' Alice said shyly.

'There, what did I tell you, she's too good to be true. Really Alice, you should be ashamed of yourself and your whole generation. Why when I was at the Byblos when I was about your age...well, let me just say, I never ordered a non-alcoholic drink.'

'Oh, I don't think you should accuse Alice of being representative of her entire generation. In deepest Sussex where I live most of the time, the pubs are chocker with binge drinkers and the like at the weekends. Although I must say, my own grand-daughter is very abstemious. Alice, I hope you will come to La Ciotat and meet Amber... she's a painter.'

'I'd love to,' Alice looked across at Grace who, with her back to the bright sunshine pouring in the window, looked very beautiful. It was obvious that she was flirting with William and that he was thoroughly enjoying it. Now, thought Alice, as she raised her glass to them, I am playing gooseberry to septuagenarians. 'To your very good health!'

'To the good times at the Byblos!' Grace responded, sipping an evil looking bright green cocktail. 'Did you know St. Tropez in the sixties, William?'

'Indeed, my late wife and I spent several holidays down here. The Byblos was way beyond our means, then, but we knew of it and heard all the scandals. I remember some very topless times and you, Grace Devine, were surely the most beautiful star in the universe.'

'Well, that's very sweet of you, William, but the real queen of St. Trop was Brigitte Bardot, there's no denying it. I can remember her sitting by the pool here, wearing a simple little Provençal print cotton shift, her hair tied back with a peasant scarf… very lovely. I remember thinking that times were changing. Of course, this whole hotel had just been built in her honour. A charming guy from Beirut, Jean-Prosper, completely infatuated with B.B, built it in the style of a palace from A Thousand and One Nights. Just imagine, nearly fifty years ago and the myth still hangs in the air. Ah yes, B.B. was a real beauty of the sixties.' Grace looked pensive for a moment and then raised her be-ringed hand to her hair, silvery blonde in the bright light, 'But I think I have won the race… I really have worn a lot better than her. Now, are we going to eat lunch? Give me your gentlemanly arm, William and we'll go through to the Rivea, shall we?. I particularly like their wild sea bass with those tiny spiky artichokes. Come along, Alice, don't forget your little parcels.'

Alice walked behind Grace and William Marsden as they made a slow procession to the restaurant. She almost laughed aloud and could have applauded at Grace's performance… she was holding on to William's arm and looking up at him with her blue eyes shining. The difference in their heights gave Grace a child-like appeal as she nodded in agreement to everything William said. Alice wondered if she should slip away and leave them to lunch together… whether they would even miss her? At that very moment, Grace turned round and beckoned to Alice.

'Do come along, Alice, catch up now… we're all starving.'

Alice moved forward to join them as they sat at a table overlooking an inner courtyard. Certainly, she thought, the gooseberry was very hungry and very lucky, too.

32 *'She spluttered, swallowing water as she hurriedly surfaced'*

Alice woke early and laid in bed, thinking how Sunday was now a less interesting day than a weekday. Was this what her mother had meant when she told her that if she found a job she liked then she would never have to work. Certainly working with Grace was like one amazing luxury holiday. There were moments when Grace became somewhat high-handed, but it never offended Alice, in fact, she enjoyed it. Grace's belief in her own self-importance was fragile in a strange way. Alice smiled up at the ceiling as she thought back through the lunch at the Byblos. William was obviously an intelligent and self-assured man and he seemed totally charmed by Grace's capricious conversation. Before they parted they had arranged for Grace and Alice to stay at William's newly renovated hotel in La Ciotat. Alice had agreed happily but all the time she was thinking... surely Guy will be back by then? There hadn't even been a text message yesterday and Grace had heard nothing more. His silence was becoming painful and Alice felt her throat constrict as she thought about it. Impatient with herself she jumped out of bed and peered through the blind. Yes, Jason was already in the pool, pushing his way through the blue water with hardly a ripple. Alice went to find her swimsuit and was annoyed to find that she had forgotten to hang it to dry. Then, she remembered her new bikini. She hadn't even tried it on. She pulled open the little paper carrier and quickly slipped into the bikini. Without a doubt, it was a perfect fit. The brief bikini bottom was tied with two neat bows and the top with shoe-string straps, was cut to a deep v-shape and fastened in the front with a clip under another bow. Never had Alice seen her cleavage to such advantage. 'Yes, you're very clever, Suzie from Bristol, Brigitte Bardot, look out!' Alice twirled in front of the mirror, delighted with her purchase and smiled, remembering Grace's derogatory comment about the famous B.B's ageing. Then, she grabbed her towelling robe and ran round to the pool.

Jason saw her immediately and raised a hand out of the water to wave at her. Then he stopped swimming and his blonde head came out of the water for long enough to give a long wolf whistle. Alice laughed and dived into the deep end. As soon as she entered the water she felt her bikini top snap and come right off. She spluttered, swallowing water as she hurriedly surfaced and held her hands over her breasts. Jason looked round and immediately pulled himself out of the pool and ran to fetch her robe. He held it out to Alice and stretched out an arm to pull her up from the pool. She almost laughed to see that he had his eyes screwed tight shut. Then, he slipped the robe around her and patted her shoulders for a moment. Alice blinked the water out of her eyes and saw, there, at the far end of the pool, was Guy Bond. For a brief second their eyes met and Alice stood still in shock, her cold nipples jutting out and pointing straight at Guy. Then she pulled her robe around her and took a step toward him. He turned and disappeared round the end of the cottage. Jason was standing behind her, with his eyes still closed. Alice was rooted to the spot, water dripping off her, the cold air chilling her skin and her mind racing through the disastrous scene. Then, she ran, around the pool, along the pathway beside the cottage and out to the front driveway. Her bare feet hurt on the gravel as she ran vainly after Guy's Land-rover. Before she could reach the end of the olive grove she saw the gates swing open and, with a flurry of gravel, Guy drove away at high speed. She reached the gates as they closed again and she hung onto the iron railings, shivering with misery. Smoke and Cloud joined her and she felt their warm bodies leaning against her as she stood, staring through tears, at the empty road. Then she saw the security guard coming back toward the gates after his tour of the grounds and she turned and ran back to the cottage.

'Hmm, for a quiet, good girl you certainly do get yourself into some pickles, don't you?' Grace was sitting drinking her small cup of coffee and Alice sat opposite. The dogs were sprawled out, sound asleep in front of the log fire. The room was darker than usual as the afternoon had turned to cloud and a light rain fell against the huge windows. Alice had forced herself to go to Sunday lunch at the villa, as arranged the night before. Unable to swallow the food that Minnie served she had sat, miserable and forlorn, trying to make some conversation. After lunch, Grace had asked her to come into the salon and Alice had told her the events of the morning. Fighting back tears she said,

'But Grace, it was all so innocent, my bikini broke and Jason behaved impeccably… he even screwed up his eyes tight closed.' Alice gave a sob as she remembered the moment when she had looked up to see Guy watching them, Jason standing behind her with his hands on her shoulders. Her, shrugging on the towelling robe, her cold, bare breasts pointing full front at Guy.

'Hmm, but you have to see it from Guy's point of view… he has been away for a week and returns to find you standing half naked with one of the best-looking men God ever created. I mean, I quite believe you and it was all just a horrid coincidence that he should arrive at that moment…hoping, no doubt to surprise you. To find you… well, what can more can I say? Another tit exposure moment, rather like mine. I warn you, it can be life-changing.'

'But I don't want to change my life, it was simply perfect, working here for you and meeting Guy… the prospect of working together on the screenplay for your biopic…' Alice was lost for words and put her head in her hands and wept. The dogs both jumped up from their place by the fireside and came over to her, licking her hands and nudging her with their soft noses.

'Oh dear, poor Alice, yes, '*a pair of star-crossed lovers*' indeed.'

'Romeo and Juliet,' Alice wailed, 'and look how they ended up!'

'Now, you mustn't upset the dogs, here take my handkerchief and mop up your tears. In my experience, it is quite useless to cry… never gets you anywhere, ruins your eye make-up, leaves your nose and eyes red and your throat sore. Of course, I have had to cry in films, more times than I can recall but… in real life… no, definitely not worth it.'

Alice looked up and took the handkerchief that Grace was holding out. It was delicate fine lawn with a lace edge and lightly perfumed.

'Oh, I can't use that, it's too lovely. Sorry, Grace, I know I am supposed to be working for you not off-loading my problems. I have a tissue in my bag.' Alice sniffed and patted the dogs. 'Isn't it sweet how they try to console you when you cry?'

'Hmm, I suppose so, though I suspect they like the salt in your tears, too.'

Alice gave a weak smile, 'Grace you are such a realist.'

'I know, hard as my perfectly manicured nails! Now then, let's think what to do next. You could, of course, simply call him and explain the whole thing.'

'Certainly not!' Alice sat up straight and stuck out her chin defiantly. 'Why should I? First he doesn't understand that I can't break off my work with you and he swans off to Greece… next he completely mis-reads my actions at the pool. Who does he think he is?'

'Hmm, well, I really didn't expect that outburst. Maybe you're right though. I can see he has foolishly jumped to the wrong conclusion, but the circumstances were rather… err, well, extenuating, to say the least?'

'I can't help that… there is no way I am going to ring him and make excuses.'

'Very well, then you will have to put the matter out of your mind until he comes back to you.'

Alice slumped back against the sofa cushions, 'But supposing he never does?'

'Hmm, well, you can't expect me to have all the answers, can you? I imagine I may hear from him next week about the contract that Bernie has sent him for the screenplay. That should bring some response. What was it your clever mother advised you? If you don't know what to do then try to hang on for a while until the right answer becomes obvious. Sound advice, I should think. Alternatively, we could ask Madame Clare?'

Alice sat forward again, 'Ask Madame Clare, what do you mean?'

'My astrologer, dear Madame Clare, she comes in once a week, usually a Wednesday, as you know, but I could ask her to call tomorrow. I'll get Marie in for our manicure, too. We're booked in at the Hotel de la Plage in La Ciotat on Tuesday, so it will all work out very satisfactorily. Marie can try and do her best with your nails and Madame Clare… yes, yes, we'll ask her to read your horoscope.' Grace looked at Alice, her blue eyes piercing the distance between them. 'I expect you're thinking all this reading the stars is a load of tosh, but you know, she has come up trumps for me, several times. She used to work with Nancy, I think.'

'Nancy? You don't mean Nancy Reagan, do you. I heard that she used an astrologer during the Reagan administration… surely you don't mean…'

Grace interrupted, 'Well, what do I know? There are so many people that say they work with famous people…who knows? But, as I said, she does have an uncanny way of seeing the future.'

'Well, if you say so… thanks, I mean, it's very kind of you, of course. But…

'That's settled then, tomorrow morning at ten. Come along after breakfast. Now I need my rest so you'd better trot off now, but shall we watch a film later tonight… about six? It's such a dull day.'

Alice wandered slowly back down to her cottage, the dogs trailed behind her catching her mood. Even the Provençal sun had given up on the day and the clouds hung low and heavy as the first large drops of rain began to fall. The olive trees were dark and sombre in the half light and the whole world around seemed ready to weep with Alice.

33   *'Phases of the moon and all that stuff about the stars'*

Madame Clare, the astrologer, sat at the dining table at the villa, her hands folded in front of her. She was everything that Alice had not expected. Dressed in a sombre grey suit with a soft white silk shirt, she could have been addressing a board of directors.

'Unfortunately, without the exact detail of the time of your birth it will be very difficult to work out your detailed chart, Alice.' Madame Clare looked at Alice severely, her voice very low and with a strong, strange foreign accent. 'Obviously, with your birthday in October you will be well aware of all the normal characteristics of your sign.'

'Yes, of course…' Alice hesitated, feeling Madame Clare's dark eyes upon her, 'well, actually… I should say no… I don't really have any idea at all.'

Madame Clare did not smile or even look surprised. She gave a deep sigh and briefly closed her heavy-lashed, almond shaped eyes. 'The true Libran enjoys calm and peace. They avoid conflict or confrontation. Libra is a sign of the air, ruled by Venus and the planet of love. You have a talent for seeing the best in people and you appreciate beautiful objects and the wonders of nature. This week, with the full moon, you are liable to be indecisive. This is one of your problems.' Suddenly, Madame Clare reached out and took Alice's hand in her own. Alice had a brief moment to be thankful that her nails had just been expertly manicured. 'I see you are troubled in some way, but it is a passing trouble, you will resolve it in your own way. I am not a clairvoyant, but I do see, for no reason that I am aware of, I see something floating away… blue water rippling… a rift… but, I'm sorry, I can't say more. You should ask your mother for the exact time of your birth and then we can talk again.' Madame Clare gave the vaguest of smiles and released Alice's hand. There was a silence and then Grace spoke,

'You see, Alice, you have nothing to worry about, just a passing trouble. Now you run along and ask Minnie to bring us a pot of mint tea, would you? Then we'll meet again later.

Alice stood up hurriedly, feeling that she was emerging from a dream or sleep. Madame Clare's voice had a calming effect, almost to the point of hypnotism. She thanked Madame

Clare and went through to the kitchen, pleased to find Minnie there by the Aga.

'Minnie, Grace asked if they could have a pot of mint tea… I'll take it in if you like?'

'Don't you worry, dear, I'll do it right away. What did you think of the wonderful Madame Hot Air Clare then?'

'I don't know, really. She certainly has a very commanding presence, I think she almost hypnotised me just now… I suppose she did make sense. It's hard to say.'

'Load of rubbish, in my opinion. Phases of the moon and all that stuff about the stars. She leads Grace a right dance sometimes.' Minnie sniffed disapprovingly, 'I can never believe Grace falls for it. But I think they have a good old gossip together about some of the clients that Grace knows.'

'Well, it was all very peaceful and sort of calming. Anyway, I suppose she did say things that meant something to me, but they could be…oh, I don't know, anything really. She has a very strange voice and her accent… I don't know, it's not exactly French.'

'You're right there!' Minnie laughed as she poured the kettle over the fresh mint leaves, 'Gerald and I think it's an accent that comes from being born south of the river Thames and just been Frenchified. That's what we think, anyway.'

'Really, you don't think she's English?' Alice stretched her eyes wide in surprise as she looked at Minnie. 'I must say she does sound sort of phoney. I suppose Grace might have let slip some clues about me when they were gossiping before I arrived. But anyway, Grace loves it all and, after all, what's the harm in it? Now, the manicurist is definitely Italian. She told me she was born in Genoa. She's really sweet.'

'Let's see your nails, then… at least there's a bit of sense in having a posh manicure.'

Alice stretched out both hands for Minnie to inspect.

'Lovely, just right… that natural shine is perfect for you.'

Alice turned her fingers and admired them herself, 'I am really delighted with the effect. The varnish is called 'French Manicure', funnily enough, and it's such a lovely, pearly colour.'

'Suits you, ducks. Anyway, I'll take this tray through now. But have you got a minute to wait for me, Alice? I'd like a word about our Jason. There's some coffee in the pot if you want.'

'Thanks, yes, of course, I'll wait.'

Alice sat at the kitchen table and poured herself a milky coffee. The dogs looked up at her lazily from their place in front of the range. Alice gave a big breath out, 'It's all right for you two dogs! I don't know, why can't my life be simple?' The dogs wagged their tails and stirred, then went back to sleep. The kitchen was warm and comfortable and Alice sipped the hot coffee and wondered what Minnie was going to say about Jason. She had been so pre-occupied with enjoying her day out in St. Tropez and then the catastrophe at the swimming pool that she hadn't given any more thought to Jason. She wondered how she could help him and whether he would return to his silent retreat from the world or if there was a solution. Minnie came back into the kitchen and sat next to Alice.

'Jason has told you all his troubles then, Alice?' Minnie looked miserable and, somehow, a little older than usual. 'He's a good lad, really he is… it's just not fair.'

'So, you and Gerald came to his rescue, really?'

'Well, it wasn't us really, was it. Grace was the one that sorted everything out. The police were just doing nothing to help after they had all the information they needed. Jason was right double crossed, not just by his friends but by the cops as well.'

'So now Jason has seen this Brad, Jeb's brother and thinks he's after him… I mean why? Why would he come all the way down here to the south of France.'

'Well, Jason fitted his little brother up, didn't he. A gang like that, they don't let a grass get away with it… it would be a matter of pride with them.'

'I see, well, I think so, anyway. So now Grace has a guard patrolling the gate and the perimeter… I mean how long can that go on?'

'Well, Grace said it was the first thing to do and then I know she spoke with someone in Nice… I heard her on the phone for a long while. I think he's some sort of private detective.'

'So will he search for this Brad? But what if he finds him?' Alice shuddered at the thought of coming face to face with a man so intent on harming Jason, a man with HATE tattooed on his forehead.

'Well, then he can call in the French police because it seems there is already a warrant out for his arrest… something to do with drugs.'

'Drugs, oh my god, Minnie, it's all so scary, isn't it? Poor Jason, we were just having such a good morning out. I thought he was agoraphobic or something? I had no idea the trouble he was in.'

'Aggra-whatsit? You mean fear of going outside or something? Oh no, he's always been a lovely boy.'

Alice smiled sadly and finished her coffee. Jason certainly was a lovely boy… and that must be what Guy was thinking too.

Minnie suddenly stood up and went over to the Aga, 'Oh, I nearly forgot… this is yours. Jason brought it up from the pool.' Alice looked up in surprise as Minnie held out the top of the blue and white gingham bikini. 'He told me what had happened… ever so upset, he was. Always thinks he brings bad luck wherever he goes. I tried to talk with him, but he went off in a dark mood. Took the dogs out early this morning and cleared a whole area behind the villa for a new vegetable patch or something. I don't know, the troubles that poor boy gets into.'

'So he told you about Guy Bond turning up?'

'Yes, well I knew he was back because Gerald had let him in the gates. With all the new security, there has to be a phone call through to the Villa now before the gates are opened.'

'Yes, of course.' Alice looked down at the bikini top, now dry and neatly folded. She examined the shoestring straps and then the fastener. Nothing broken. Now, all she could think was that she just hadn't fastened it properly at the front. A careless moment, a hasty action that had changed everything. Was this what Madame Clare had actually sensed… the blue water… a rift? Not Alice's future but the events of yesterday's disastrous morning swim. Perhaps Grace had told Madame Clare and the whole session was a trick. It would certainly be a lot more useful if she could be told the future and not a past calamity. If only she had known. She wiped a tear from her eye as she thought how nearly it had never happened. If her usual swimsuit had been dry, if she had never gone to the market in St. Tropez… she sighed and stood up to leave the warmth of Minnie's kitchen. Minnie looked at her sympathetically,

'Cheer up, ducks, the course of true love never did run smooth, now did it? I'm sure your Mr Bond will be back.'

'Midsummer Night's Dream,' Alice answered without thinking, as she saw, in her mind's eye, the look in Guy's eyes before he turned away. She knew Minnie was trying to be kind, but it was hopeless to think that Guy would ever return.

'You have been very good for me, Alice, insisting I should go out and about more.'

Alice nodded in silent agreement. She had learnt that Grace was quite capable of putting any spin on whatever she said or thought. There was no point in trying to tell Grace that all the outings had been completely her own idea. The truth was that Alice felt so low in spirits that it had been quite an effort to even get out of bed that morning. If Grace hadn't planned this stay in William Marsden's hotel in La Ciotat she was quite sure she would still be under her duvet in bed. Not only her utter grief at losing Guy's love but the worry of the problem that shrouded Jason and his life at the Villa la Vie en Rose. Alice looked across at Grace, as the old Bentley rolled south along the coast road. Even though she had just been talking, Alice was surprised to see that Grace was fast asleep, her head resting comfortably on the headrest. Alice envied her this remarkable ability to snatch a brief nap and awake fully revived. She caught Gerald's eye in the rear view mirror and they both smiled. He was obviously very used to driving the beautiful, sleeping Grace. It was true that even in sleep she had the beauty that could only last on good bones. Grace had high cheekbones and a delicate nose over the most perfect mouth. Hardly a wrinkle showed on her face, but Alice knew that Grace carefully chose high-necked dresses or blouses and usually wore a scarf. Maybe her neck did show her age? Alice looked away and caught her own reflection in the car window. How miserable she looked. She brushed her hair away from her forehead and smiled at herself. This just wouldn't do... she could not and would not let Guy Bond ruin her time here on the Côte d'Azur. She determined to forget all about him... and how his dark, brown eyes looked at her across the swimming pool... so hurt and so sad and burning into her memory. There, it was all rolling in front of her again like the repeat of a film, a film she no longer wanted to watch. She blinked away the tears that were always ready to fall and concentrated on looking out of the window. She could not allow herself to be miserable when she was being driven in a Bentley to stay at a hotel on the beach. No, it just would not do. She felt like Alice in Wonderland giving herself stern advice. *'I give myself very good advice, but I very seldom follow it.'* How true that was. Her mother had read her both the Alice books when she was a child, in fact, she had never asked her mother, but she wondered if that was why she was called Alice. She had phoned her mother before leaving the Villa, but it had been a difficult call. They were so close that somehow her mother had guessed that Alice was feeling miserable. As Alice had never even told her mother about Guy there was little point in trying to explain. As for Jason's story and the new sentry on duty, Alice had kept all that completely secret. She knew her mother, and no doubt nice Mike too, would want her to come straight home, back to the safe Surrey suburbs. In the end, she had let her mother think that she had just slept badly and might be getting a cold. If only she could do as her mother advised and just take an aspirin for the pain of losing Guy. Alice sighed and once again decided to take in the scenery. It was a brilliant day, the sun had come back in full strength and there wasn't a cloud in the sky. She looked at her phone, not a single message and the time showed nearly noon, so they must be getting quite near now. Gerald had told her it would be just over two hours. Just then, Gerald pulled into the toll booth, paid with a card and took the exit off the motorway. Grace awoke,

'Good, we're nearly there now, pass my beauty bag, Alice, chop chop!'

Alice opened the flap in the back of the seat and passed Grace her bag, smiling at the way Grace could wake and immediately be in imperious mode.

'Mirror, dear, mirror!' Grace clicked her fingers impatiently and Alice hurriedly passed her the long-handled mirror.

'Good, that's better, I must say a little sleep has done wonders for me. You should try it, Alice, you look like a miserable little urchin. Brush your hair and brighten up, do! Anyone would think we were going to a funeral. Ah yes, I know what will cheer you up,' she raised her voice, 'Gerald, pass Alice that parcel on the front seat, will you. Be careful!'

Alice took the large, brown paper parcel and went to hand it to Grace.

'No, it's not for me, silly girl. It's for you… now hurry up and open it.'

'For me?' Alice felt a ripple of childish excitement as she untied the string bow and the brown paper fell open to reveal a silver shoe box. 'Oh, Grace!' Alice drew in her breath as she took the lid off the box and found three pairs of pumps lying side by side in tissue paper. 'Oh my god, I've never seen anything anywhere like them. They are so, so beautiful.' Alice took each pair out and examined the fine stitching and soft leather lining.

'Which colour do you like best?' Grace asked, almost as excited as Alice. 'I love the pale blue, but the white are so perfect and then the turquoise green could be just right with what you're wearing today, what do you think?'

'I just don't know what to say. I love them all, I've never seen anything so beautifully made.'

'Try them on, quickly, we're dropping downhill now into La Ciotat.'

Alice hastily slipped off her loafers and put on the turquoise green pair of pumps. She gasped and looked at Grace, 'I can't believe it, they fit like gloves and they feel so light and sort of silky. Oh, goodness, they must have cost a fortune. I only meant to buy one pair, the pale blue. Do I owe you lots of money?'

'Don't be ridiculous, they are a present, of course. You couldn't possibly afford them on the wages I pay!' Grace gave a low laugh, 'I loved the turquoise green, perfect for spring weather and then, well, I thought you should have white, you know how I love it… and so good for the summer months.'

'Thank you so much, they are all beautiful. I'll wear the green now, you're right, they are perfect with this dress.' Alice put on the new shoes and looked down at them. 'Why do you always wear white, Grace, if you don't mind my asking?'

'Why? Do you think I should wear purple? Like that annoying poem? Grow old disgracefully, you mean?' Grace glared at Alice.

'No, no, not at all. You always look wonderful in white, I just meant… well, why always white?' Alice struggled to find the right words. Then Grace laughed at her,

'Hmm, don't look so worried. You haven't offended me and it's a perfectly good question that I shall try to answer politely. Let me see, hmm, for one thing, it does simplify life. No problem with wondering what goes with what…' Grace stopped and her face looked sad as she continued, 'but, do you know… I think the real reason is that when I was a child and just wanted to play, you know, how children get grubby playing… well, my mother was always so angry if I spoilt my clothes and she would always shout 'never put you in white.' Silly really, but I always felt good wearing white and I hated her saying that. I resolved that when I could choose my own clothes, then, I would wear nothing but white on white. I dare say an analyst could make a lot of it,' she laughed again, her face lighting up with fun 'but here we are. Well, well, the Hotel de la Plage has had quite a facelift.'

Alice looked out the window and saw they had pulled into a circular drive in front of marble steps leading to the hotel entrance.

Before Gerald had time to get out the car and open Grace's door, Alice saw William Marsden hurrying down the steps to greet them.

Grace noticed too,

'There's William, my goodness, he must have been waiting right by the door. Hmm, he looks very handsome in his Panama hat and blazer, very old school. I just hope he doesn't fall down the marble stairs trying to look sprightly.'

An hour later they were sitting in a large orangery that ran along the back of the hotel. It looked over a luxuriant garden of oleanders and palms, then down to a fine sandy beach and the sea.

'Now tell me, William, how did this all come about? How did you move from your clever cardboard boxes into the hotel business?'

Grace was sitting in a white wicker chair under the fronds of a palm tree, her back to the sea. Perfectly placed with delicate, flattering shadows falling across her face. Once again the lighting was perfect and she had set her scene.

35   *'you left the film world so mysteriously'*

'Why don't you go for a walk around La Ciotat?' Grace leaned across the table as lunch finished, 'You need to get some colour in your cheeks, Alice.'

'Hold on a minute,' William held up his hand and smiled at Grace. Alice watched with interest as Grace smiled back. Could it really be that Grace was letting someone else give the orders? She was almost simpering as she waited for William to continue, 'Excuse me, one moment, but I thought I'd ring my grand-daughter, Amber. She has an apartment and an atelier on the top floor and usually takes a walk after lunch. I'm sure she'd like to meet Alice.' He spoke briefly into his phone and then looked at Alice. 'Amber's just coming down if you can wait.' He smiled and Alice could quite understand why Grace was so bemused. William Marsden was not only handsome, but he had a quiet commanding manner.

'Thank you, that would be lovely. Did you say she was a painter?'

'Yes, she works in her studio on the top floor when she's not out and about with her easel and paints. I have a little apartment up there, too. It's lovely to spend time with her, but she works long hours.'

'Hmm, are they her water-colours in the foyer?' Grace asked, leaning forward to regain William's attention. 'Such wonderful work, I noticed the paintings as soon as I came into the hotel.'

'Yes, they're all Amber's work. I am probably biased, but I do think they're very good.'

'Does she sell at a gallery? I should love to buy a few to add splashes of colour to my white walls at the Villa.'

Alice looked at Grace in surprise but before she could say anything, William stood up, saying,

'You can ask her yourself, here she is, my grand-daughter, Amber.' William stood up and held out a chair at the table. 'Amber, this is Grace Devine, who needs no introduction, and her young friend Alice Shakespeare.

They all shook hands formally and the girl, her striking auburn hair catching the winter sunlight, leaned forward and held Grace's hand a little longer than the rest. 'This is such an honour, Miss Devine, I can hardly believe I am holding your hand in mine. I have seen all your films. I hope you don't mind, I've brought the hotel's *livre d'or,* I was wondering if you would sign it? It would be wonderful to have your name in our guest book.'

'Give it here, 'Grace held out her hand rather disdainfully and looked at the book, 'My goodness, it's the original from when the hotel was opened in 1925. Fancy that?' She flicked quickly through the pages, 'I feel quite overwhelmed with the past. My name must be in here somewhere…'

'Oh, it is, I put a bookmark on the page for you.' Amber leaned forward and turned the pages back, 'Here, this is your signature.'

'My dear girl, I refuse to look… I dread to think how long ago it must have been and I can't even remember which of my many disastrous husbands or lovers I would have been with at the time.' Grace took the gold pen that was attached to the spine of the book and scrawled her signature across the latest page in the book. 'There, now we are back to the present day, much to my relief. You are young enough to be a fan of old movies, but for me they are better forgotten.' Grace laughed melodiously, 'Really, I'm surprised anyone of your age would ever have heard of me.'

'But you're so famous… and then you left the film world so mysteriously, so suddenly. It created such a mystery around your name.'

'Hmm, well, it didn't please my agent, I can assure you, he is still trying to recover. The simple truth is that I saw that times were changing. Right here on the Côte d'Azur, Brigitte Bardot had removed her top and taken the world by storm, I was telling Alice the other day. And that was before it became fashionable for girls to have thighs the same width as their knees. The new age of the anorexic waif was yet to come. But I certainly didn't want to become out of fashion and then I had a very good offer in a completely different world. I invested my money and ran for the hills behind Mougins. No mystery, really, just a fast disappearing act!'

'Well, it takes courage to give up a life one knows. You were a top billing star…everyone's darling,' William looked at Grace with interest, 'How did you manage to give up on all that?'

'Very easily, I can assure you. I have a natural talent for being idle and spoilt. Now, why don't these two young and lovely girls go for a strenuous walk and you and I, William, perhaps we could totter round the hotel gardens?'

William sprang out of his chair and held out his arm to Grace, 'It seems to me that I have the fortune of walking with the loveliest girl of all.'

'Really William, don't be ridiculous!' Grace gave one of her lowest and most seductive laughs and took his arm.

Alice stood next to Amber and watched as Grace and William walked slowly along the conservatory and out to the terrace. As Grace walked outside, she raised her hand to shield her face from the bright sunlight. Immediately, William grabbed one of the parasols from a table and held it over Grace. She looked back at the two girls watching and called out, her voice clear and resonant,

'Quite a Pablo moment!' She gave another deep rich laugh, 'I remember seeing Pablo with Françoise on the beach in Cannes… and their horrid little Dachshund…'

Alice looked at Amber and they both laughed out loud as Grace's voice died away in the distance.

'They seem to be getting on very well.' Amber said, wrinkling her brow, 'I've never seen my grandfather so… well, I don't really know the word… sort of…smitten?'

'Grace is quite a character. There's something about her that should be annoying but, in fact, is completely delightful. Do you really want to go for a walk? I mean they just sort of organised it between them. I quite understand if you want to carry on with your painting.'

'Amber stretched and yawned, 'Goodness no, I've been working too long today as it is. I began at first light and I get to the point where I overdo it. Knowing when to stop is the hardest thing. Would you like to come up to my flat for a cup of tea or coffee?'

That would be great, thank you. I love the hotel. I took my bag up to my room before lunch so I've seen a bit of it. The decor is in fabulous style… I don't know, is it art deco?

'Yes, the place was practically derelict when Grandy, that's William, my grandfather invested in it. There's a partnership with this young couple who already had a hotel in the hills near Aix. The wife, Calinda, has all the vision… the decor is all researched from the first days when the hotel was opened in 1925. When we bought it, well, it had a faded beauty but it was all peeling pink crumbling plaster and worn out bathrooms. Of course, the location is amazing, with the gardens straight down to a sandy beach. But it was Calinda who brought it back to its original glamour. She was once a supermodel in London. You may have heard of her.'

'Oh my god, the famous model Calinda? Of course, she disappeared off the scene in rather the same way that Grace did years before. So she runs this place?'

'With her husband, François. It's a pity they're not here at the moment… nor my boyfriend, Luc, he's away, too. He plays the flute in the Nice orchestra. They're playing in Paris tonight.'

'Goodness, you all lead such glamorous lives. I'm just in my first job since leaving university, working for the amazing Grace.'

'Must be fun. Believe me, hotel life can be very demanding. Not at this time of the year but you can imagine the craziness of the summer season. Here's the lift. I'll show you where we all hideout.'

The heavy decorated lift doors slowly opened and Alice stepped inside, 'So were the lift doors original or did you have to find them? The tulips and arched lines in the brass are so beautiful, absolute works of art.'

'All original and very difficult to restore as we had to change the entire working of the lift. It's good to meet someone who appreciates it all. Most of our guests just breeze in for the thalassotherapy in the spa… all sea water treatments and all incredibly successful. Personally I'd rather just swim in the sea. Do you like swimming?'

Alice was overwhelmed with a sudden rush of misery as she remembered her last swim at the Villa. 'Yes, I swim most mornings at Grace's place, she has an outdoor pool with heated water and…' but it was no good, she tried to keep talking, but tears were rolling silently down her cheeks.

Amber reached out and put an arm round Alice's shoulders, 'I'm so sorry, whatever's the matter?' She looked at Alice anxiously as the lift doors opened and they went into a large, bright studio. 'Don't cry, nothing can surely be that bad… why don't we have a cup of tea and you can tell me all about it.'

'I'm glad you like them, Mum, the parcel must have arrived really quickly then. I only posted the table mats a few days ago.' Alice looked mournfully out the window of her cottage at the driving rain. It seemed like just a few days ago that she had been in the market at St. Tropez and bought her mother a present and then… bought the fateful bikini. Since their return from La Ciotat the days had slid past quietly.

'Mike and I use them at supper time. It brings a little of your Provençal sunshine into our lives here. We absolutely love them, thank you, darling. A market in St. Tropez, you said, how glamorous.'

'I know, it's fabulous!' Alice strived to make her voice upbeat, 'You and Mike will have to get down here some time so I can show you around.'

'We can't wait, but Mike can't get away for another three months at least. He has to get a locum, of course, and now that I am running all the admin, I would have to get a replacement too. Our lives just seem to get busier and busier.'

Alice sighed with relief and hoped her mother hadn't heard, she carried on quickly, 'Well, sounds like you're enjoying yourself, too. You've always liked hard work.'

'Well, you may be right. I suppose I have to agree that I do enjoy working and this job is very rewarding indeed. I meet all sorts of people and face all sorts of life problems. It's very involving and I think if I didn't work with Mike it wouldn't be the same.'

'I'm sure you're right, Mum. I can imagine you lighting up the whole surgery and cheering everyone up.'

'Well, I hope you're right, dear. Anyway, how are you?'

'Oh, I'm just fine and dandy,' Alice crossed her fingers behind her back, 'I'm having a great time and meeting new people now that Grace has decided to go out more. I made a good new friend the other day, a girl called Amber who lives down here and paints the most amazing water-colours.'

'That's good. I'm so glad you have someone of your own age to talk to… Grace sounds a wonderful person, but she is old enough to be your grandmother.'

'She's been so kind to me, Mum, in fact, it is a bit like having a grandmother or maybe more a fairy godmother. You know we went to that shoe-maker in Nice, well, she bought me three pairs of the most beautiful soft leather pumps… it's like wearing gloves on your feet, honestly!'

'Goodness, you are being quite spoiled, Alice. She must really appreciate your work. How's the biography going along?'

'Well,' Alice paused, trying not to think about the screenplay that she had hoped to work on with Guy, 'there's been a bit of a hold up with all our jaunts and outings… I expect we'll get back to it today though.'

'Good, it sounds such interesting work. Well, better go now, dear, the surgery opens again at two today with a well woman clinic. Thank you again for the table mats and all your lovely letters. Bye, darling!'

'Bye, Mum.' Alice blew out a long breath of relief as she switched off her phone. At least she hadn't let her mother guess how miserable she felt. She was glad the Provençal sun shone on her mother's table as it certainly wasn't out in Provence. Glad too, that her mother had found a new and interesting life. There was no need for Alice to worry about her being lonely, now that she was with Mike. She sighed as she thought about what her mother had said…what was it? Yes, something about having someone of her own age to talk to… well, that was fairly awful. Somehow, she had opened her heart to Amber who had proved to be a sympathetic listener. But how embarrassing to have broken down in tears and told the wretched story of the snapped bikini. To Alice's surprise, Amber had listened very seriously and then told her about her own disaster story… she had actually been jilted at the altar. That was so awful that Alice had dried her tears and both girls had then gone for a long walk along the beach to recover their equilibrium. Still, Alice thought now, it was all right for Amber, she had now met a man who loved her. There didn't seem to be a happy ending in sight for herself. Checking the time she realised she would be late for her afternoon work with Grace if she didn't hurry. Quickly tidying up her room she grabbed her laptop and an umbrella and ran up to the Villa.

37   *'one of my husbands, rather a sweetie before he took to drugs'*

Alice took her usual place on the sofa opposite Grace and stroked Smoke and Cloud who had lazily come over to greet her before returning to their fireside place. Everything seemed normal except Grace. She was sitting upright on the sofa and holding a folded piece of blue paper in her hand. Alice's heart missed a beat as she realised it was another letter from Guy. Grace was not waving it aloft and smiling but just sitting quietly still and holding it folded in her hand.

'Do you want to read it?' Grace went straight to the point and then held out the letter.

Alice shivered slightly even though the room was warm with sunlight and the heat from the log fire. 'No, it's a letter to you. I don't want to read it, thank you.' Her voice sounded strange to her own ears as though someone else was speaking.

'Shall I just tell you some of what it says then?' Grace's voice had none of its usual vibrance and she continued without waiting for Alice to reply. 'It affects us both so you have to know that Guy Bond has decided to go over to California and pick up some work he has there and so, he says, regretfully has to turn down the offer of working on my biopic screenplay.' Grace then threw the letter down on the glass table between them and looked at Alice, her blue eyes now piercing and determined, 'So that's that and we shall both have to get on with it.'

Alice took a deep breath before drawing on every ounce of her courage she replied in an even voice, 'Yes, it seems so. I'm sorry if any of this is my fault.'

Grace threw herself back on the sofa and drew up her legs, resuming her usual reclining position. But anyone could have told that she was anything but relaxed, in fact, her shoulders were rigid and her face angry. 'Wretched man, waltzing into your lovely young life and upsetting you. It's too bad.'

'It was all just a dreadful misunderstanding.' Alice quickly wiped a tear away as it rolled down her cheek. 'Anyway, what about your screenplay? Will you find another writer?'

Grace turned and looked at Alice, 'You have guts, Alice, I'm pleased to say. You look so fragile, but you have an inner strength. I've seen it in you more than once. We'll get over this together, don't you worry. I know you are much too sweet to believe me, but there are a great many men in the world… I know, right now that's hard to believe, but it is true. Admittedly it is very hard to find the right one, like looking for the proverbial needle, but there is someone out there in this beautiful universe who is made for you. Whether it is Guy Bond or not… in fact, there are probably hundreds of them but you just don't meet them. Oh dear, I had better stop… my consolation and advice seems to be going in the wrong direction. Anyway, to answer your question about a replacement writer… Bernie has already spoken on the phone this morning.'

'Goodness, have you found someone already?'

'My dear girl, of course not, it may be just as hard to find me a writer as for you to find your heart's desire in the form of a handsome prince. Sad to say, there are more frogs that will never be kissed into princes than you could possibly believe. In fact, I could probably give you more advice on kissing the wrong men than most women. Now there I am quite an expert… I have kissed so many men on screen. Mostly very handsome, of course, which made it bearable…those screen kisses would usually turn very real and continue off screen… but I have non-kissed many unattractive men as well. I walked off the set for a week once over a screen kiss. My co-star was an ugly man who thought he was god's gift and he was taking our screen kiss much too far down. I remember my producer trying to persuade me back on set saying that even an ugly man can look beautiful in love… absolute rubbish, of course. Finally, I did go back on set after I had eaten some very garlicky salami.' Grace gave a low-pitched, bubbling laugh at the memory, 'But I have never been able to love a man who is not A class handsome. But there, you see, that is absolutely why I shouldn't give advice… my history is disastrous.' Grace sighed audibly, 'As for screenwriters, well, the search must go on.'

Alice smiled at Grace's words mad rush of words and began to recover a little, 'What did Bernie suggest then?'

'Oh, he's getting a bit desperate and, of course, like you my dear, he thought Guy Bond was the answer to his prayers. Now, he wants me to meet with the writer he suggested a long while ago. A sorry character, I thought. Mind you, it's a hard life, being a screenwriter… not much acclaim. Do you know there are fewer stars for writers on the Hollywood Walk of Fame than there are for animals? The whole industry relies on writers but tends to neglect them. Your Mr. Bond is something of an exception.'

'So, will you? Will you meet this other writer?'

Good god, no. Never in a month of Sundays. I knew him in the past, no, he'd be quite hopeless for the task…just a stupid little poodle-faker who writes romantic drivel.'

Now, Alice actually laughed aloud and the dogs stirred and looked up, 'Whatever is a poodle faker, Grace?'

'Oh, some little creep who fawns around rich and elderly women. Pampering to their every whim.' Grace sniffed disapprovingly and closed her eyes.

'Sounds ideal!' Alice replied, giving Grace a wicked smile.

'Cheeky girl!' Grace flashed her eyes open and then laughed, 'Ah, I see your spirit is returning. Now then, as we are both somewhat emotionally jaded I suggest you get on with some work that you have seriously neglected.'

Alice looked at Grace in alarm, 'Neglected my work, sorry Grace, tell me more.'

Now it was Grace's laughter that filled the room, 'Oh, my poor little Alice Shakespeare, don't look so worried. I mean, quite simply, that you promised to read to me and I think this dreary afternoon would be an ideal time to start. Tell me, what did your mother read to you when you were a child?'

'That would be more easily answered by what didn't she read to me. We read everything we could get our hands on… a regular weekly visit to our local library and always our full quota of borrowed books. But our all time favourite, one we would return to again and again, was, Alice in Wonderland.'

'Of course, how lovely your childhood sounds, Alice. I don't suppose my own mother even knew about public libraries. By the way, you haven't seen my own library yet, have you?'

'Your own library?'

Well, of course, I may have been dragged up in the grime of Walthamstow but I have learnt not to be a complete philistine. I began to collect books years ago and one of my husbands, rather a sweetie before he took to drugs, he left me his own collection when he died. Go through that door at the end of the salon and you will find the library. Go on, Alice, you don't need a ticket or a magic key. Go on with you!'

Alice stood up and the dogs followed her, their paws tip-toeing on the marble floor. She opened the white door that was hidden as part of the wall and went through. She found herself in a long narrow, windowless room completely filled with shelves and shelves of books. Soft lighting came from above each shelf and there was a simple white table in the centre, high like a rostrum. Alice began to read the titles, running her fingers along the spines of the books.

'See if you can find Alice Through the Looking Glass… it's a red leather book, a double volume with Alice in Wonderland. It should be on a top shelf on the left with all the first editions.' Grace's voice carried through from the salon and Alice looked up to the top shelf in amazement. She found a narrow white ladder that slid along the shelves and moved it toward a row of leather-bound books. There, in a corner of the top shelf she found the double edition, just as Grace had said.

'Have you found it?' Grace's voice was impatient now, 'Bring it through, chop chop.'

Alice went slowly down the ladder, holding the book carefully. The dogs looked up at her as though waiting to see where she would go next. She turned and went out of the library and the dogs rushed ahead, happy to get back to the fireside.'

'Good, you've found it. I knew I had a copy.'

'Not just any copy, Grace, this is a first edition.'

'Well, of course, I know that but after all, you can't judge a book by its cover, however lovely the squidgy red leather is… so, will you read to me, Alice?'

'From this book?'

'Well, I don't have the paperback or a version on Kindle if that's what you mean? Don't be ridiculous, Alice, of course from that book, what else?'

'It's just so rare,' Alice opened one of the books carefully, 'Oh my, this is an illustration by John Tenniel.'

'Well, I sincerely hope so, or it wouldn't be a first edition would it. Now, what do you think? I remember Alice in Wonderland quite well, but perhaps you would read Through the Looking Glass?'

'I'd love to… maybe I should wear white gloves or something?'

'Tosh, I may like wearing white, but gloves for reading, don't be silly. The book has survived very well since 1867 and unless you spill your tea over it, I am sure it will enjoy being opened.'

'*Weak tea with cream in it?*' Alice laughed as Grace pulled a questioning face, 'It's a quote from the book. My mother used to say it nearly every time I asked for a drink when I was little. We used to have a game of quotes. Try to catch each other out.'

'Hmm, that's why you're so quick at recognising quotes. Ahh, Alice, if only I had your upbringing I would probably be queen of England.'

'Well, you seem to have made a very good job of being recognised queen of the movies.'

'Ah, but what's that in the scale of things?'

'William Marsden seemed very impressed.' Alice looked at Grace with another wicked smile.

'Hmm, sweet William. He may do very well, I shall have to see, but right now, good gracious girl, can't you just read to me?'

Alice opened the book and held it carefully in front of her. The dogs settled by the fire and Grace leant back on the sofa.

'In fact, there is a White Queen in this story, Grace… maybe that would suit you?

'I expect she's a wicked old harridan.'

'Well, actually the White Queen lives backwards, through the theme of the looking-glass. She cries out in pain before she pricks her finger on a brooch and also, she claims to be more than a hundred and one years old …'

'Well, you'd never catch me doing that, now would you? Anyway, of course, no-one would possibly believe I was that old…'

'… and the White Queen tells Alice '*Why, sometimes I've believed as many as six impossible things before breakfast.*'

That's my absolute favourite quote in the whole book.'

'Alice, are you determined to be a plot-spoiler? Will you please just begin? Read, girl, read!'

Alice very carefully turned to the first page and began, '*One thing was certain, that the white kitten had had nothing to do with it: it was the black kitten's fault entirely. For the white kitten had been having its face washed by the old cat for the last quarter of an hour (and bearing it pretty well, considering); so you see that it couldn't have had any hand in the mischief.*'

Smoke and Cloud rolled on their sides and stretched out as Alice began to read. Smoke gave a large yawn as though a book about kittens had to be the most boring book in the world.

Alice looked through the slats of the shutter on her bedroom window. No sign of Jason in the pool and rain was still slanting down from a dark sky. She sighed, she missed her early morning swim, but she just didn't have the courage to go back to the routine. Jason seemed to have given up too. She hadn't seen him at all yesterday, but Minnie had told her that he was staying in his room, playing music and gaming. Alice pulled on her track suit, deciding that, rain or not, she would make herself go for a jog through the olive grove. Just as she was leaving the cottage the air was filled with the ear-splitting noise of the Villa burglar alarm. Alice covered her ears and looked around. Nothing seemed to be happening so she began to run up to the Villa. On the way up she met Gerald,

'What's happening, Gerald?'

He shook his head and raised his hands in the air and continued to run as fast as he could toward the villa. Alice ran ahead and reached the kitchen at the same time as Jason. His face was panic-stricken as he shouted over the deafening noise of the alarm,

'What is it, Alice, what's happening?' Alice shook her head and pushed him ahead of her into the kitchen. There they found Minnie on the phone, one hand clapped to her ear as she tried to listen. She looked round as they came in, followed by Gerald.

'I was trying to call the guard at the gate, but he doesn't answer,' she shouted and then, suddenly, the alarm stopped ringing and there was a haunting, echoing silence. Grace came into the room, looking small and scared and clutching a white kimono around her.

'I've turned off the alarm and called the police. Lock all the doors and stay in the villa. Where are the dogs?'

There was another silence, heavier and more frightening than before. Alice ran to the back door and gave a long, loud whistle. They all waited, staring out of the kitchen door into the rain, but the dogs did not appear. Alice turned to the others,

'I'm going to run round the grounds to see what's happened'. Before they could stop her she ran off down the drive and toward the gates. She ran as fast as she could, the rain beat into her face but she could soon see that the gates were still closed. She stopped, brushed her wet hair back and looked around then whistled again. Still nothing. She ran to the perimeter fencing and began to follow it closely as it wound uphill. Before she had gone more than a few hundred metres she found a gaping hole cut into the wire fencing. Then, as she drew closer, she saw a piece of paper in a polythene bag fastened to the jagged wire with the dogs' white leather collars. She looked around, her heart beating fast and then she snatched the bag from the fence, unbuckled the collars and clutching everything inside her jacket, she ran as fast as she could back to the Villa. When she reached the kitchen she found Grace and Minnie sitting at the table. Alice, out of breath, held out the note and the dog collars to Grace.

'I found all this fixed to a gap in the fencing, The wire has been cut… it's addressed to you.' As she spoke, Gerald and Jason came back into the kitchen.

'The dogs! Where are the dogs? Did you find them, Alice?' Jason said, his voice desperate.

'No, no, just this note and…' Alice suppressed a sob, 'and their collars.' She pushed back her wet hair and sat next to Grace, who had pulled the white piece of paper out of the plastic bag. She held it out to Alice. 'Please read this quickly, Alice, read it aloud. I think we all have an idea of what it will say.'

Alice took the slip of paper and read aloud, her voice hoarse and shaky,

'If you want your dogs back safe wait quiet no police.' The words were pencilled in large capitals across the lined piece of paper. Alice laid it down on the table and they all looked at it in horror. Grace spoke first.

'Pass me the phone, Alice, now, quickly.' Alice grabbed the house phone and passed it to Grace who dialled quickly,

'*Gendarmerie? Bonjour, re-bonjour… je m'appelle Grace Devine, Oui, oui … absolument mon erreur, pas de probleme ici… chez moi, La Villa La Vie en Rose… c'etait une fausse alerte, excusez moi. Oui, oui, tout va bien merci, merci, au revoir.*'

Grace set down the phone and looked at them all in turn as though willing them not to say anything. Then she stood up and Jason moved forward and took her arm as she went toward the salon.

'Thank you, Jason, now please, everyone, we need to think and I want you all to meet me in half an hour in the salon.

Minnie, please make us all a little breakfast. I want to lie down for a few minutes.' She patted Jason on the arm and said quietly, 'Now, I think at last we shall be able to sort this all out. Be a good boy and just stay put and I'll see you again in a minute.'

Minnie came over to Grace and took her arm, 'I'll see you to your room, Grace.'

Gerald and Jason stood in the kitchen and looked at Alice.

'Grace does speak French!' Alice said, almost to herself and then added, 'Let's go!' she said quickly, 'I'll show you where the fence is cut and we can try and find that useless guard.'

They hurried down the drive, the rain still pouring relentlessly. Alice showed them the jagged cut in the metal fencing.

'Well, that would certainly have triggered the alarm, all right.' Gerald said as he pushed through the undergrowth and examined the cut wires.

'It's Brad, isn't it?' Jason's voice was low and he sounded near to tears.

'We don't know anything yet, Jason. It could be anyone… maybe someone from that gang of olive pickers?' Alice rested a hand on his arm. 'Grace is right, we need to think carefully, but right now I think we should go down to the gates and see if the guard is around or what. I just don't understand where he can be.'

'A security guard like him would be easy meat to Brad. Either he's been paid off or they've slugged him. I know it's Brad that's done this.' Jason looked at Alice, his face more miserable than ever. 'The dogs, Alice, the dogs…'

'I'm going to get the dogs back, Jason, you just watch me. Brad may be a thug, but he can't be very clever, can he? How would he have HATE tattooed on his forehead if he had any brains at all? He's a criminal and he's made himself instantly identifiable. We are going to find him and the dogs.' Alice spoke firmly to try and reassure Jason, then realised that she believed herself. She turned to Gerald, 'Do you think you could call in someone to mend the fencing?'

'Yes, yes, I will right away. I know the firm that installed it all.'

'Why don't you go back to the villa and give them a call. Tell Minnie that Jason and I are on our way back. We'll all need a hot drink.'

'Right you are.' Gerald looked relieved to have something to do and hurried off.

'Now, Jason, I need you to watch my back. I'm scared out of my wits, but I think we ought to go down to the gates and see if we can find the guard. Are you up for it?'

'I'll go on my own, Alice, you better go back to the villa, too.'

'No, I'm coming with you, but let's hurry.'

They ran together down the drive to the gates. Jason pressed the side gate button and the gates slowly swung open. Taking a deep breath, Alice cautiously walked through with Jason at her side. They looked in both directions, but the road was completely empty. The rain was falling so fast that the surface of the road was running with flood water.

Jason stood in the middle of the road and said, 'I'm going to run right round the outside fencing. You go back now, Alice.'

Alice looked up at Jason, surprised at the new tone of confidence in his voice. The rain was trickling down his face as he looked back at her. 'It's OK, Alice, I'll be OK.'

'I'm coming with you. I have my phone. We'll just check it out, right? Let's go.'

They set off at a steady jog and soon reached the gap in the fencing. They stopped and looked at the ground outside the fence. The grassy verge was muddy and trampled, the heavy rain had obliterated any signs of footsteps, but there were obvious car tyre marks in the mud. They looked at each other in silence and then ran on following the line of the fence but finding nothing more.

Back in the warmth of the kitchen, Minnie passed Alice a towel, hot from the Aga. 'Better dry your hair a bit, Alice, you'll catch your death. Hadn't you better take off that wet track suit?'

'Thanks, Minnie, no, I'll be fine. I'll dry my hair and just take off my jacket.'

Minnie took Alice's jacket from her and hung it on the Aga rail. 'Gerald phoned that security company. They said the guard had called in sick and they were trying to find a replacement. Sounds fishy to me.'

'I knew it, that's Brad, he's paid him off, hasn't he.' Jason sat down at the table and put his head in his hands. 'This is all my fault, I've brought my bad luck to the Villa, to Grace. She's been so kind to me and now the dogs.'

'That's quite enough of that, Jason.' They all turned to see that Grace had come back into the kitchen. 'There is absolutely nothing to be gained by talking in that way. Now then, Minnie, I thought we could have some breakfast in the kitchen for a change.' She sat at the table looking as immaculate as ever, now in a neat white wool suit with a high-necked ruffled, silk blouse. Jason jumped up and held out a chair for Grace at the end of the large kitchen table. She sat down and Minnie poured her a coffee. Gerald came back into the kitchen, wet through and looking very tired. 'Gerald, you had better sit down and have one of your big mugs of sweet tea. I'm sure Minnie has a pot on the go. Now, how about you, Alice, I notice you ignored my instructions and went down to the gates.'

'Well, I had Jason with me… we checked the perimeter and apart from tyre marks in the mud we didn't find anything more. No sign of the guard.'

Gerald sipped his hot tea and said, 'The security company are trying to wriggle out of responsibility, The guard had called in sick and they said they had tried to call here to tell us they were sending a replacement as soon as possible. Made me see red, that did.'

'Hmm, well it seems fairly obvious that they are corrupt.' Grace appeared calm, 'Ring them again after breakfast Gerald and tell them not to bother. What's the point?'

'And I called the fencing chaps and they are sending someone out to repair the gap this afternoon.'

'Hmm, also rather pointless if anyone can cut through it, but thank you, Gerald, it does have to be done. Now then, sit down all of you and have some breakfast. An army can't run on an empty stomach. We have a battle on our hands, it seems.' Grace looked round at them all, suddenly looking very tired and vulnerable. There was a brief silence as they all thought about the dogs… and then the phone rang.

'I'll take it,' Alice jumped up from the table and went over to the dresser where the phone lay, flashing and ringing. She picked it up and saw *'unknown number'* on the screen, then she said quietly.

'Good morning, La Villa la Vie en Rose, *qui parle?* Yes, I understand, yes I will tell her. Yes, in half an hour. I'll be here.' The phone went dead and she turned to face them all staring at her from their seats at the table. 'It was a man with a low voice. He is going to call again in half an hour to give us instructions.' She put the phone down carefully on the table between them all. 'He said he wanted ten thousand euros in cash'

'Not more?' Grace answered quickly, 'I thought they would want more than that.'

'He called the ten thousand his expenses,' Alice took a deep breath, 'what he wants is the diamonds.' Alice looked at Jason. 'He wants Jason to bring the diamonds and he is going to call in half an hour to tell him where to go.'

Jason stood up, pushing his chair back from the table and running his fingers back through his hair, 'But I don't have the diamonds, the police have them. I've told you all.'

Grace looked up at Jason, 'We know, Jason, we all know and believe you, but it seems that this man, presumably the tattooed Brad does not believe you. Sit down, Jason, we need to think quietly before he calls again.'

'It seems to me,' Alice spoke slowly, 'that we should call the French police back now, straight away.'

'No, no… I am not risking that.' Grace answered, her voice rising in anger, 'don't you see, they could be as corrupt as the English police… not to mention the security company. We can't risk anything happening to the dogs.'

'You're probably right, but… as we don't have the diamonds… what can we do? What were these diamonds like, Jason?'

Jason sat down again at the table, 'I have no idea, absolutely no idea. All I heard was afterwards and talking with the police… it seemed that they were a stock of rough cut diamonds ready to be taken to Hatton Garden. The jeweller in the Mile End Road was handling them and dealing in drugs on the side.'

Gerald turned to Alice, 'Well, that much was in all the papers. They made a lot of it at the time, but it was the drug ring they were after.'

'Rough diamonds… what do they look like?' Alice asked, looking round the table.

'I've seen rough diamonds,' Grace said, 'they're not like diamonds, really, just yellowish grey pebbles, not round... more like gravel, I suppose.'

Alice ran out of the kitchen and came back in a moment with a handful of small stones. 'Like this?' She held out the palm of her hand with a few small chips of gravel spread out for them to see.

'Alice, is that the gravel from my pot plants?' Grace asked, 'Are you thinking what I think you are thinking?'

There was an intake of breath from everyone around the table. Minnie spoke first, 'It could work, supposing we wash the gravel and make it a bit shiny then put it in one of your posh black velvet diamond jewellery bags, Grace?'

'The thing is...' Gerald spoke slowly, 'the point is, he is expecting you to have the diamonds, Jason.'

'And he can't be the cleverest criminal on the planet to have HATE permanently on his forehead.' Grace looked round the table as though hoping they would all agree.

'Exactly my thoughts, Grace.' Alice nodded, 'How stupid he must be. How would he know if the stones were diamonds or not?'

Grace nodded slowly in agreement, 'Gerald, would you please check the safe and see how much cash there is in the cashbox and bring me one of the black velvet bags.'

Gerald hurried from the room and Alice sat silently, looking at the gravel in her hand and then at the clock on the wall. The kitchen seemed horribly quiet and empty without the dogs sprawled in front of the range. How could she possibly be thinking that her crazy idea would work and how would they ever get the dogs back safely from a man like Brad?

Gerald came back into the kitchen and broke the silence, 'You have more than thirty grand in euros, Grace, and I brought this bag.' He passed a black velvet pouch to Grace and she pulled open the drawstring and tipped out a necklace. It lay curled on the white scrubbed wood table, glinting in the light.

Alice gasped, 'Oh my god, that does look like I expect diamonds to look, it's so beautiful but somehow...evil.'

'Ah well, we all know now that diamonds can have brought misery, blood diamonds. When I was given this, diamonds were just a symbol of extravagant love, I suppose. I never cared for this particular necklace anyway,' Grace pushed the necklace with her finger. 'I would happily give it to the wretched Brad in exchange for my dogs.'

Then the phone rang. They all jumped and Grace nodded at Alice who answered and pressed the speaker-phone so they could all hear, 'Hello,' she kept her voice low and controlled, trying to conceal the horror she felt at talking to the man on the other end of the phone. Was he the man with the HATE tattoo? Was he with the dogs now? Was he looking after them? Where had he taken them? The questions rushed into her head, one on top of the other, but all she could do was to listen. 'Very well. No, we have not called the police. Not yet, but we want the dogs back before the end of the day. We have the money and the diamonds.' Alice heard a gasp on the other end of the phone and the man's voice changed a little,

'So the young bastard did have them all the time… I knew it. Right, tell him to bring the diamonds and the cash tomorrow. I'll call again when I know where… and he has to come alone'

'That's not going to happen… first we want the dogs back before nightfall and second, I shall be driving him.'

'I said alone.'

'You can hardly be scared of me, I'm a young woman. I shall just be driving. We don't want to risk being stopped by the police on the way… Jason no longer has a driving license. Thanks to you.'

'That's enough of your lip, all right you can drive him you stroppy slag, but any funny business and the dogs get it. They're a handful of trouble anyway.'

'You'd better look after them or there's no deal.'

'The sooner we meet the sooner they'll get fed then, right? We'll meet at five today and I'll let you know where in my next call.'

'Whatever you say, we're ready with the cash… and the diamonds.'

'Yeh, the diamonds.' Then the phone went dead. Once again Alice laid it on the table and silence fell.

Gerald stood at the side of the gates as Alice drove through. He waved a hand in farewell and Jason, sitting beside Alice in the Mini, waved back. They pulled away slowly, turning uphill, the rain still pouring down so fast that the windscreen wipers barely cleared the glass.

'You were so clever on the phone, Alice. How did you get him to agree to meet at the lay-by you knew?'

'I didn't really need to persuade him at all. He didn't really seem to have any idea where to meet and just said in the forest…I told him about the lay-by where I met Guy once. It's a big pull-in and the first one on the left as you reach the forest coming from Mougins. He seemed to get it and be quite relieved to be told where to go. I knew he was stupid.'

'Not as stupid as me,' Jason's voice was miserable, 'If I hadn't been so stupid none of this would be happening.' He slapped the leather bag on his lap.

'For god's sake stop beating yourself up, Jason. You're not stupid you're just too nice and you got taken in… that's all. End of story.'

'I keep thinking over and over it all. Why I ever got involved with Jeb and his brother… I just think I was desperate for friends at the time… it was like you had to be in a gang to survive or something.'

'It's all in the past now, Jason. You have a lovely girlfriend and you're learning French. There will be good times ahead for you when we get over this. Now, let's concentrate. You have the bag ready, the money in the envelope and the diamonds… well, OK, the gravel… in the velvet bag. I'll stay in the car, as we agreed and any sign of trouble you just get back to the car and we drive off, OK?'

'But what about the dogs?'

'All going well he will hand over the dogs as you give him the bag. He'll have a job holding them once they see you. You'll have that slight advantage.'

'True, they'll be pulling at the lead by that time. Yeh, I hadn't thought of that. Trust you to think ahead, Alice.'

'Are you scared, Jason? You don't sound it.'

'Funny you should ask, I don't feel a bit scared. I'd like to kill Brad right now with my bare hands. Do you know what, Alice? It's really difficult to be scared when you're around.'

'Well, that's great, I guess, and I see your point about wanting to kill Brad but, Jason, we really don't want more trouble. Just get the dogs back and then we can think what to do about the low-life with HATE on his stupid head. Leave me to worry about that after. OK?'

'Yeh, we just want the dogs back, I know.'

Alice turned on the Mini headlights and peered into the gloom ahead.

'I hadn't reckoned on it getting dark so early though. It's dusk already at five to five. With this rain, there'll be no moonlight so I'm going to keep the headlights on full beam when you get out of the car. OK… we're exactly on time and we're nearly there now so we've no time left to change our minds about anything anyway. Are you ready? The lay-by is just up there on the left.'

Alice slowed down and signalled. 'There's a white van already parked. Do you think that's Brad?'

'Sort of van he'd use, I suppose. Yes, he's getting out… park up, Alice, let's do it!'

Alice pulled quickly over to the kerb and Jason jumped out before the car had come to a halt. She left the engine running and peered into the stream of light coming from the headlights, the raindrops spiralling and sparkling around the outline of Jason directly in front of her. The windscreen wipers continued to sweep back and forth. Alice hastily wiped the steam forming on the inside of the glass and then she gasped as she saw a man, even taller and bulkier than Jason, wearing a black tracksuit and holding the dogs on a rope. She gripped the wheel, desperate to run to the dogs herself. She watched as Jason walked slowly toward the man and, as she had foreseen, the dogs began to bark and strain at the rope. The man yanked the rope back, but the dogs still pulled forward. Then through the space in the misted glass she saw that the man was carrying a knife. Suddenly, she was out of the car and without a moment's hesitation she gave a piercing whistle. Both dogs stopped still for a moment, raising their heads high, then jumped up and twisted violently around. Both slipped their heads free of the rope and galloped at full speed toward Alice. Brad, stumbled as the dogs escaped and Jason threw the leather bag with full force at his head. The bag opened and the money and gravel scattered across the car park. Brad looked bewildered and held his hand to his head, then bent to pick up the velvet bag and a handful of money. Jason launched himself at Brad and fell on top of him, pinning him to the ground. Alice ran forward and kicked Brad's hand and the knife span out of his reach. Jason was struggling to keep Brad down and then managed to get his knee onto the back of Brad neck. Suddenly all the breath seemed to go out of Brad and he lay still, wheezing and gasping for breath.

'Don't kill him, Jason, just keep him down. I'll think of something...' Alice looked around, wondering if they could possibly man-handle Brad into the back of the white van. At that moment, a Landrover pulled into the lay-by, a familiar grey Land-rover, towing a horse box. Before she had time to believe her own eyes, Guy had jumped out of the Land-rover and run over to them.

'What the hell's going on?'

'This man stole Grace's dogs... Jason has just tackled him to the ground... help us, please help us.' Alice spoke desperately as Jason still leant over Brad, one knee over his neck.

'Looks like Jason is killing him to me... but OK, hold on. Jason, don't let him stop breathing... I've got a spare rein...' Guy didn't finish speaking but ran back to the Land-rover and returned holding a long leather leading rein. Guy leaned over and yanked Brad's hands behind his back and began to tie them. Brad groaned aloud and made a feeble attempt to struggle,

'Well, he's not dead, anyway!' Guy looked up at Alice with a brief smile as he continued to tie the reins around Brad's wrists and then down and around his ankles. Finally, he pulled a tight knot. 'That should do, OK Jason you can let him breathe a bit now. He's not going anywhere. I saw a gangster tie someone up just like this on a film set once. I never expected it to come in useful.' He stood up and brushed off his hands on his jeans. 'Now what?'

Alice let out a deep breath and looked at him, 'Thank you, Guy, I don't know what we would have done if you hadn't turned up right then.' He smiled back at her and she suffered a pang of misery as for a brief second she recalled their time together when he had been smiling at her with such love in his eyes. Then Jason slowly stood up, one foot firmly planted in Brad's back and said,

'Alice, do you think you should pick up Grace's money, it's beginning to blow around the car park... and where are the dogs?'

'I saw them jump in the Mini when I ran over to you,' Alice managed a weak smile, 'they ran straight past me and got in the back.'

Jason gave a wide smile, 'They never have liked the rain. We've got them back, Alice, we did it. We effing well did it.' He turned to Guy, one foot still holding down Brad, looking every inch a heroic warrior, and held out his hand. 'Thank you, sir, for your help. When this is all over I'd like a word with you about Alice.'

'Right,' Guy shook his hand, 'No trouble, understood, but… well, what do we do next?'

They all looked down at the large body of Brad lying at their feet. Alice spoke first, 'Jason, you should take the dogs and the Mini back to the Villa. I'll phone Grace to tell them you're on your way now.'

'But I don't have a driving license.'

Alice laughed aloud, 'Oh Jason, you kill me! I think in the circumstances that it's a risk worth taking.'

'But I can't leave you here with this heap of dirt.' Jason pushed his foot down into Brad's back and Brad gave a rasping grunt.

'I have an idea. Hold on a minute.' Guy ran back to the horse box and they waited while he led his horse out and tied it to a tree. Then he got into the Land-rover and backed close up to where Brad lay on the ground, 'There you go, one portable holding cell. We'll lock him in there and call the police.'

'Excellent idea!' Jason looked at Guy in admiration and immediately began to drag Brad toward the van. 'You take his feet, Guy and Alice, you hold the door back.'

Struggling to pull and drag Brad, the two men managed to finally roll him up the ramp and into the horse box. Brad made a few weak attempts to struggle, but he seemed to have lost all hope. As Jason gave him a final push onto the floor of the horse box, Brad muttered and swore, 'Diamonds, where's the diamonds, you git?'

'No diamonds mate,' Jason leant down and spoke close into Brad's ear, 'the pigs took the diamonds on day one and all we had here was a bag of gravel…oh yes, and your travel expenses. Well, you won't be needing that where you're going as they take you away for nothing.' Jason stood up and looked down at Brad, 'To think I was scared of you…' He pushed the toe of his trainer into the side of Brad's stomach. It was not even a kick, more a nudge of disgust, 'you fat lump… no muscle, no brains and HATE written on your stupid head. Should make an identity parade a bit easier, shouldn't it? Bye now.' Jason jumped out of the horse box, pulled up the ramp and slammed the door. Guy turned the key in the lock and both men looked at each other before turning to Alice.

Alice shook her head, raindrops flying from her long, blonde hair, 'Don't look at me… seems like you're managing very well. Now, I would like to get out of the rain.'

'Why don't you take the dogs back to the villa, Alice? I'll stay here with Guy.' Jason looked at her doubtfully.

'Because I shall make a much better job of explaining all this to the police… and you really do not need to get involved, Jason. You've done your part, now get safely back to the villa with the dogs.'

'Anyway,' Guy opened the passenger door of the Landrover, 'Alice can take shelter in here while we wait for the police.' He frowned at Jason and Jason suddenly nodded and smiled.

'Oh right, get it, yeh, I'll be off then.' He ran back to the Mini and they watched as the dogs greeted him and he made a great fuss of them.

Alice jumped in the Land-rover gratefully and immediately phoned the Villa. It only took her a few minutes to explain what had happened and to tell Gerald, who had taken the call, that Jason would tell them all about it once the dogs were safely home. Then she put away her phone and looked at Guy who was sitting in the driver's seat. 'What about Cassie? Is she all right over there?'

'She'll be fine, I've thrown a waterproof blanket over her and it's not too bad under the trees. I'll call the police now. I'll just tell them that this thug tried to steal your dogs, right?'

'Thank you, yes, that would be good.' Alice had begun to shiver, the adrenaline seeping away and leaving her shocked and exhausted. She listened as Guy spoke rapidly into the phone and then he clicked his phone shut and turned to her.

'You're cold, Alice, you're shivering. Here, I've got a rug on the back seat. Put this round you. Wait a minute, I've got a thermos of tea on the floor your side.' He reached over and brushed against her leg as he found the thermos. Alice had a strong desire to reach out and touch his head, stroke his dark hair, but the moment passed and she sat motionless, her emotions jangled and confused. He poured her a cup and she drank the hot, strong tea while an awkward silence fell between them. Then Guy spoke quietly,

    'Your bluebell perfume, Alice. Being so close to you again, it's driving me mad…' He turned to her, once again his dark, brown eyes burning with desire, 'I came back, Alice. I don't know what there is between you and Jason, but I want you to give me a chance. What we had just seemed so perfect and I'm not going to give you up without a fight.' He stopped and suddenly smiled, 'Not that I think I'd have a snowball's chance in hell of beating Jason in a fight… I'd probably end up with his knee on my neck… that's if I hadn't had the chance to run or jump onto Cassie and gallop away… but seriously, Alice, please give me a chance.'

    'Oh Guy, you've got it all so wrong. There's never been anything between me and Jason… I mean we're just friends, really good friends.'

    'But that morning at the pool, he had his arms around you and you were half naked…that's not just friends.' Guy turned away from her and slammed his hands angrily on the steering wheel.

    'No, no… my new bikini had just come off in the pool… I dived in and it came right off. Jason realised and ran to get my robe. He held it out to me with his eyes tight closed. Didn't you notice that?'

    'I wasn't exactly looking at Jason's handsome face… your cold nipples pointing straight at me, your beautiful wet hair shining like gold in the rain… are you seriously thinking I was looking at the super-hero?' Guy turned back to face her again, a small glimmer of understanding in his expression. Alice blushed, the warm tea coursing through her and her heart beating with a rush of emotion. She put down the empty cup and turned toward Guy and reached out for him. Then they were kissing. He smothered her face with kisses until their mouths met. She held his head in her hands and he pulled her toward him and whispered in her ear. 'I've wanted to tell you I love you since the moment I first saw you…' his words were suddenly interrupted by a loud thumping noise from the back of the horse-box. They drew apart and looked at each other and then burst out laughing.

    'Oh lord, I'd quite forgotten about Brad!' Alice looked at Guy, her eyes stretched wide.

'Me too, this is an unusual situation… err, not the most romantic of places to tell you that I love you… but well, I can't wait any longer. Who knows what will happen next… your life is so frantic that I have to seize my moment with you.'

Alice raised her hand and rested it over his lips to stop him saying another word. 'I love you, too, Guy' Alice said quietly and then there was another barrage of thumps from the horse box and the Land-rover actually bounced up and down a little. 'Do you think…' Alice's words were lost in the strident sound of a police siren.

'Thank goodness, the police have got here quickly.' Alice pushed back her wet hair and looked out of the window.

'I don't know, I was just beginning to enjoy myself. Best time I've had in more than a week. You stay in here, Alice. I'll go and sort out the cavalry.'

'I think I will then if you're sure.' Guy stroked her hair gently and kissed her forehead. Alice watched as he strode across the car park, splashing through the puddles to meet the police. For a moment, she wasn't sure if she would laugh or cry as relief washed over her.

'For a clever writer you do speak such rubbish'

'I want to thank you all for coming here, rather early for a Sunday morning, but, as you know, my usual lunch guests will descend soon enough, like gannets.' Grace stood at the head of the kitchen table and looked around with a delighted smile. The rain had stopped and the morning sun was filtering through the long kitchen window behind her, turning her ash blonde hair to gold. The scene was once again perfectly set. 'And not just to thank you for joining me for coffee, but a huge thank you to you all for saving my dogs, Smoke and Cloud.' At the sound of their names, the two dogs, wearing their new white collars, looked up and lazily wagged their tails before returning to doze in front of the range. Grace waved a gracious hand around her as she continued. 'Now, in the style of the end act of an Agatha Christie mystery, I shall speak to each of you in turn. First, I shall thank my dear Minnie and Gerald. As always, or maybe even more than usual, their loyalty and kindness saw me through the dark hours when I thought my dogs had gone forever.' She shuddered, maybe it was a theatrical gesture but her face showed real distress before she continued brightly, 'next to Jason and Josette.' As her name was mentioned, Josette looked up quickly and began to shake her head, 'Don't interrupt me, Josie, be a good girl, I am in full flow now... I know you are going to say you have done nothing, but my goodness, you are so wrong. You have helped our beautiful Jason back onto the tracks and, without you in his new life, I very much doubt he would have found the courage that he showed that dreadful day in the forest. *'La vie est une fleur dont l'amour est le miel.'* Grace turned to glare at Alice, 'Victor Hugo, in case you don't recognise the quote, my dear Alice, and yes, very well, I confess I do speak French but only in moments of dire necessity. *'Speak in French when you can't think of the English for a thing—turn out your toes when you walk—and remember who you are'*... Grace held up her hand to stop Alice from replying, 'Alice Through the Looking Glass!' Grace laughed, 'Alice has taught me a very good game of quotations, one that her mother, whom I hope to meet soon, taught her. But I must continue, *'le denouement.'* Grace smiled and nodded meaningfully at Alice. Somehow they were both well aware that it was Alice who had goaded Jason to his new found confidence and bravery. Looking at Jason and Josette, sitting close together and so happy in each other's company, Alice was glad that Grace included Josette in her speech. Certainly it was Josette that had given Jason hope for the future. And speech it certainly was… in the emotional and all-encompassing style of a star accepting an Oscar rather than the finale of an Agatha Christie mystery. Now, wiping a solitary tear from her eye with a lace-edged handkerchief, Grace turned to Jason, 'Now, I come to you, Jason. You've come through some hard times and we have been lucky to have you here at the Villa la Vie en Rose, sheltering, hiding but most of all working so hard for me. Yes, now, you have tackled your demon in the form of the loathsome and well-labelled, Brad… you brought him down and saved my dogs at the same time, how can I ever repay you? In fact, I am a woman who does not like to be in debt so I do have something up my sleeve, but… we'll come to that later.'

Jason looked at Grace, his handsome face wrinkled in puzzlement. Alice wondered what Grace was up to and almost laughed. Jason had good reason to be worried, she thought, knowing now Grace's scheming and generous nature. Jason was looking at Josette and then he looked across at Alice. He smiled and immediately the frown cleared and his face, so symmetrically perfect, had all the charm of a movie star. Grace had now reached out her hand and rested it gently on William Marsden's shoulder. He was sitting next to her and looking at her in what could only be described as adoration. 'Now, don't you interrupt me, William Marsden, or I shall forget my words… and that just wouldn't do. I know you are thinking that there is nothing that I should be thanking you for but you are very wrong. My sweet William, you have defeated my long-held determination never to fall in love again. Yes, girls and boys, I take this opportunity as if you haven't already guessed, that William and I are an item. I refuse to say more and this new-fangled term, an item, suits me very well. I like being an item, William's item.' She blew him a swift kiss with an elegant wave of her hand and William caught her hand and kissed it to a round of applause. 'Now, I told you not to interrupt, I am a woman in mid-speech,' Grace took her hand away from William and clasped both hands together but then gave him a sweet smile before she continued, 'And talking of items, brings me to the young man sitting on my left. Guy Bond, or, as I call him to Alice, the talented Mr Bond. Well, 007 he may not be but he arrived on the scene in what can commonly be described as the nick of time. Jason had floored the tattooed Brad, but then what?

This is the scenario… Alice has the dogs, my money is fluttering around the car park and the diamonds, well, gravel thanks to Alice, scattered around worthlessly. There is a knife somewhere on set, kicked away by my shy but ever-resourceful Alice… but, what indeed next? Along comes our dashing knight to the rescue, not quite on a white charger but at least with a horse box which turns out to be a most handy prison. Mr Bond rapidly writes the next scene by calling the police and convincing them that they should arrive on set at the speed of light. Why do they turn up so promptly? Because, it is revealed that our tattooed dog-napper is already wanted by the Toulon police for drug smuggling. Pleasingly easy to be identified… the hateful Brad will moulder in a French prison for a suitably long time. As if that is not enough to thank you for, Mr Bond, I now need to thank you again as you have agreed to the delicate and truly daunting task of writing the screenplay of my long and rackety life. Yes, I think I owe you my heartfelt thanks, Guy.'

Guy nodded and half stood as he gave a small bow to accept the applause from everyone round the table. Grace held up her hand again for silence,

'Now, at last, I come to my new young friend and companion, Alice Shakespeare.' Grace looked at Alice and her bright blue eyes filled with tears. 'Alice, I don't know where to begin. You have come into our lives at the Villa la Vie en Rose and brought youth and beauty to us all. You have breathed new life into me and brought me back into a world I thought I wanted to forget. As for all the rest of the story,' Grace looked round the table, 'I think we all know how much you have done and I will simply have to say, thank you, as words finally desert me.' Grace suddenly laughed, a perfect low-pitched laugh, 'That has to be a first, I am lost for words.' She sat down and now everyone was clapping and cheering. The dogs jumped up at the commotion and began to chase each other in circles round the table. In the pandemonium a bell rang and Gerald stood up,

'That's the gate bell, must be the first lunch guests, Grace. Jason and I will see the cars in and get them parked up.'

'My goodness, how time flies when I make a speech. William, will you come through with me… I am not ready yet to meet guests. Alice would you and Guy see people into the dining room and the salon. Alice, there are two special guests you will be very pleased to see. Now, Minnie and Josette, I know you have everything prepared so please begin with the canapés. I shall join the party in half an hour or so. Grace took William's arm and swept out of the kitchen.

Alice and Jason looked at each other across the table and laughed, 'Grace is up to something, isn't she?' Jason said.

'I think so,' Alice agreed slowly nodding, 'She had that wicked gleam in her eye. What was that about some guests I'd be pleased to see? And what did she mean about you… something about having an idea up her sleeve. Oh dear, Jason, watch out!'

'I know, anyway, we all have our orders! I'm going to run down to the gates… you stay by the villa, Uncle Gerald and get them parked up, no need for you to come all the way down the drive.'

'Thanks, lad, that'll suit me. I've put the Bentley and the Mini away so there'll be more room… goodness knows how many Grace has invited though. She seems to be back in her old style, full party mode. We'd all better watch out, I reckon.'

'Don't I know it,' Minnie stood up and tied on her apron, 'Grace ordered canapés for more than thirty. That's quite a few more than our usual harpies and hangers-on. Gannets, she calls them. I know old Madame Fleurenne is coming over with her son and daughter-in-law, at least they're good friends… and Bernie Goldman, he hardly ever misses an invitation, always trying to keep on at Grace about her career… at her age!'

'Better not let her hear you say that,' laughed Gerald, 'Age is a four letter word in Grace's world. Anyway, better get going. They'll be queuing at the gates by now. Come on Jason… all or nothing you are boy. Put young Josette down now, her Mum will be here soon and she'll see to you.'

Jason was standing, towering over Josette and attempting to tie the back of her apron strings whilst kissing the back of her neck. He jumped at Gerald's words and reluctantly gave Josette a last kiss and made for the door. 'I've already met Josette's Mum, Uncle Gerald, and I have her full approval to date Josie, so there, see!'

'Something must have gone wrong with the translation then.' Gerald reached out and slapped Jason on the back as they left the kitchen. Minnie looked after them both with a fond smile,

It does my heart good to see them both so happy.' She wiped a tear from her eye with the back of her hand, 'Now look, what am I like, crying when I'm so happy? Come on Josette, I'll show you how I set out the salmon roulade. Alice has already made a lovely job of decorating the table with mimosa.'

Alice and Guy stood together in front of the range, the dogs sprawled at their feet.

'They certainly don't look any the worse for their dog-nap adventure, do they?' Guy said, looking down at the sleeping dogs.

Alice took Guy's hand and was about to reply when Gerald popped his head back through the kitchen door. 'First guests at the front doors, Alice, will you see them in, they've just parked.'

'Yes, I'll be there.' Alice, still holding Guy's hand went quickly out of the kitchen and through to the main entrance door. She stood with Guy on the doorstep and waited for the guests to walk round from their car. 'I wonder who will be the first guest? I don't suppose I shall even know them…' the words died in her throat and suddenly she was running to meet her mother. Alice ran into her mother's arms and they hugged for a long moment, 'I had no idea… Mum, this is such a great surprise, when did you get here? You look so well.' Alice realised that her stepfather, Mike, was standing politely back, waiting for Alice to greet her mother first. She turned to him and kissed him on both cheeks, feeling so happy that she managed to give him a small hug, 'Mike, this is so great! I had absolutely no idea.'

'Well, you have to thank Grace for organising us… she phoned the other night and told us you had been very busy but this weekend was a special celebration. We're not even sure of what!'

Alice's mother interrupted him, 'Mike managed to get a locum at the last minute and took a week off. Then we couldn't get flights but somehow Grace managed to get us last minute train tickets and sent them by courier. So here we are! Isn't it all so beautiful here, Alice, what a wonderful place! Now, are you going to introduce us?'

Alice was made aware that Guy was also hovering discreetly in the background. She turned quickly to Guy and grabbed his hand, pulling him forward to meet her mother and Mike.

'Mum, Mike, this is Guy Bond and… well, we love each other!' The simple words slipped out and, in the general excitement seemed all that needed to be said. Guy shook hands with Alice's mother and then Mike and they all went into the Villa.

There was only time for a short excited conversation between them all before other guests began to arrive. Guy had talked seriously to her mother for a few minutes, explaining about his work and how he had met Alice at the last Sunday party at the Villa.

It just can't be only a month ago, surely? I suppose I've just ended my month's trial then?' Alice said in shock. 'So much has happened, it seems so much longer.'

'Not to your mother, I assure you, Alice,' Mike smiled at Alice as he spoke, 'she has missed you so much at home. When your letters arrive she reads every word through and then, in the evening after dinner, she reads them aloud to me.'

Alice looked at Mike, he really was a very nice man and her mother looked so very happy, 'Mum reads aloud very well, doesn't she? I've been reading to Grace and I try to read like Mum. But, oh dear, my letters can't be that interesting.'

'Oh, but they are, you describe Provence and daily life so well… although I do always get the feeling you're not telling me everything that's going on.' Her mother looked at Alice and then at Guy who said,

'Alice has certainly had an adventurous month in her Provençal wonderland…'

Alice interrupted Guy, 'Well, I'll tell you more later but I've just seen some more guests arriving… it's the de Fleurennes… I have written about them, Mum, they have the Château near Grasse, the perfumery. I must go and greet them.'

For the next half hour, Alice was busy greeting guests and helping Josette to serve the canapés. She was pleased to see that Guy persuaded Jason to come into the dining room and help pour drinks. She was looking round the room, making sure everyone was served when the door opened and Grace made her entrance. Leaning on William's arm and followed closely by Smoke and Cloud, she walked into the sunlight. Alice almost gasped aloud as she saw that Grace was wearing a velvet dress in bright emerald green. At her neck was a sparkling emerald and diamond choker and, most surprising of all, on her feet were flat green pumps, very similar to Alice's own. The soft velvet dress clung to her remarkable figure and, even in the bright sunlight, she looked like a beautiful young woman. There was a spontaneous round of applause as she made her way through her guests and over to a seat by the window, next to Madame

Fleurenne. She waved the applause away and silence fell as she spoke,

'Dear friends, thank you all for coming today. This is the second speech I have made this morning so this will be very short. One must never over-do a performance. However, I want to introduce you all to my new friend, William Marsden.'

William raised a hand and looked around the room, 'I know you are all thinking that I must be the luckiest man in the universe… and I have to admit it's true. I can hardly believe I am here, with the brightest star in the constellation on my arm. In her speech earlier this morning she said we were an item. All I can say is that I am one very lucky item.'

There was more applause and then general conversation was resumed. Alice began to relax and helped herself to a tiny pastry canapé. Just as she had popped it in her mouth, she heard a voice in her ear,

'So, it seems a lot has been trending on since last we spoke.' It was the easily recognisable voice of Bernie Goldman. 'What have I been missing? Just look at our lovely Grace in bright green, I'd never have believed it… and that's William Marsden if I'm not mistaken… I've seen his noble face on a list of the one hundred richest self-made men in Britain… if I'm not mistaken… and, believe me, Alice, sweetie, it's the sort of think I know.'

Alice hastily swallowed her canapé and replied, 'I certainly do believe you, Bernie. Isn't it good to see Grace so happy… she looks marvellous. I thought she said you were in Los Angeles?'

'Oh I was, I was. She persuaded me to get my sorry ass across the Atlantic… she said she had something important to discuss… and well, here I am, red-eyed and awaiting her orders, I guess. I mean why change a habit of a lifetime?' Bernie laughed and crammed a large, cheese croissant into his mouth and carried on talking, 'I'm not sure if this is breakfast or dinner, but I'm starving and Minnie's food is worth crossing the pond for any time, never mind what Grace has been plotting for me.'

'It must be about the screenplay, surely. I think she's back on track with that.' At the thought of working on the screenplay with Guy, Alice felt her stomach flutter in excitement and she looked across the room to where Guy was standing, talking to her mother and Mike. She realised he had been looking at her and their eyes met. She almost laughed aloud at the thought of their eyes meeting across a crowded room. At the same moment, Guy flashed a smile at her and she was almost sure he was thinking the same. There seemed to be an electric current between them, a magnetic force that drew them to each other and transmitted their thoughts. But Bernie was still talking, now mopping his face with a napkin and searching for something more to eat.

'No, we've had long talks about the biopic on the phone… that seems all tied up again and I've sent the contract back to Guy Bond. I'm just keeping my fingers well-crossed this time, especially as he has been nominated for the *priz du scenario* this year in Cannes. Hopefully, he'll sign up this time and we can get going… there was quite a hiccough over that… Grace wouldn't tell me why but she refused point-blank to work with anyone else. She can be very, what shall I say, outspoken? Two other screenwriters that I told to get in touch with her had their noses put well out of joint. Probably never speak to me again… but that's Grace, bless her.'

Alice was about to reply and especially to ask more about the *prix du scenario* when, from her seat by the window, she saw that Grace was beckoning to them. Bernie quickly put down his plate and they made their way through the crowd of guests to Grace. She held out her hand as they approached and Bernie took it in his,

'Grace baby, you look a million dollars, and in green… what's going on here?'

'Well, Bernie, late as usual so you missed my welcoming speech, quite unforgivable and I refuse to bring you up to date. One day you will learn to be punctual.'

'Well, I did fly in from California, Grace, give me a break!'

'Excuses, always feeble excuses. However, I shall have to forgive you as I have a business proposition to put to you.'

'Anything you say, Grace, you know I am the proverbial putty in your elegant hands. Come on then, tell me what's up your green sleeve then.'

'Well, just look around the room and see who stands out amongst the crowd?'

Bernie swivelled round and then turned quickly back to Grace, 'The tall, blonde guy with all the muscles… is he a new star that I missed out on?'

'Not quite, but almost.' Grace turned to Alice, 'Would you ask Jason to come over for a minute, Alice.'

Alice made her way back through the guests and over to Jason who was standing near the buffet table next to Josette.

'Jason, Alice wants a word with you.'

Jason quickly put down the tray of glasses that he was holding and followed Alice over to Grace.

'Ah, Jason, there you are… I want you to meet Bernie Goldman. He is my agent and he seems to think that you have potential to be the next star in his galaxy. What do you think about that?'

Alice watched Jason as he tried to take in what Grace was saying. She could well imagine Jason's handsome face in close-up on a big screen, betraying every emotion. Now, he was the perfect example of bewildered surprise. One blonde eyebrow lifted quizzically, his cornflower blue eyes puzzled and his lips slightly parted as though words failed him. Well, Alice thought to herself, trying not to laugh, certainly he was speechless. She stood close beside him and said, 'Why that's the most amazing and yet obvious idea ever. Jason, you even told me that you loved drama when you were at your academy, you were in that Shakespeare festival, weren't you?'

'Drama? You've been to drama college?' Bernie's voice raised a few decibels but still Jason made no reply, 'Grace, you know I think you have something. This big guy has the James Dean magic appeal. Yes, yes, so tell me Jason, what's your background?'

Jason looked from Alice to Grace and spoke at last,

'Background, er, well…'

Now Grace interrupted, 'Bernie, you're just going to love his background. A bad boy dragged up in the slums of London… you could make so much of that. A more troubled youth you would be hard to find, very Jimmy Dean, yes, I see where you are coming from… you're so clever, Bernie.'

Alice looked at Grace as she carried on weaving her plot. Bernie and Jason were easily caught in her gossamer web. She moved away quietly and made her way over to Guy who was now listening intently to her mother,

'Oh yes, Alice was always so good at English, always top in her class at school.'

'Mum, can't you try and be a bit more embarrassing? No photos of me as a kid with my front teeth missing?'

'Well, now you come to mention it…' Alice's mother pretended to look in her handbag.

'Oh, I've seen that photo,' Mike added, as they all laughed, 'I thought I'd post it on Facebook one day soon.'

Alice looked at Mike and could suddenly see what her mother saw in him… yes, he was nice but funny, too, and very quick to react to her mother's style of humour. Then she looked at Guy, chatting so easily, full of confidence, so relaxed, his brown eyes now looking at her as he reached out his hand and drew her close to him.

'I'd love a copy of that. I have a photographer friend who could blow it up really large for our wedding reception. By the way, Mrs Shakespeare, I haven't mentioned it to your beautiful daughter yet, but I do intend to ask her to marry me soon. Well, that is as soon as she forgives me properly for a mistake I made a few weeks ago.'

'Guy, behave yourself,' Alice leaned into Guy and looked up at him fondly, 'For a clever writer you do speak such rubbish.'

'Ah well, that's why I can write film scripts so well… fluent verbiage, known as dialogue. But, I mean it you know… and it's no good squirming,' Alice had wriggled as he held her close to him, 'I shall win your heart, you just wait and see. It's written in the stars.'

Alice's mother looked at them both and then smiled and nodded, 'Maybe so, I think it may well be so, but remember '*It is not in the stars to hold our destiny but in ourselves.*'

'All's well that ends well.' said Alice.

'We are all of us stars, and we deserve to twinkle.

Marilyn Monroe

Have you read my other titles?

ROMANTIC THRILLERS
Perfume of Provence
Provence Love Legacy
Provence Flame
Provence Starlight
Provence Snow
Dreams of Tuscany
Moonlight in Tuscany

WINE DARK MYSTERIES
Well Chilled
Skin Contact
Lingering Finish
Rich Earthy Tuscany

I wrote Provence Starlight because it just happened. My plan was to write a Provence Christmas book… but Alice and Grace just came on the scene and took me over for a while. I now definitely intend to get my skis on and go off piste. Hope you will join me in fictional chalet land this Christmas, Kate

'words are the voice of the heart'

Printed in Great Britain
by Amazon